Also by Jean Rezab

RICHMOND SIBLING SERIES

Chokecherry Valley Comfort
Chokecherry Valley Joy
Chokecherry Valley Love
Chokecherry Valley Faith

OTHER BOOKS

In This Place Together
The Prediction

www.jeanrezab.com

In This Place Together

Jean Rezab

This book is dedicated to my mother and grandmother.
Two strong women who inspired my love of reading and
writing by their great example.

CHAPTER 1

Sapphira kept her veiled head bowed as she walked slowly past the guard, up the stairs, and into the synagogue. She felt his stare, but he didn't stop her. He had to be wondering why a heavily veiled, pregnant woman arrived at worship long after the sun had set on the city.

Why had she volunteered to be the one to go into the synagogue? When she suggested stealing the scrolls to make money to save Aaron, Gideon had followed her lead. She had started to have second thoughts, yet Gideon had promised her they wouldn't be caught.

She jumped at a sudden creak that sounded in the old building and stood silently waiting for another sound, but none came. The lack of air under the layers of veil emphasized the heat of the evening. Lifting it for a moment, she took a deep breath, which didn't cool her. The smell of old blood from burnt offerings, along with the scent of incense, made the air stale and heavy.

She must hurry and complete what she'd come to do. Gideon would be waiting. The children and Aaron slept while she lingered. If she got caught, Aaron would find out what she'd done and be disappointed that she'd felt it necessary to steal for him. He was resigned to his death, but she would not give up until she had no choice.

Shadows covered the walls with even darker areas between candlelit wall sconces. So many offerings had been given here. She shuddered and quickly found the scrolls. When she'd planned tonight's events with Gideon, he'd instructed leaving the larger scrolls in place. She chose a few of the smaller ones, making sure to get the written scroll handed down through Moses' line, a copy of the Ten Commandments.

She gathered them up and placed them in a pouch Gideon had made for her to wear under her gown. With only a few buttons to open, she was able to hide the scrolls in pockets that made her look pregnant. The soft material of the pockets also kept the scrolls from becoming damaged. She was forced to lean forward to keep from bending the fragile scrolls. This added to her image of a pregnant woman but made her steps awkward as she tried to hurry.

The constant creaking, shifting, and moaning of the building worked on her nerves. When the scrolls were hidden on her person, she hitched in small breaths and felt faint. Why, oh why, had she decided to do this? Perhaps it wasn't too late to change her mind. Was this the only way to get money to help Aaron? There must be another way. Would Gideon keep his promise once she gave him the scrolls? Could she be sure he wouldn't tell anyone that she was the one who stole them?

Why didn't God heal Aaron as she prayed for him to get well day after day? Aaron was a good man, who had been faithful. Would Aaron suffer because of this? Sapphira had not had a choice. Aaron's only chance was to see that rich Jewish healer, and he cost money they didn't have.

Sapphira tried to walk normally toward the entrance while carrying the hidden scrolls. The wooden dowels poked her stomach. After hesitating for a moment to gather courage, she opened the door and exited the synagogue.

The guard watched her as she shuffled down the synagogue stairs. He turned away, and she took a deep breath. Hurrying would make him suspicious, so her steps remained measured, her head bowed to appear as if deep in thought. Her limbs trembled, and her back ached from trying to keep the dowels from poking her and moving so she wouldn't damage the fragile scrolls. She feared he could sense the truth, but there was no way he could know, and no reason for him to go into the synagogue and suspect what she had done. No one would enter the synagogue until tomorrow morning.

Besides, she was heavily veiled, and tomorrow they'd be looking for a pregnant woman, not a slim, respectable woman with two children and a sick husband.

Just as she reached the bottom step, the guard turned around and started walking toward her. She instinctively clutched her stomach, and he stopped. She stood, debating what to do. Start walking again? Or wait? Though she knew he couldn't see her fear, perhaps he sensed it. Perhaps he thought she was afraid he would attack her. A thought that occurred to her since she'd been too preoccupied with the theft and not other dangers.

He waved her on, and she wasted no time. No longer afraid of what he thought, she rushed from the synagogue gates and down the road and turned onto a side street out of the guard's sight.

She hurried the mile through Naraah's deserted roads, panting as she stayed out of sight whenever she detected human movement, afraid of the consequences that might befall her and furious at herself for getting into this predicament. Taking longer than expected, she reached the back alley where Gideon waited for her outside of his house.

When he saw her, a greedy glint appeared in his eyes. That was all she could see in the dark, but she had the impression his lips curved in a smile behind his red, bushy beard. Sapphira unbuttoned the special pouch on the side of her dress to give him the scrolls, happy to be rid of them. He wrapped the items in a blanket and placed them in an empty bag.

Breathing a sigh of relief that her part was done, she flipped the veil off her face, letting it hang down her back. She debated walking home alone or asking Gideon to escort her. Her experience with the guard at the synagogue made her leery. "Will you show me home?"

"Yes. It's on the way to where I'm going next." He bent over the bag, closing it. She couldn't tell anything else from his voice. "When will I get my share of the money? You know about Aaron, and we need the money soon."

He stood up, sneering. "I won't be sharing the money with you."

She didn't understand. "What?"

He took a step toward her and grabbed her arm. "I said, I won't be splitting any money with you."

She tried to pull away, but his hold was too tight on her arm. She started to struggle, realizing the danger she was in. She had never cared for Gideon but hadn't feared him until this moment. She kicked at his shin, but her sandal barely grazed his leg.

Gideon laughed, his eyes cruel. "There's no one here to save you."

"Let her go," commanded a voice from behind them.

Gideon dropped her arm and whirled around to see who had spoken.

Sapphira scrambled away from Gideon and tried to peer around him. The voice was familiar, but she couldn't identify it.

"What are you doing here?" Gideon demanded.

"Come here, Sapphira."

Sapphira crept closer but still couldn't see around Gideon. "Who are you?"

"It's Elam. Come around. Gideon will let you through."

She hesitated. Elam was Gideon's father. She trusted him. But would Gideon let her by, or would he grab her again?

"Gideon won't harm you. You can come."

She edged around Gideon, but he just stood there, staring at his father. She reached Elam's side. Elam looked at Gideon. "We'll talk later."

As Sapphira and Elam left the alley, she kept looking back, but Elam walked steadily on, ignoring his son.

When they were a few streets away from Gideon, Elam spoke. "Are you all right?"

"I'm fine. How did you happen to be there at the right time?" Did Elam know what she had done?

"From inside the house, I heard Gideon's laugh."

Sapphira shuddered. Gideon's laugh had been pure evil. "Thank you for saving me."

They walked until they were nearly at Sapphira's house, and then Elam stopped in the street and faced her. "Stay away from Gideon. You were lucky tonight, but next time there might not be anyone to stop him."

"I will." Sapphira had learned her lesson. "Do you know why I was there?"

Elam scratched his chin beneath his beard. It was the same scruffy thatch as Gideon's, only Elam's was gray. "It's none of my business."

"I thought it would help Aaron, but it was a waste of time." She felt like crying. "I'm so tired."

"We all want to help."

"You helped me tonight. And you're helping Omar and the rest of the men with the harvesting. Thank you."

Elam looked down at his feet, and she thought he might be embarrassed. He was a quiet man and rarely spoke. She thought of him as gentle and kind. Unlike his son.

She turned toward home, and the rest of the way they traveled in silence. Once they reached her front door, she thanked him again, and he left.

She stood outside for a few minutes, gathering her scattered thoughts. She wished she felt as confident as when she'd set out from home a while ago. Where was the exhilaration she'd expected after accomplishing her goal? Where was the relief that she was closer to hiring the Jewish physician who would help cure Aaron? She had stolen the scrolls, and only Gideon would benefit. Where could she find the money to pay the physician?

Would Aaron's physician Demetrius talk to the Jewish physician? She and Aaron weren't Jewish themselves, so he probably wouldn't come see Aaron. And as Aaron's current physician, would Demetrius be receptive to another physician seeing Aaron?

Her shoulders sagged with weariness. Hopefully, Aaron hadn't noticed her absence. She'd slipped him some extra laudanum before she'd left, hoping he'd get a good night's sleep for once.

She went inside, removing the veil and breathing in relief when she found Aaron sound asleep. His lack of coughing was a rare event these days.

CHAPTER 2

Sapphira stood outside the door of their small, three-room, mud-brick house. Why did Demetrius want to see Aaron alone today? Usually, they listened to the physician's instructions together.

The day's stifling heat caused mirage waves above the cobblestones in the U-shaped road. Doors stood open in the mud-brick houses lining the road as people tried to get as much air flow as possible. But the air was still, and the dry, dusty air burned her eyes.

Next door, Leah was probably making bread. Sapphira could share her fears with her friend, but she didn't move. Demetrius would be out soon with news of Aaron.

She could hear the pounding of a hammer on pine or cedar as the carpenter further down the road worked. She lifted her thick black hair away from her neck and held it up, feeling the perspiration dry as more formed and took its place.

Aaron was close to the end. That was what Demetrius thought.

The door behind her squeaked open. She turned, and Demetrius gestured to her from the doorway.

"Come in."

She slid past his tall frame and into the house.

Instead of lying down on the mat, Aaron sat on the floor with his back against the wall. The room was plain with tiled floor and colorful rugs her mother had made with sheep's wool and many different dyes. Sapphira's and the children's mats were folded up against one wall. Sapphira was grateful there was a quiet room where Aaron could rest. He could no longer make it to the rooftop to lie in the cooler air, but he said he was cold most of the time anyway.

He struggled to rise from the floor, coughing all the while. His thin frame shook with the effort. He had lost several pounds since the start of his illness. Perspiration beaded on his forehead, and his long dark hair hung lank and lifeless around his narrow, pale face with its sparse beard.

She rushed to him. "Stay there."

He waved her away and finally stood. "I'm fine. Let's go into the kitchen."

Sapphira followed Aaron as he made his way bit by bit into the kitchen, and Demetrius followed.

They had tiled their small kitchen floor the previous year before Aaron became ill. It was the same tile as in the sleeping room. The ten-foot, simple pine table and chairs barely fit in the small room. A narrow chest with no legs stood along the wall where Sapphira usually spent the morning kneading bread and preparing stew or vegetables. A bowl for washing sat on the corner of the chest, and a clay jar of clean water for drinking sat on the floor at the end of the narrow chest.

Today, Sapphira sat at the low, long pine table with Aaron beside her and Demetrius across from them. The tile floor was slick beneath her sandals as she sat and listened to Aaron cough.

She couldn't wait any longer for the news and braced herself. "What is the news?"

"He doesn't have long. His consumption is advanced." Demetrius glanced at Aaron and then looked at the table.

He gave her time to compose herself. She didn't need much time. She'd suspected such news for a while. Her hands were shaking. What would she do without Aaron? "Are you sure?"

"Yes." The sympathy in his eyes confirmed his words.

"How long…" She couldn't finish.

"Soon. About a week or two."

"A week." Sapphira stood up, and the room whirled around her. She steadied herself against the wall.

Aaron reached for her and caught her hand in his. She grasped it, feeling his cool firm touch.

"You're strong, Sapphira. You'll get through this," he said.

She didn't feel strong. "I'll be fine," she agreed, squeezing his hand and letting go.

Demetrius couldn't do any more for Aaron. It was now up to her. She would talk to Aaron when Demetrius had gone. "Thank you for what you've done," she said to Demetrius.

"I'm sorry I couldn't do more." Demetrius walked around the table to them. "I'll still come around daily and see you both."

Sapphira walked over to the chest, picked up a cup, and used the dipper to fill it with water. She offered Demetrius a drink. He refused. She drank deeply from the cup.

As Demetrius was saying goodbye, Sapphira said to Aaron. "I'll be back in a moment."

She followed Demetrius outside and closed the door.

As they stood outside the door, he waited for her to speak.

Gathering her courage, she took a deep breath and let it out. "Do you think there's a chance that the Jewish physician Tobias, the son of Uri, could help Aaron? I mean, you've done a great job, Demetrius, and I trust you, but is there anything he could do?" She fell silent, embarrassed by her own desperation.

Demetrius's eyes held only kindness. "I've talked with him in the past on various illnesses, and he's been very helpful." Demetrius paused, and she knew what that pause meant. He was trying to find a way to tell her there was no hope. But she refused to give up.

"So, you'll talk to him now? See if he'll come to Aaron?"

"I'll talk to him." But his eyes were guarded. "You have to be prepared, Sapphira."

She knew what he meant. "Do I need to give you money for him? I could ask Omar, although I don't think my brother will lend me the money."

"No payment is necessary. I'll talk to the physician."

"Thank you." She watched him walk away with his head bowed.

Sapphira went into the sleeping room where Aaron lay on the mattress with his head propped up to reduce his coughing.

When she knelt on both knees beside the mattress, Aaron took her hand in his. "I know how hard this is for you."

"And what do you think?" She blinked back tears as she studied Aaron.

"I think he's right. I'm sorry he couldn't do anything more. I'm sorry for what this means for you. I know how you don't care to stay with Omar and Naomi, but you and the kids will probably have to move in with them."

Sapphira didn't tell him she had no intention of staying with her brother and his wife.

"Where are Caleb and Rachelle?" he asked.

"They're with Leah. Demetrius told me he would have news today, and I took Rachelle over to play with Ruth. Caleb wanted to work with John and Thatcher." Leah, her husband John, and their son Thatcher all lived next door to Sapphira and Aaron.

"I don't think we should tell them what Demetrius said, do you?" Aaron asked.

"Definitely not Rachelle, as she's only five. I think we might have to consider telling Caleb."

"He's just a boy." Aaron started coughing again. When he finally stopped, he lay still, gasping for breath.

Sapphira took hold of his hand. "He's almost a man. His thirteenth birthday will be in a few months." Aaron might not live that long. "I think Caleb already knows."

"Whatever you think is best."

Was she to make all the decisions now?

CHAPTER 3

Sapphira left the town of Naraah behind as she walked to her brother's house. He and his wife lived about a mile away. As she walked along the dusty track past a grove of olive trees, she listened to the birds sing. She didn't smile at the sound as she normally would but plodded along the path, preparing her approach to Omar. He would be overbearing, and she needed to get him to see that Aaron's only chance lay with the local Jewish healer. A defeatist attitude would accomplish nothing.

When Sapphira arrived, Naomi stood outside her front door, beating the dirt from a rug, and they greeted one another.

"I've come to see Omar."

She could see him out in the field with the other workers. Omar was taller and broader than most of the others. He noticed her, said something to Elam, and started walking her way. Sapphira also noticed Gideon out in the field watching her. She shivered.

"Is it Aaron?" Naomi asked.

Sapphira turned to her sister-in-law. "Demetrius has only given him a week or two at most. I need to do something."

Naomi nodded but said nothing.

Sapphira could see the pity in her eyes.

Omar stopped about six feet from her. "I need to talk to you." His voice sounded sharp, which didn't bode well for her errand.

"What do you need?" She would let him have his say first.

"Let's talk in private." He glanced at Naomi.

She took the hint and, with a nod at Sapphira, went into the house and closed the door.

Sapphira gathered her composure as she joined her brother.

"This won't take long," Omar said. He walked about a hundred yards from the house.

"What did you want to say that Naomi can't hear?" Sapphira's heart beat faster. Omar wanted privacy only when he was going to tell her something he knew she would find objectionable. "It's about Aaron," Omar said, not looking at her.

Either her brother was giving her time to compose herself or trying to decide how to broach whatever he wanted to say to her because he was silent for a few minutes.

"What?" Sapphira asked.

"With Aaron…" His voice trailed away.

This wasn't like her brother at all. He was usually very sure of himself. Very sure of what he wanted to say, what was right, and what she should do.

"This is difficult for me to say because I like Aaron."

Was that a tear in his eye? Maybe. Or maybe the sun was striking him in the eye.

"I know you do. I appreciate that you let me marry Aaron. He's taken good care of me."

This shored up Omar's courage. "Yes, he's been a good provider. That's what I want to talk to you about. Gideon will also be a good provider."

He looked at her, awaiting her response.

"What do you mean 'also'?" But she knew. She had been expecting Omar to eventually reveal his plans for her once Aaron could no longer care for her.

"Gideon will make an excellent husband for you when Aaron is gone." His words gathered speed as he got to the point. "Yes, he will be the perfect replacement and will take care of you. As Naomi's cousin, he's already part of our family."

Perfect? Gideon perfect? If only her brother knew how Gideon had attacked her in the alley. But there was no way to tell him without revealing the whole story. Would Omar even care enough about her to save her from Gideon's vileness? She didn't know.

"No." Sapphira didn't know whether to cry or stomp her foot. "Aaron is still alive. How can you possibly have a substitute already lined up for me? No one will replace Aaron. No one. Do not ever speak to me about Gideon again. Not now. And not when Aaron is…"

She turned back toward the house.

Omar followed. "You need to think about the future. You cannot live alone."

She whirled around. "I won't be alone. I have Caleb and Rachelle."

"A twelve-year-old and a five-year-old will not be enough."

"They're all I need." She reached the closed door. "Do not bring it up again, Omar."

He pushed against the door so she couldn't open it. "You're not being realistic. I have the right to marry you to whomever I choose. I choose Gideon."

He walked away.

She entered the house without responding to him. He wouldn't hear what she was saying anyway. He'd already made up his mind. Her legs were shaking as she sat beside Naomi, who stared at her open-mouthed. She realized she was shaking all over.

Naomi put her arm around her. "What is it, Sapphira? What has Omar told you?"

"He's going to force me to marry Gideon." She turned to Naomi. "Did you know what he was going to say?"

"No." Naomi shook her head. "He didn't tell me. I would have told him to wait, but you know Omar. It wouldn't have mattered."

"Wait? I never want to marry anyone besides Aaron. I know Gideon is your cousin, but I don't ever want to marry him." But she was afraid that Omar had the power to make her marry Gideon. She couldn't let him force her. She couldn't think of this right now. She only had energy to focus on Aaron. The situation with Gideon could wait.

"I know," soothed Naomi, patting Sapphira's arm. "You and Aaron are a love match."

"Aaron's only got a week or two left to live. I know I've already said that." To her own horror, Sapphira burst into tears again. She needed to stop falling apart. "Demetrius told me there is little time left. And to think Omar is already planning Aaron's replacement."

When she'd stopped crying, she sat for a few moments before an idea came to her. "I know Omar wouldn't like what I'm going to ask you, but I'm desperate and going to ask you anyway. I need to see the Jewish healer here in Naraah. I know that we're not Jewish, but his reputation as a healer is the best."

Naomi opened her mouth to speak, and Sapphira stopped her.

"Before you say no, please listen to me. Demetrius has promised to talk to him on Aaron's behalf, but I can't help but think I should offer him money or something. What do you think?"

Naomi patted Sapphira's clenched hands. "I understand your need to hang on to Aaron, more than you know. I'm not familiar with Jewish customs, so I don't know what is best when approaching the healer. You should ask Leah or John to go with you, as they are relatives of Demetrius. They might have more influence than you do. I'm sorry, but I won't be able to go with you."

Sapphira realized she'd put Naomi in an awkward position. Omar was her husband, and he could punish Naomi. The suggestion to see the healer was as far as she could go without repercussions. "I won't tell Omar that you said that. Thank you for your encouragement. I'll check with Leah and John if Demetrius has no luck."

Naomi nodded. "Thank you.

CHAPTER 4

Elam visited as Aaron sat on the bench at the long table in the kitchen. Today, he'd been too tired to get up and eat with Sapphira and the children before they'd left for Naomi's house. He forced himself to eat small bites of his breakfast of bread and figs.

"Sapphira said you wanted to see me?" Elam said.

"Thank you for coming," Aaron said.

Elam's large stomach touched the table as he leaned forward to listen. He was a big man with masses of reddish-gray hair and a full gray beard. His dark eyes sized Aaron up, and Aaron knew that look. That look everybody gave him these days. A look of concern, wondering how much longer he had.

"How's the harvest going this year?" Aaron asked.

"The crop's fairly good. Drying's swift due to the dry weather, but it'll be all right. We're about half done." Elam shifted on the pine bench. "You didn't call me over here and interrupt harvest to discuss the crops, did you?"

Aaron put down his uneaten bread. "I need you to take care of her, Elam."

"You don't need to ask. You know I'll do anything I can for both of you."

Aaron bowed. "Thank you. Demetrius doesn't give me long, and I trust him."

Elam's solemn dark eyes held Aaron's. "I'm sorry to hear that. Demetrius is a good physician. He treated Gideon a few times when he was younger. You know Gideon's a bit wild and isn't always careful."

"Gideon does things without thinking about them first. He looks so much like you, but you've always been steadier." Aaron hesitated before he continued. Once he asked, it wouldn't be something kept to himself. He took the plunge. "I need you to follow Sapphira."

Distress crossed Elam's timeworn face and highlighted the deep pouches under his eyes. "Oh, you don't want me to do that."

"I do. Follow her. See where she goes, what she does. She tends to act before she thinks, and now that Demetrius has told me I don't have much time, I'm afraid of what she'll do. I need you to watch her." He tried to keep the anxiety out of his words, knowing he sounded like a desperate man, maybe because he was a desperate man. He might seem out of his mind to his friend, to the closest man he'd ever had to a father figure since he'd last seen his own father.

Elam shook his head before Aaron finished. "Surely, you do not think she is with another man. Sapphira loves you more than anything."

"No, no. That's not what I mean at all." Aaron ran his hand through his thinning hair, his head covering going askew. "I'm afraid for her. I'm afraid she will get into some sort of trouble. She's angry. Angry at me for dying on her. And she's desperate for me to see that Jewish healer here in town. I've heard her asking Demetrius to bring him here." He met Elam's troubled gaze. "Please help me."

Elam scratched his scraggly bearded chin, eyes doubtful. "She'll catch on to what I'm doing. I'm not easy to miss in a crowd."

Aaron patted his arm. "She'd never think I'd have someone follow her. If she saw you, she'd think it was a coincidence. She slipped out of the house at night. What if something had happened to her? I can't take care of her as sick as I am."

"I suppose I could. But I think she will know."

He ran his shaking hand through his sparse hair again. "I don't care if she does. I need to make sure she's all right. I trust you with her life." He knew what he was asking of Elam. A betrayal of Sapphira. Both of them betraying her. But she was too important, and in her anger, she would do many silly things. In the past, he had been there to help and protect her. Now, he couldn't. His own experience with anger brought him only fear for Sapphira.

CHAPTER 5

Sapphira spent a sleepless night worrying about Aaron and trying to forget her brother's threats about marrying her off to Gideon. After putting food on the table for Caleb and Rachelle, she took a small plate of bread to Aaron, where he rested on their mat.

After getting him a cup of water, she sat on the floor near him. "I'm getting a few things at the market this morning." She hated lying to Aaron, but she wasn't telling him where she was really going because he would tell her it was no use. "Can I leave Rachelle here?"

"Yes. Is Leah going with you?" He nibbled at the bread and took a sip of water.

"I think so. Since I realized this morning that we needed a few things, I haven't asked her yet."

"She can leave Ruth here." He picked at the bread without eating.

Sapphira bit her tongue. She was not telling him to eat, though she wanted to tell him he needed to keep up his strength. Since Demetrius's last visit, Aaron seemed to give up any will to live. She had enough determination for them both. He might be ready to quit, but she wasn't.

"I'll see if Leah wants to leave Ruth here or bring her with us." She stood up. "Is there anything you need before I go?"

"No, I'm fine." He smiled at her.

She leaned over and kissed him. "I'll tell Rachelle I'm going."

After she'd given Rachelle a hug and kiss goodbye and seen Caleb out the door on his way to help Omar, she went next door to talk to Leah.

Leah agreed to leave Ruth with Aaron and Rachelle. Thatcher had already gone to work with John.

Sapphira walked along with Leah. They each carried a woven basket for anything they needed to bring home. Sapphira knew it was time to tell Leah of her plan. She'd hesitated because Leah's quiet nature would make this request difficult.

She stopped on the street near the blacksmith's forge.

Leah stopped beside her. "Do you need something here?"

"No, I wanted to ask for your help. You know that Demetrius has said Aaron only has a short time left. I asked him to approach the physician, Tobias, the son of Uri, and see if he would visit Aaron."

"That's good, isn't it? I know you want to make sure everything can be done, and Demetrius will talk to him if he said he would."

"I know he will, but I need to talk to the physician myself, so I know I've tried everything to get him to see Aaron."

"Won't Demetrius be angry that you don't trust him to convince the physician?"

"I don't think so." She glanced at Leah. "You know Demetrius is starting to have feelings for me. I'm trying not to encourage him."

Leah patted her shoulder. "I know you're not encouraging him and that you love Aaron. It's hard for Demetrius to see anyone suffer. It makes him a good doctor, but it makes it hard on him."

"I can't worry about that right now anyway. Aaron's all that matters." Couldn't Leah see that? Couldn't everyone see that? There was so little time.

"Where are we going this morning?"

"We're going to see the physician."

Leah grabbed Sapphira's arm. "He's a great man in this town, but we can't go there without an introduction and an appointment."

Sapphira put her own hand on Leah's. Calm determination had settled over her, and she knew this was the right move. "I'm going. If you walk with me most of the way and stay near, I'll go up to the door by myself. I would appreciate your support."

Leah sighed and let go of Sapphira's arm. "I understand, but I don't agree. I'll go with you. All the way to the door."

Sapphira hugged her. "Thank you."

They didn't speak as they walked. Sapphira was practicing her speech as they strode along the cobbled streets. Everyone knew where the physician lived, which was about a ten-minute walk for them. Not far in distance, the houses were larger as they entered the area of town where Tobias lived. She knew several of the town's wealthiest people lived in these houses. Her determination to help Aaron contributed to calming her nerves.

They had reached the beginning of the street where he lived, and Sapphira stopped. "Do you want to wait here?"

Leah's hands were clenched together in front of her. "No, I'm coming."

Sapphira nodded and took a deep breath. "Here we go."

When they reached the physician's door, Sapphira knocked firmly. A moment later, the door opened, and a beautiful, young woman with her black hair tied behind her head and a head-covering stood before them with a welcoming smile. "Can I help you?"

Her pleasant greeting surprised Sapphira into momentary silence. She'd been expecting a gruff gatekeeper.

"Are you all right?" asked the woman.

Sapphira gathered her composure. "Yes, I'm sorry. I would like to talk to the physician if I could, please? My husband, he's sick, and I don't know where to turn." She felt tears near the surface.

"Come in, please." The woman moved aside and ushered them into a small room with two chairs on each side of a small carved table against one wall. Another wall had two more chairs, but the rest of the room was bare of furniture. The floor beneath their feet was sturdy oak. A few woven wall decorations finished the look of the simple room. "Have a seat, and we will talk."

Sapphira and Leah sat down, and the woman pulled one of the other chairs to the table so she could sit in front of them.

"I am Esther. Tobias, the son of Uri, is my father."

"This is my friend Leah, and my name is Sapphira. I'm sorry to come by without an invitation from you or your father."

Esther smiled again. "That is fine. Few people who come to him let us know ahead of time. You said your husband is sick?"

"Yes. He's been attended by Demetrius, who, I believe, knows your father?"

Esther nodded. "Demetrius has been here many times. Yesterday, he came to speak to my father. Was he going to talk to him about your husband?"

"Yes. Aaron is my husband's name. Demetrius said he would speak to your father and see if there is anything further that can be done. You see, my husband doesn't have much time, according to Demetrius, and I…" She looked down, unable to go on.

"You want my father to see for himself if anything else can be done. I would do the same thing if I were facing your situation."

Sapphira raised her head at Esther's words. "You would?"

"Oh, yes." Esther's musical laugh matched her smile. "My father calls me his impatient daughter on many days. But I'll tell you a secret." She glanced toward the doorway leading further into the house, then leaned forward and whispered, "My father is more impatient than I am."

Sapphira smiled at Esther and noticed Leah's stunned expression. "Leah is very patient with me and my ways." She sobered. "But do you think your father will see Aaron?"

"I will go ask him." With that, she rose from her chair and hurried out of the room.

Sapphira grasped Leah's hand. "I think he will see Aaron. I have a feeling."

"Esther is very kind. She reminds me of you."

"I like her."

They waited and waited some more. Sapphira started doubting the outcome. Soft, quick footsteps sounded, and she looked at the doorway, hoping for good news.

Esther reappeared, her smile subdued but still in evidence, and Sapphira stood up in her excitement. Surely there was good news, or Esther would be frowning.

"My father spoke to Demetrius yesterday, and they agreed he would see Aaron. He plans to stop by with Demetrius tomorrow, if that is all right with you?"

Sapphira smiled at Esther. "That is great news. We look forward to seeing him. Will you please tell him thank you for his generosity? We are appreciative that he will go out of his way to do this."

Esther nodded, and her expression turned solemn. "God's will is unknown, Sapphira, but you will get through this period. You are a strong woman." She showed them to the door.

After thanking her numerous times, Sapphira and Leah left.

When they had turned off the physician's street on their way home, Sapphira stopped. "I don't like the way that conversation ended."

"What do you mean? She said her father would see Aaron. Isn't that what you wanted?"

"It was the way she said, 'God's will.'"

Leah looked puzzled. "But you know they are Jewish, right? They will speak of God."

"That's not what I mean. When she came back from talking to her father, she was still smiling, but it wasn't the same luminous smile as when we arrived at her house. I think she's a very happy person and likely to smile, but something her father said caused her to be more subdued. I'm afraid he's already made up his mind about Aaron and he agrees with Demetrius."

"He hasn't seen Aaron yet. You can't think that her father's given up on him already just because Esther acted a little different at the end of the visit. She was still smiling."

But not the same smile, Sapphira thought.

"He's coming, Sapphira. Hang onto that thought."

"You're right. He's coming." She began a brisk walk toward home. That was all she could do for Aaron today.

CHAPTER 6

The Jewish physician had arrived early in the morning with Demetrius. Sapphira had sent the children to Leah's house and sat in the kitchen while the men talked to Aaron. She sewed a patch of Caleb's clothing, trying to catch up with her mending but never seeming to reach the end. There was always something to fix.

Her hands were idle as she sat staring at but not seeing the fabric to be mended. What would be the news? How would this end? The longer it took, the more her anxiety mounted. She heard only a murmur now and then despite the small house. Then she heard the physician saying a Jewish prayer. Interesting. Neither she nor Aaron were Jewish. Maybe it was something the physician did, no matter the religion of the sick? She didn't know. She'd had no prior experience in the realm of illness.

Her parents had died quickly when she was a young girl. Omar had raised her with practical efficiency and with little feeling. During a trip to a neighboring town, Demetrius had met Aaron, and they became friends. Demetrius had convinced Aaron to move and work for Omar when Omar needed help. It was then that Omar had set up Sapphira's marriage to Aaron.

Sapphira was grateful for the way everything had turned out in the end, though she was unsure when Omar had first told her she was to

marry Aaron. But when they met, she had instantly
fallen in love with Aaron and wanted marriage to be
Aaron's idea, not Omar's. When she learned Aaron
loved her too, she was happy.

She heard shuffling in the other room, and
she knew they were finished. She put the garment
she'd held in her lap on the table and stood up as
she heard the outer door close after Demetrius and
Aaron wished the physician a good day.

She entered the room where Demetrius had
taken a seat on the floor beside Aaron's mat. "What
did he say?"

The two men looked at each other, and then
Aaron spoke. "It's no use. I'm not going to get
well."

She stood frozen in place. She had so hoped
that this physician would be the answer.

"Sapphira?" Aaron struggled to his feet,
coughing and holding onto the wall for support.

She couldn't move. It was like she'd come
to the end of all feeling. Was this death while
living? This blank nothing?

Demetrius steadied Aaron as he made his
way to Sapphira and put his arms around her.

She heard the door close and vaguely
realized Demetrius had left them alone. She felt the
warmth of Aaron's thin body around her and heard
him murmuring he loved her. She sank to her knees
on the floor, and he followed. How long they sat
there with her head resting on his chest she didn't
know. Gradually, feeling returned—not the feeling
of despair that she forced down—the feeling of
Aaron and this moment with him.

CHAPTER 7

The next day, Sapphira arrived at Naomi and Omar's house before the heat of the day. They lived on a little farm outside of Naraah and raised sheep and goats. Omar had inherited the land and holdings from their father when he'd died. Then Sapphira lived with Omar and Naomi. Once Aaron entered their lives, Sapphira married him a year later.

Today, she'd left Aaron sleeping restlessly and brought Rachelle and Caleb with her. Caleb had been impatient with the slow pace of their mile walk, and she'd finally let him run ahead to join his uncle Omar and the others working in the fields.

She enjoyed the cooler morning air and the chance to get out of the house. Rachelle skipped beside her along the dirt path, happily chatting about the birds squawking and what she and Ruth would do once they reached Naomi's house. Sapphira half listened and nodded once in a while, which was all Rachelle needed to keep chattering.

Why had Aaron wanted to talk to Elam the other day? If he wanted to know about the crops, wouldn't he have talked to Omar? Of course, she would prefer talking to Elam rather than her brother, but that was her problem, not Aaron's.

Aaron had always been sympathetic to Omar, even though Omar could be cruel. She'd often seen Naomi in tears when Omar scolded her, and Sapphira had been the recipient of many of her brother's reprimands as she was growing up. He'd been the man in the family since he was seventeen and Sapphira was twelve. He often employed their father's overbearing methods when Sapphira committed some infraction.

Their mother had never interfered. She'd always said the man was the head of the family, and his word was law. Her mother had passed away only a year after Sapphira's father, and then it was only her and Omar until Omar married Naomi at eighteen. If something happened to Aaron, she could not move back into his and Naomi's house.

She hated leaving Aaron alone for so long when he was so sick, but this was the last opportunity she had to build up some food reserves.

Sapphira and Rachelle entered Naomi's home, calling out as they entered. "Greetings, Naomi."

They walked into the kitchen, which was twice as big as Sapphira's own kitchen.

Naomi stood at the table, ingredients for their bread-making session spread out on the table in front of her. She was a tall, homely woman with coal black hair, a broad face, and a dour disposition. Yet, when she smiled, which was seldom, she looked beautiful. Rachelle had developed a deep fondness for Naomi, which had been surprising to Sapphira because Rachelle was shy by nature. But Naomi's rough manner didn't affect Rachelle. She saw a good heart beneath Naomi's shell, and living with Omar couldn't be easy.

"Leah will be coming over soon with Ruth," Naomi said. "She's bringing some figs to add to the bread. It's something new I'm trying."

Usually, their flatbread was a simple barley flour and water combination with a few herbs to give it a little taste.

"Can I help?" Rachelle asked, holding onto Sapphira's hand.

"Yes, you can measure out the flour."

Sapphira and Rachelle washed their hands with water that was set aside for that purpose and then joined Naomi at the table.

Naomi's kitchen contained most of the furniture handed down from Sapphira's parents to Omar. The table, made from yellow tan cedar, had ornate thick legs with scroll designs meandering up the legs. A wide, long dresser matched the table and was tall enough for four big drawers where Naomi kept her bowls and utensils. The drawers also had fine scrollwork designs embedded on the outside. Sapphira enjoyed the sharp scent of the cedar from the table, which always brought back comforting thoughts of her mother.

A beautiful large cobalt blue pitcher sat on the floor in a corner of the room next to a small table with a bowl for washing. Sapphira envied her the pitcher because it was so large that water could be available whenever needed. Sapphira always seemed to run out of water at inopportune times and needed to go to the well for a refill.

Naomi handed Rachelle a metal cup from the table. "We need three of these cups of flour. You pour one cup of flour into the bowl. I'll stir, and then I'll tell you when I need the next one."

Naomi pointed to another bowl filled with dough. "That one could use some kneading."

Sapphira nodded and went over to the bowl. Sticking her hands into the warm sticky dough, she caught the scent of flat dough and caraway seeds. Slowly, she kneaded the ingredients with her strong hands and enjoyed the feeling of accomplishment as the dough became less sticky and more solid.

Naomi started stirring her own bowl, occasionally motioning to Rachelle to add more flour. "Did you hear about John's current job? The roof is so bad it will take him days to thatch it."

"I heard. Caleb wants to help him. I told him it depended on what Omar needs from him." She didn't want to offend Omar, and with Aaron unable to work, Caleb needed to take his place helping with the livestock and crops. After all, their money and livelihood depended on Omar's charity for the moment. While Aaron co-owned the livestock with Omar, she was uneasy with the situation. When something happened to Aaron, Caleb would inherit Aaron's portion, but Omar would be in control until Caleb grew to adulthood.

She heard footsteps on the rough path outside and then a gentle knock on the open door. "Hello, Leah and Ruth. Sorry I can't stop to hug you. I'm a little busy here."

Leah stepped into the kitchen with Ruth. Leah's gentle manner was reflected in her general appearance and sweet smile. She was a small, slight woman with long, light brown hair. It was straight and wispy. Ruth was a smaller edition of her mother.

Naomi took the sack of figs from Leah and reached down to hug her. "It's good to see you. Thank you."

"You're welcome." Leah looked at the table and their progress. "I'm a little late, but you seem to have things well in hand."

Rachelle put down the cup that held some flour. "Mama, can Ruth and I go outside?"

"Yes, but stay within sight of the house."

The girls hurried out of the room, squealing with delight.

Leah reached for a bowl and started tearing up the figs. "I spoke to Demetrius this morning. That's why I was late. I was just leaving our house when he came out of your front door, Sapphira."

"He's been good about checking on Aaron every day. I don't know what we would have done without your brother." She checked the consistency of the dough she was kneading. Just a little more handling and it would be ready for the fire. "I hope he wasn't angry with me for talking to the physician."

"No, he said he would have done the same thing. He only wants what's best for Aaron. And you."

Leah's mention of Demetrius's interest in her wasn't a subject Sapphira wanted to discuss in front of Naomi.

"The Jewish physician?" Naomi picked up the remainder of the flour Rachelle had left and dumped it into the bowl.

Leah glanced at Sapphira, and Sapphira nodded. Naomi and Omar would find out anyway.

"Yes, he came to see Aaron yesterday. He couldn't do any more for Aaron than Demetrius could." Leah shrugged sadly at Sapphira.

Naomi frowned. "I'm sorry to hear that."

"I'd do anything to get Aaron well." She squeezed the bread dough more vigorously than necessary. "He's given up, but I can't…" Tears threatened again, and she was so tired of emotions whirling through her.

Leah patted her shoulder and went back to tearing up the figs. "We're here for you. Let John and me know if you need anything."

"You're our family, Sapphira. If something happens to Aaron, you and the children are welcome here." Naomi smiled shyly.

Maybe she hadn't been fair to Naomi. She looked like she meant what she said. "Thank you both. I appreciate it."

Used to the rhythm of working together as it was a regular occurrence, they silently went about their cooking.

Naomi was the first to speak. "Demetrius must be very excited about what he's hearing about Jesus of Nazareth."

Sapphira was astonished at Naomi words. What possessed her to bring up such a controversial subject? Jesus of Nazareth was the most talked about man in the country, and his disciples were many. No one could decide if he was a miracle worker or a fake.

Leah quit dicing. "As a physician, Demetrius is always interested in the healing process. He thinks Jesus of Nazareth is a miracle worker. Yesterday, he told me this incredible story about Lazarus in Bethany. Did he tell you?"

"I don't think so. I don't remember that name. He did talk about Jesus of Nazareth curing the blind and deaf and even some people with leprosy. Was Lazarus one of them?" Sapphira asked.

"No, Lazarus was Jesus's best friend, and he died."

Sapphira stopped punching the dough. Jesus's friend died? That wasn't good news. "What do you mean?"

"Lazarus was sick. His sisters had sent messages to Jesus of Nazareth to come and help cure Lazarus, but Jesus didn't arrive soon enough, and Lazarus died."

"That's horrible." Naomi's mention of Jesus of Nazareth had sparked Sapphira's interest. Maybe he could cure Aaron, but not if he had let his own friend die.

"Yes, it was. That isn't the end of the story, though. Jesus came back to Bethany and commanded Lazarus to come out of his tomb. And he did! Can you imagine? They're saying he brought his friend back to life." Leah finished the figs and pushed the bowl toward Naomi to add to her dough.

Naomi had been quiet throughout the story, which was interesting because she'd brought up Jesus of Nazareth in the first place. "Do you think they're exaggerating?" asked Naomi. "No man can bring another man back from the dead. Not unless he's God. And Jesus of Nazareth is not God."

Sapphira didn't argue with Naomi. She didn't care if Jesus of Nazareth was God or not. If he brought Lazarus back from the dead, he could help Aaron. And if he had brought Lazarus back from the dead, he probably was sent from God.

Naomi added some figs to the dough that was ready to be baked on the fire. "I'm surprised you're here so long today, Sapphira. Don't you need to get back to Aaron?"

"He was resting when I left." A plan was beginning to form in her mind. Aaron had asked her not to involve any more physicians in his care, but Naomi's mention of Jesus of Nazareth gave Sapphira another idea. And she was going to find him. Because her plan involved Leah, she needed to get her alone to talk. Naomi would feel obligated to tell Omar, and Sapphira didn't want him to stop her.

"I have some things I need to take care of after we're finished with the bread. After today, I probably won't be able to join you in the mornings as I have in the past." She took a deep breath. "Demetrius tells me it won't be much longer. Did he say anything to you this morning?"

Leah nodded. "He mentioned that to John and me, too. I didn't want to bring it up and upset you."

Sapphira punched more dough and scraped the side of the bowl with her fingers to get all the flour added into the mix. "I don't know what to think most days. I try to stay focused on the moment. Leah, can you help me with something this afternoon? I have an errand to run and need to have someone with me."

"Yes. Where…" When Leah saw Sapphira's motion to not ask, she stopped.

"Naomi, would you be able to watch the children for us this afternoon?"

Naomi stopped adding water to the dough she was working on and looked at Sapphira. "Shouldn't you be with Aaron?"

Sapphira couldn't make out Naomi's expression. Was she upset? Condemning Sapphira for leaving Aaron alone? "Just this afternoon. Then I won't leave Aaron again."

She didn't add that, with the end so near, no one could pry her away from Aaron after her task this afternoon. She hoped Naomi and Leah would follow the plan.

Naomi smiled her beautiful smile, which Sapphira rarely saw. "Of course. I would try and find Jesus of Nazareth, too, if I were you."

Sapphira realized her mouth hung open and closed it firmly. Naomi had been leading her to Jesus of Nazareth. Then she grinned at Naomi. "Thank you! Please don't let Omar know. He wouldn't understand."

Naomi nodded.

Perhaps Naomi wasn't such a difficult person. Maybe Sapphira had been a little judgmental all these years and needed to be more friendly and understanding of Naomi. After all, Naomi's lot in life hadn't been as pleasant as hers. Naomi came from a nomadic family and had been given to Omar with little ceremony. Naomi's uncle Elam and cousin Gideon had come to live with her when she married Omar, and they were her only family. In that way, she and Naomi were alike. Omar was Sapphira's only living relative.

When the women had six bowls of dough nearly ready, Naomi announced she would start the fire. When she was outside and out of hearing, Leah leaned toward Sapphira. "What do you need?"

"I'm going to the Friends of Jesus meeting this afternoon, and I need you to go with me. Would you, please?"

Leah frowned. "Why do you want to go there? Who is this Jesus of Nazareth after all? Are his miracles even real? Maybe he's a charlatan," she whispered.

"It's Aaron's only chance. Don't you see? Jesus of Nazareth can heal him. How am I going to find Jesus otherwise? These friends of his will know where Jesus is. I need to find him. I don't care about anything else."

"That's blasphemy! Sapphira…" she stopped as Naomi came back into the kitchen.

"The fire's started." Naomi grabbed two of the bowls of dough.

Sapphira and Leah each grabbed two bowls and followed Naomi outside to the firepit to bake bread. They placed the dough in a hole formed in the pit at the right depth to allow the fire's heat to cook the baking bread.

Although Naomi ignored the tension between the other two women, Sapphira was sure that Naomi felt it. Leah kept glancing at Sapphira when she thought Naomi wasn't watching. But Sapphira knew Leah would go with her to the meeting of the Friends of Jesus. That's what friends did. Leah stood by her when she needed something. And that something was a someone this time. She would go to the meeting, and surely the people there who were friends of Jesus of Nazareth would know how to find him. Somehow, she would get Aaron to

Jesus of Nazareth, and Jesus would heal Aaron. Her plan would work.

CHAPTER 8

After asking around town, Sapphira learned the meeting of the Friends of Jesus was being held at Henrietta's house. She was not a woman that Sapphira knew outside of the synagogue where Sapphira had stolen the scrolls, of which the connection made her slightly uneasy. She shuddered again at the thought of Omar's announcement that Gideon and Sapphira would marry on Aaron's death.

Henrietta was a woman who organized the part of the Jewish church that the men didn't oversee. The town was small enough to recognize most people by sight, but certain parts of town didn't mingle with others. Henrietta did not live in Sapphira's part of town, but when they'd met in the market, Henrietta had been a haughty, suspicious woman and made Sapphira uncomfortable and annoyed.

Leah joined her on the trip to Henrietta's house and kept silent the entire walk. Usually, this treatment would have made Sapphira defensive, but she didn't have the energy today. She'd seldom slept the past few days as Aaron's coughing tended to keep her awake. If this weren't her only chance to save Aaron, she would have stayed home and held his hand all day and annoyed him. He felt bad enough without her clinging to him all day. It was probably a good thing that she had something to keep her occupied today.

As much as she hated leaving Aaron, she needed the distraction of this short break from the constant worry and fear of his imminent death. She was ashamed of these thoughts but was too weary to prevent them from surfacing in her mind.

Henrietta's house was on the north side of Naraah, about a ten-minute walk from Sapphira's house. As they came closer to their destination, Sapphira grew more agitated. What if the Friends of Jesus didn't know how to find Jesus of Nazareth? What would she do then? She couldn't let herself think that way. Someone would know. She took a deep breath. This would work. She pulled herself together. This was only the first step. Next, she needed to convince Aaron to go with her to see Jesus. And convince Leah, John, and Elam to help her get Aaron to where Jesus was. She took another deep breath. One thing at a time.

Her sister-in-law had been great to watch the children. Sapphira still couldn't believe Naomi had been so helpful in mentioning Jesus of Nazareth. She had probably misunderstood Naomi for a long time, which made her sad. Once things calmed down again, she would make the effort to really get to know Naomi.

Henrietta greeted them with her chin in the air and showed them into the house where the Friends of Jesus were meeting.

The barn room where the animals were housed in Henrietta's house was clean, cleaner than Sapphira's own barn room since she'd taken over the cleaning once Aaron became sick, but the musty smell of hay and manure told her definitively where they were. She looked at the group of twelve—eight men and four women—sitting on the floor around the roughhewn table.

Gideon was one of the men. What was Naomi's cousin doing here? Had Naomi known? He was a friend of Jesus of Nazareth? Something was wrong.

After a questioning glance at Sapphira and Leah, Henrietta left them and went back to her watch at the front door.

Sapphira was relieved at the brief greeting. She didn't want to go into details with Henrietta. However, on second thought, perhaps Henrietta could have told them where to find Jesus, and she and Leah could have left. As she looked around, she realized it was too late. Others were looking at them, and she didn't want to arouse their curiosity any further. She and Leah found a place in the back corner and waited.

Gideon stood up.

He spoke eloquently for an unkempt man. His red beard sprouted like a haystack. "I say we take him from the synagogue while he's healing people. He has no right. Did God heal my mother? No."

At least a few of the people around the table jumped at the explosion of his "no." But there were a lot of murmurs of agreement at the suggestion of grabbing Jesus of Nazareth.

What was Gideon saying? They wanted to capture Jesus? Why? Sapphira shivered and hugged her arms around her middle. She was used to Aaron's gentleness, and Gideon had a way of looking at her at times when he thought she didn't notice.

The others who were gathered around the table were a random lot. Sapphira only knew a few of them from when she was a young girl attending services at the synagogue with her parents before they passed away and Omar stopped taking her to the synagogue. A few others she knew from seeing around Naraah. None were friends of hers or Aaron's. Lydia, one of the women, was a rigid Jewish woman and Henrietta's close friend. She would certainly follow Henrietta's example. Lukas was another member of their synagogue, but Sapphira didn't know anything about him. The other two she knew were Tarad, who scared her as much as Gideon, and James, who was quieter and unassuming. Several of the men were angry that a man such as Jesus of Nazareth was getting all the attention and eating with tax collectors and other sinners.

"We must capture and turn him over within a fortnight," Lukas said.

"What's the hurry? He's been preaching for a few years," Henrietta asked.

Sapphira would never have thought Henrietta would be someone who agreed to capture a man and turn him over. To whom? These were enemies, not friends, of Jesus of Nazareth. The irony of a traitor herself within a group of traitors amused her. There wasn't much to amuse her these days. She pushed her dark curly hair back from her face. The air in the barn was warm and sticky, making the air clog in her nostrils and her hair stick damply to her nape.

"You're so cautious. We'd never get anything accomplished if we listened to you," Tarad said.

Lydia spoke up. "I'm a God-fearing woman, I am, and I don't expect any leeway given to me. Why should he heal those people on the Sabbath and get away with it? We'll have our way. He won't get away with this." She half rose from the straw, her face flushed with perspiration.

"We all seem to be in agreement as to the necessary steps to take to halt these atrocities," Tarad said.

While Gideon was merely frightening, Tarad was downright scary. Facial scars covered most of his face. They were from the lash of whips and knives in various stages of healing. They weren't from one fight, but many. Did Henrietta really understand what Tarad and these other men were capable of doing? They were going to kill Jesus of Nazareth, a man who had done many good things—and Sapphira needed him alive.

Although she'd been sidetracked with the surprise of the real meaning behind this meeting, she still needed to know where she could find Jesus.

"I know someone who will turn him over to the soldiers," Tarad proclaimed.

Sapphira shuddered. She didn't want to know the man if he was someone Tarad knew.

"Where are we going to find him?" Gideon asked. He looked at Tarad with an expression that was almost like worship.

"He will be traveling from Bethany to Ephraim during the next few days. We will find him along the road. I'll talk it over with my friend."

His coarse laugh sent a shiver down Sapphira's spine. She had forgotten Leah was beside her until she gripped Sapphira's hand. Leah's face was white. Sapphira squeezed her hand. They had to do something.

Maybe this would work to her advantage. Leah would now want to help find Jesus of Nazareth to warn him, and in the process, she would be helping Sapphira take Aaron to find Jesus. Her stomach cramped. Jesus helped people, and she was using knowledge of his possible capture and imprisonment as a steppingstone to help Aaron.

Gideon leered at her throughout the meeting, and she knew he would bring up the meeting when he saw her again. As long as he didn't tell Aaron, she'd be fine. Any extra stress for Aaron might hasten the end, and she didn't want to be the source of his anxiety.

CHAPTER 9

After a trip to the outdoor market for spices and other necessities, Sapphira returned home with Leah. While Leah went to collect Rachelle and Ruth from Naomi's house, Sapphira went home to check on Aaron. She left the door open to let in the afternoon breeze.

Caleb looked up from where he sat on the floor beside Aaron. He was quiet, almost shy, but he loved to tell jokes, and he kept her laughing. He had her wavy black hair, but they kept it short.

"What took you so long, Mama?" he asked, getting up from the floor and taking the packages from her hands.

"You know how it is." She smiled at him. "People get to talking when they see me, and it takes a long time before they say goodbye."

He grinned, and his smile, so much like Aaron's, brought tears to her eyes.

"Who did you see?"

She pretended to think for a minute, and he tapped her arm. "You know!"

"I do."

She laughed with him. He always asked her, and she always pretended to think. "I saw James at the vegetable stall at the market. He asked about you." She knew that would please him. His smile widened as she knew it would. Caleb always told her he wanted to run a stall at the market when he was older. "And I saw Gideon and Henrietta." She didn't mention where she'd seen them.

He frowned. "I don't like Gideon. He's mean."

"Caleb, that's not how we talk about people," Aaron said. His voice lacked his usual authority. He was not strict with the children and spoke gently when they needed to be reminded to be kind and courteous.

Sapphira wasn't surprised by Caleb's feelings about Gideon, but they concerned her. Caleb spent a lot of time with Gideon while working with Omar and Elam on their property and dealing with the animals. Without Aaron, Caleb would be constantly scolded and ridiculed by Omar and Gideon. Elam would help in defending Caleb, but he could only do so much to mitigate the damage.

The consequences of Aaron's illness got more complicated daily. She needed to convince Aaron to see Jesus of Nazareth so he could be healed, and they could return to a normal life. Aaron helped in the house sometimes, but more and more, he was too tired to do anything. In the past two weeks, his coughing seemed to never stop. She pushed away the fear.

"Gideon helps us out, so stay clear of him when he comes around," she said to Caleb.

"I do. I like Elam, though."

"Good. He's a nice man. Do you need to go back out and help them today?"

"Yes, Elam sent me home to stay with Dad until you returned."

She wondered if Elam had seen Gideon treat Caleb poorly in the fields today. Is that why Elam sent Caleb home for a while?

"I'll put these packages in the kitchen and then go. I'll see you both later," Caleb said.

When he was gone, she looked down at Aaron. He had his eyes closed, but she knew he was awake.

"He is doing well," Sapphira said, sitting on the floor by Aaron.

He opened his eyes. "Yes, he's turning out to be a fine young man. Did we have any influence on him?"

She smiled. "Maybe. I think he was born with a conscience and to know how to do the right thing on every occasion. We're lucky. Rachelle is sweet, and Caleb is obedient."

"Don't get too satisfied. They're still children and could make any number of mistakes yet."

"I'm sure they will. How are you?"

He frowned. "I'm a bit tired of that question. First Demetrius, then Caleb. Now you."

"You're a bit bad-tempered. Did you eat anything today?" She stood up. "I'm sure you didn't."

"I'm not hungry. I'm tired of lying here."

"Yes, definitely irritable." She was surprised to hear herself imitate Aaron's bad mood. When had she dared to criticize Aaron even slightly? Not before he'd become ill. He'd always been a generous, kind, and caring husband, but his words were law. She'd learned that from her father and brother and her mother's subservience. Aaron had never demanded she treat him that way, but she had anyway.

The last few months of Aaron's illness had changed her and their relationship. They'd never really talked about what would happen after Aaron became sick. They both believed it would pass, and things would get back to normal. Here they were, months later. Even if Jesus healed Aaron, they would not be the same people, and their marriage would never be the same.

That night, a month ago when she had finally given up on Aaron getting well had been dark and chilly, and Aaron had coughed more than usual. She'd stood outside their front door on the chilly cobblestone and begged God to make Aaron well. She'd bargained, offering him sacrifice after sacrifice, but when Demetrius had come the next day to check on Aaron, he'd offered no hope.

"He's not getting well. It's only a matter of time." Demetrius had been Aaron's friend for years and his physician for the past four months. The pain in his face at the gravity of the situation was evident.

Her world had changed and shrunk with those four words. "He's not getting well."

"What are you thinking about?" Aaron asked.

Was now the time to ask him about Jesus of Nazareth? Then she heard the steps on the cobblestone outside. Leah was back with Rachelle.

"We'll talk later," Sapphira said.

She gathered Rachelle into a hug and thanked Leah, who shot her a questioning look. Sapphira shook her head.

"Leah, can you help me in the kitchen for a moment? I won't keep you long."

Leah followed her, and they stood by the table in the far corner.

"I haven't told him about Jesus of Nazareth yet," Sapphira whispered. "Don't let John talk to Aaron until I have a chance to convince him."

"We have to warn Jesus about his enemies," Leah whispered back.

"I know, but first I have to convince Aaron that Jesus can heal him. We'll talk later. The girls won't keep him occupied for long." She could hear Ruth and Rachelle telling Aaron something about sheep, and then Rachelle came into the kitchen and got some water.

"I'll let you know later," Sapphira said to Leah.

When Leah left with Ruth, Sapphira went back into the kitchen.

Before she could decide how to approach Aaron, Rachelle came in and hugged her leg. "Mama, I helped Daddy. I got him a drink." Her dark eyes shone as she looked up at Sapphira.

"That's good, honey. I'm sure he liked that."

Rachelle nodded her head vigorously, her black curly hair tumbled about her face. "He did."

At the sound of a cough, she saw Aaron standing in the doorway between the kitchen and the sleeping area. Her heart raced. After thirteen years together, her heart still soared at the sight of him. She'd married him for love, even though their marriage had been arranged. "Should you be up walking around?"

Sapphira instantly regretted greeting him that way. Since he'd become sick, they'd had more arguments about his health than they'd had during their marriage about anything else. Before he'd become ill, she'd never questioned his decisions.

"I'm fine. I wanted to be with you and Rachelle. I'm tired of my mat." Aaron shuffled over and hugged her.

"Let's sit down." She couldn't help it; she wanted to take care of him.

Fortunately, Rachelle caught her attention. "When are we eating, Mama? I'm hungry."

Aaron sat down on a bench at the long pine table and watched them.

"As soon as I get it ready. Until then, you can talk to Daddy or help me."

Rachelle looked back and forth, clearly unable to decide what to do, until Aaron said, "Go help your Mama."

Her look of relief made Sapphira laugh. She was happy to let the little girl distract her from everyday grownup responsibilities.

Rachelle helped Sapphira make a snack of bread and honey for them all. Though Aaron still claimed he wasn't hungry, he ate most of the bread, and Sapphira sighed in relief.

She looked over at Aaron, and his eyes met hers above Rachelle's head. He smiled, and tears came to her eyes. Whatever happened, he loved her.

#

Sapphira had finished cleaning up the kitchen when someone knocked on the door. When she went into the sleeping area, Demetrius stood by the front door.

"Sapphira, I've come to see how Aaron's doing this afternoon." He stepped into the house and looked down at Aaron on the sleeping mat. "Hi, Aaron."

"Thanks for coming back. You can't neglect your other patients for me, though."

Demetrius sat down on the floor beside Aaron. "They get enough of me."

Sapphira knew he was a dedicated physician and continued to examine every patient he had so he could help each one.

"Would you like something to drink?"

"I'll check on him first."

"I'm right here." Aaron's objection mirrored his earlier frustration. He seemed to be more querulous today.

She walked to the kitchen door. "I'll finish up some things while you're talking." She didn't have anything to do, but she left them alone.

She heard the murmur of voices but didn't step close to the door to listen as she usually did. Demetrius had already told her the outcome, as had the Jewish physician. Jesus of Nazareth was the only answer left.

She picked up a tunic she'd left on one end of the bench by the table and started mending a hole. Caleb was hard on his clothes. He ripped the material on posts or fell, creating holes where his knees scraped the rocky ground. Rachelle was no easier on her clothes. She was glad Rachelle enjoyed being outside. She didn't feel the need for her daughter to be the lady that Sapphira had been forced to be at a young age.

Another knock sounded on the door, and Sapphira jerked, poking herself with the needle. She hadn't heard the sound of steps on the cobblestones. She stood to see who had come and saw Demetrius standing by the front door.

"Who is it?" she asked.

Demetrius stepped aside, and Gideon stood there, his red hair bushier than usual. The breeze from outside brought in the scent of dung and dust.

His insolent gaze roamed her body. "I've come to let you know we're starting to clear the north field. Caleb will be home at nightfall. I wanted you to know."

"Thank you for informing us." She looked down at Aaron.

Gideon's gaze followed hers, and he saw Aaron lying there. His expression changed. Sympathy replaced insolence.

"Aaron. Good to see you." Gideon nodded. Then he quickly glanced at Demetrius, and a smug smile edged his lips before he looked back at Sapphira. "Good day." He turned and left.

She shut the door after him and looked at Demetrius. "I don't like that man." She sighed. "But he has helped us with the fields while Aaron has been ill. Without his help and his father's, I don't know what we would have done."

"I would help you," Demetrius said.

Sapphira shook her head. "You're a physician. There are other ways you've helped, and I'm grateful to you for everything you've done for

Aaron. You've been his friend, and that has helped him as much as your care of him."

Demetrius bowed his head. "Thank you. I doubt that I deserve such praise when I haven't been able to do anything."

The frustration in his voice was plain to her. "He needs a miracle."

She looked up at that. "I've prayed, and nothing's happened." She couldn't keep the bitterness from her voice.

"God doesn't always answer in the way we expect." Aaron's voice startled her. She'd been caught up in thinking that Jesus of Nazareth was the miracle she'd prayed for, and now she needed to talk to Aaron. With Demetrius here, it might be best. Aaron might listen to her if she weren't the only one talking to him about Jesus, and Demetrius might be intrigued to meet Jesus.

Energized, she sat down cross-legged by Aaron and gestured Demetrius to join them. When he'd sat down, Sapphira plunged into her plan.

"I know you've been patient in spite of me going to talk to the Jewish physician to ask for help." She kept the disaster of stealing the scrolls to herself. "I know miracles are rare, but I have an idea. I'd like you both to listen to what I have to say without interrupting."

They both nodded. She could tell Aaron wasn't surprised that she had another plan.

"Leah and I went to a meeting today. A Friends of Jesus meeting."

"You what?" Aaron yelled.

She jumped. That was the loudest he'd spoken in ages.

"We went to a Friends of Jesus meeting."

"Do you know who they are, Sapphira?" Demetrius asked. "They're a very bad group of people, and you shouldn't associate with them."

Aaron frowned at her.

"I didn't know that before the meeting today, but I do now. I didn't go to join. I only wanted to ask them where to find Jesus of Nazareth. I thought they were his friends. I didn't realize…"

"That they weren't really friends?" Demetrius didn't seem surprised.

So, he'd known. But she hadn't thought to have Leah ask Demetrius about the group. She'd been in such a hurry to see what she could find out about Jesus and where she could find him. Now that she'd told Aaron and Demetrius, however, Gideon didn't have any power over her. Except for the stolen scrolls.

"No, they aren't his friends. In fact, they want to kill him." She shouldn't have said that last part.

"Kill him?" Aaron sat up and started coughing.

She moved to help him, but he waved her away.

When he could talk, he said, "Who was there? Who plans to kill him?"

"Tarad did most of the talking. He said Jesus was being blasphemous and sacrilegious, and he needed to be stopped. Tarad said the rumors of healing were spread by Jesus's followers and weren't really true."

Demetrius shook his head. "They are true. At least, I know some of the stories are true. I heard from a friend of a friend of Lazarus that Jesus of Nazareth really did bring Lazarus back to life."

Sapphira leaned toward him. "Do you believe it's true?"

Demetrius looked over at Aaron. "I think it's true. I believe Jesus of Nazareth can perform miracles."

"That's why I think we should take Aaron to see Jesus. Jesus can heal him. That's our miracle." She watched them and waited to see what Aaron would say.

The men looked at her and then at each other. She couldn't tell if the idea had taken hold and if they were considering it or not. She waited until she couldn't stand their silence. "If we don't go to get Aaron cured, we at least need to save Jesus."

Demetrius looked at her as if she had lost her mind. "Save Jesus? Do you have any idea how many enemies that man has? We would never be able to save him. And who is going to kill him? Did they say at that meeting?"

"They are turning him over to some other men. They have it all planned out."

Aaron shook his head. "There's no way we can make it. I'm too sick. I can hardly walk into the kitchen. And how would we even find him?"

Sapphira wasn't about to give up, even if she had to argue with Aaron all day. Demetrius hadn't said no about taking Aaron to see Jesus. He'd only said they couldn't save Jesus. "We can get Elam and John to carry you."

Aaron was shaking his head before she finished. "Carry me? How far would that be? Plus, they both have jobs they can't leave for long."

"We could hire someone to carry you," Sapphira said desperately. "Think about it, Aaron. That's all I ask. Don't give me your answer today. Think about it overnight. If you'll only agree to it, we'll find a way. Jesus raised someone from the dead. He can heal you. Please…."

"I'd like to meet Jesus," Demetrius said. He didn't look at either of them when he said this.

"They are going to kill him soon, so if you really want to meet him, you don't have much time. Are we allowing this to happen if we can stop it?" Sapphira got up and went to the kitchen. Aaron looked at her when she asked him to think about it. He'd given up on life and was ready to die.

She walked back into the room where Aaron rested. She looked down at him. "I know where to find Jesus. He can heal you. I know he can. I'm not ready for you to die yet, even if you are." She walked out the door.

CHAPTER 10

Sapphira went next door to talk to Leah. The short walk did nothing to lessen her anger at Aaron. How dare he give up on life when there was a possibility that Jesus could heal him? He hadn't even wanted to discuss it with her.

Demetrius wanted to take Aaron on the trip. She could tell by the way he said that he wanted to see Jesus. If she could convince John and Leah, they might be able to convince Aaron. They could make a group of John, Leah, Demetrius, and Elam to take Aaron to where Jesus would be. Jesus would be traveling, so they'd have to plan for their paths to intersect. But it could be done.

She knocked on Leah's open door and waited for her to appear. Leah and John's house was made from the same mudbrick as the other houses on the road. The inside of the house had the same three rooms that were similar in layout to Sapphira's house. One room was the sleeping room, one room was the kitchen, and one room held the animals that did not roam Omar's land. Omar had made a deal with John to allow his animals to graze on Omar's land in exchange for John's services as a thatcher.

Looking in at the living and sleeping area that Leah decorated with lots of earthenware pots and flowers, she waited for Leah to greet her. Sapphira hadn't had a chance to find out what Leah's opinion was regarding seeing Jesus. There had been no time between baking bread, feeding the men, and attending the meeting to discuss the options.

"Sapphira, come in." Leah stood in the kitchen doorway, drying her hands on a linen towel. "I was wiping up a water spill. Ruth is determined to do everything on her own these days. She's all grown up at six, according to her. She's in the kitchen playing with her doll and telling her stories."

"Rachelle is at home probably doing the same thing. I walked out on Aaron because he made me so mad. She's with him." Which is not the way it used to be. Aaron had been in the fields with the other men, and Rachelle had always been with Sapphira. Sapphira would never have walked out on a discussion with Aaron.

Leah held out her hand and gestured toward the chairs of pale pinewood, crafted to be curved where a person sat down. Scrolled leaves and vines carved into the wood decorated the backs of the chairs. "Let's sit down and talk. Ruth will be busy for a while, and she'll let me know if she needs something."

After they sat in the chairs in the corner of the room, Leah asked, "Are you all right?"

Sapphira bit her lip. She appreciated Leah's concern, but she didn't have time to think about how she felt right now. "I'm fine. What do you think of Jesus healing Aaron?"

"Well…don't you think it's a risk?"

"We know what's going to happen if Aaron doesn't see him. This is his last chance."

"What if we take Aaron and can't find Jesus?"

"We'll find him. They mentioned his route at the meeting. I know this is the right thing to do." If only someone could help her convince everyone else. Sapphira wished Leah was less meek at a time like this. "Demetrius wants to make the trip."

"He does?" Leah tapped her fingers on her lap.

While Leah thought about it, Sapphira held still, waiting. When Leah looked up, Sapphira said, "Yes, Demetrius said he is willing to go. I think he not only wants to help Aaron, but he wants to see the great healer. Why wouldn't he? As a physician, Demetrius would find it fascinating to meet a man who can heal people so miraculously."

"What if Aaron dies on the road?" Leah asked this gently, but she needn't have been concerned.

"He's dying anyway. This is our only chance. Omar's going to force me to marry Gideon if Aaron dies." She wanted to tell Leah about Gideon's actions the night they stole the scrolls, but she didn't dare confess what she'd done. "Caleb doesn't like Gideon, and Gideon will treat him cruelly. Please, Leah? Will you try to convince John to help?"

"Who else do you want to come along?"

Sapphira noticed Leah didn't agree to help her. "Elam, John, and Demetrius. They can take turns helping to carry Aaron, or we can find a wagon to pull behind one of the horses." Aaron weighed so little now. "Omar and Gideon should be able to manage the farm during that time. It would only be two days at the most. The trip would last about a half day. Then we would need to find Jesus, which shouldn't take very long. Others will know where he is. We'll follow the crowds."

Leah got up and put her arm around Sapphira, gave her a quick one-armed hug, and sat down again. "I think you might be depending too much on this trip and Jesus."

"Don't you believe that he could cure Aaron?"

"It's not that exactly. The trip itself will make Aaron worse. I think…" Leah didn't finish.

"That we should stay home and wait." Sapphira finished the sentence for her. She stood up and restlessly paced around the small room. The flowers stirred in jars set in each corner. Heat she hadn't previously noticed flushed her cheeks, and she fanned her hand in front of her face. If Leah didn't agree to this, then she wouldn't be able to get the men to help her. What could she say to convince Leah?

Sapphira sat down and leaned toward Leah. "What would you do if it were John? Would you wait for the end?"

"Yes, I would." She smiled gently. "But that's me, and that's not you."

Sapphira shook her head. "That's not me. I'm pregnant."

"What?"

"I'm pregnant. Aaron will never see this child."

Leah slumped back in her chair. "Does Aaron know?"

"I haven't told him yet. I will if he doesn't agree to make the trip to see Jesus." Her conscience stung at using their baby this way.

"I'll talk to John. I'll do what I can to convince him."

Sapphira smiled and leaned over to hug Leah tightly. "Thank you. You know Aaron means everything to me." She leaned back against the chair.

"You still have someone more stubborn than me to talk into this plan. You have Aaron."

"That will take time. We'll both have to do some strong talking to our men. At least Demetrius is agreeable once we have John and Aaron convinced."

#

Sapphira returned home to find Aaron and Rachelle in the kitchen talking to one of Rachelle's dolls. The dark-haired doll had an exquisite blue tunic with decorative embroidered white flowers along the hem that had been sewn by Sapphira's mother. Sapphira passed the doll on to Rachelle when she was old enough to play with it.

Aaron's breath rasped as he breathed, and she wondered why she hadn't noticed that when they were talking with Demetrius earlier.

"I thought you were sleeping. How long have you been up?" She took his arm to lead him back to his mat.

He shook off her hand and stayed sitting by Rachelle. "Don't fuss. You were at Leah's?"

"Yes, we had a nice talk." She didn't want to tell him she had spent the whole time convincing Leah how important it was for Aaron to see Jesus. Would Leah be able to convince John? Sapphira had her own work ahead of her in convincing Aaron.

He studied her face. "You're tired."

She knew she must look a mess. She'd been running around all day. The early start of making bread at Naomi's, feeding the men, the meeting about Jesus. It all ran into one long, emotional day, which wasn't over. She blinked to keep the tears away. She didn't have time to cry right now.

His concerned eyes examined her face. "You have been different lately. I've noticed. What's wrong?"

"You know what's wrong." The sleepless nights and worry broke through her control. She started crying.

He got up and put his arms around her.

Rachelle set her doll on the table. "What's wrong with Mama?" Her lower lip quivered.

Sapphira tried to pull away to go to Rachelle, but Aaron wouldn't let her go.

"Mama's tired. She needs to lie down. Come, Sapphira." He tugged her toward the mattress.

She looked back at Rachelle. "I'll be fine. Don't worry. Daddy will take care of me. You play with your doll." She lay down.

He lay down beside her and settled her head on his chest.

The comfort caused more tears to fall. He let her cry. He knew her so well. Her sobs increased, and he patted her back. She couldn't make out his words, but the murmuring soothed her. Exhausted, she finally fell asleep.

CHAPTER 11

Aaron watched Rachelle play with her doll at the table when he heard steps on the cobblestones outside their front door and then a light knock. He was weak but made his way to the door as fast as he could to keep the visitor from waking Sapphira. Stifling his cough was difficult, but Sapphira didn't wake.

Elam stood on the doorstep, waiting for him.

Aaron walked outside, shut the front door, and drew Elam a few paces away so they could talk uninterrupted. The hot day had given way to a cool evening, and Aaron felt a chill pass through his chest. "Sapphira's resting, so we'll talk out here."

"It's good to see you up and about, Aaron." Elam's reddish-gray hair bristled in the slight breeze.

"The day's been good to me." Taking care of Sapphira eased his conscience. The burden of their life fell on her more every day.

"You didn't come away from work just to talk with me, did you?" Aaron was out of breath and realized how weak his knees had become. He leaned against the wall to rest.

"I shouldn't have come until tomorrow morning." He patted the gray hair on his chin.

"This is fine. I'm sure you're busy, and I appreciate that you stopped. What did you have to tell me? Is it Sapphira?" He wanted to make this easy on Elam. He should never have asked him to watch Sapphira.

"Yes, she went to the Friends of Jesus meeting this afternoon. She went with Leah, so I thought it was all right. But then I heard some things about the group. They're not friends. They're enemies."

"Sapphira admitted she'd gone to the meeting and what had happened there. She said the group is planning on killing Jesus."

Elam bent his troubled face and looked at the ground. "That's not good. Not good at all."

"She wants me to go see Jesus. She thinks he can heal me."

At this, Elam's gaze lifted. "Possibly he could. Are you going?"

"I don't think so."

Elam gave a mighty sigh. "This troubles me to say, but you need to know. When you're gone, Omar's going to force Sapphira to marry Gideon. You know I love my son, but he's no man to marry your wife. You should consider the trip to see Jesus." With that, he walked away, shoulders stooped.

Aaron stood there, watching him go. Elam would have never said anything if the situation hadn't been dire. It had cost his friend to speak so honestly about his son.

#

When Sapphira awoke, it was dark, and Aaron wasn't beside her. She stirred, feeling guilty at dumping the work on him, but also refreshed from finally getting some rest. She heard coughing from the other room, and then the high-pitched giggle of Rachelle's and Caleb's voices. Caleb's voice sometimes cracked when he spoke, but at other times, he had the deep man's voice that would soon be his normal tone.

She heard the rattle of dishes and knew that Aaron had let her sleep, and the children were getting the evening meal ready. She should get up and help, but she didn't move. The children were content. She would be letting Aaron help—the way he wanted to help—if she continued to rest. She closed her eyes but couldn't sleep anymore.

Now that she felt better, she was ashamed of the scene with Demetrius and Aaron. What did Demetrius think of her now? That she was a fishwife. An ungrateful wretch. She sighed. Demetrius liked her a little too much, and she was beginning to feel an attraction to him, too. She couldn't let that happen.

She needed to keep some distance between them. How on earth would it benefit her to lead him on? She would soon be a widow with two children. She couldn't have him thinking she'd set her sights on him as a substitute father and husband, though he would be better than Gideon.

She felt guilty even thinking of a possible replacement for Aaron, but she couldn't raise two children on her own, and she did not want to move in with Omar and Naomi. Though she was beginning to think she'd misjudged Naomi, she didn't want to live in her house. When she'd told Demetrius not to tell Omar how bad Aaron's illness was, Demetrius had understood. She hadn't had to explain that her home was with Aaron in the house they'd built, and she wasn't moving until there was no alternative.

She stood up, not wanting to think anymore about her brother's plans for her.

When she entered the kitchen, Rachelle ran to her and hugged her. Caleb offered to get her a plate of food. Aaron examined her face, nodded with a satisfied gleam in his eyes, and then he winked at her. She lowered herself against Rachelle's shoulder to hide her expression.

Aaron hadn't winked at her in months.

Later, when the children were occupied with their games in the sleeping room, she and Aaron were in the kitchen. Sapphira mended a tunic, humming under her breath, pleased with the evening.

Aaron sat down across from her at the table. "I've been giving it some thought."

She looked up from her sewing. "Thought about what?"

He set his elbows on the table and leaned forward. "The stories we've heard about Jesus of Nazareth. The meeting you were at today."

Thrilled that Aaron had brought up the subject, she went back to her sewing. "Are you still angry at me for going with Leah?"

"No, I'm just glad neither of you was hurt. Those are some rough people according to Elam."

Her head jerked up. "When did you talk to Elam?"

"While you were sleeping. He wanted to give me an update on the field work."

"I must have been sound asleep. I didn't hear him."

Aaron reached across and patted her hand. "I'm happy that you were able to rest, and I'm not angry about the meeting. You went. It's done. I think Elam and Demetrius would go with us if we went."

She looked up again from her sewing. "You would go? What made you change your mind?"

"I haven't made up my mind, but I think we should talk about it and see if it's realistic. Plus, we must see if there's anything we can do to save Jesus. I need to think about that, too."

She knew it was hard for him to admit that he would need help. He had always been a strong man until his illness, and now he would have to depend on others. They would make it only a short way before the other men would have to carry Aaron unless Jesus stuck to the main roads.

"Jesus will be traveling from Bethany to Ephraim. That's what they said. We'll have to decide soon, or we won't be able to catch up to him and his followers."

"I know. I wanted you to know I'm thinking about going."

"If we do go, we'll need to plan, so don't wait until the last minute." Even though she said it, she didn't mean it. If they had to go in the middle of the night, she would arrange things so it would happen.

"I'm not sure I believe all the stories about him. What if we go, and he can't do anything for me? Don't you think it's blasphemous to believe anyone other than God can heal me? Shouldn't I be praying harder?"

Surprised at his mention of prayer, she put down the tunic she was mending. "Why are you praying? We've never talked about praying."

He wouldn't meet her gaze. "I grew up Jewish and left the faith when I moved here to Naraah."

"You never told me." She picked up her mending, but just held it in her hands.

"There are some other things that happened." He still wouldn't look at her.

Did he want to tell her about them? She couldn't tell, but her silence brought no more admissions. She responded. "I've prayed, too. My parents were Jewish, but when they died and Omar took over the family, that ended. I don't know what I believe anymore. We need to do something. I need you to be around for me and the children. This is the only chance we have left. I don't think it goes against God to try."

"Maybe not. But I need to pray about it."

How long had he been praying? What else didn't she know about him? What didn't he know about her?

"I'm pregnant, Aaron." She hadn't meant to tell him now.

He stared for a moment, and then a big smile broke across his face. It melted away all the pain and suffering he'd endured in the past months, and she was glad she'd told him. For this moment, they could be happy.

#

A few days had passed since pushing Aaron to decide to see Jesus. Leah was still working on convincing John. John was waiting for Aaron to make up his mind.

Aaron was finally considering the trip. After telling him about the pregnancy and her recurring inclination to cry, he treated her with more care, going out of his way to be kind and thoughtful. He had talked about warning Jesus about the men who were after him. Aaron had started talking about the trip as if it might happen. Either way, it was now a possibility. She couldn't forget that time was a factor, too. Aaron didn't have long, maybe only a week.

CHAPTER 12

Aaron woke feeling satisfied. He thought he'd been quiet enough through the night that Sapphira had finally had a good night's sleep. Suppressing a cough, he slid from his mat and went to the kitchen. The children were already up and dressed. Caleb was outside helping the men with the preparations for the day. Today was the final day of clearing the fields to plant wheat and barley.

Rachelle's sandals were on the wrong feet. He helped her switch them as she giggled quietly.

"What are you two giggling about?" Sapphira asked from the doorway. She was dressed for the day, too.

"Daddy helped me with my sandals." She lifted her feet so Sapphira could see.

"Nice." Sapphira smiled sleepily at them both and sat at the table.

"Would you like some breakfast?" Aaron was pleased to see her face relaxed for a change.

"I'll get up in a minute to work on it. Sit down." She pointed at the chair across from her. "Where's Caleb?"

"He went outside to help Gideon, Elam, and John. Leah said to let her know when you're ready, and she'll help you with the bread."

Sapphira stood up. "Then I guess I'd better get busy. It sounds like everyone is already working, and I've been lazy." She smoothed Rachelle's hair as she walked by.

"Mama's lazy. Mama's lazy." She giggled again.

Aaron squashed the helpless feeling that rose within him. He couldn't help outside. He couldn't do much inside either. The wild plan Sapphira had concocted began to seem like an option. It was his only chance. And Sapphira's only chance.

He hated his helplessness. The indignity of having his friends carry him to Jesus. Was this the right thing to do? Who was Jesus of Nazareth? Would God understand if Aaron put his faith in a healer who walked around the country preaching?

Demetrius would be an objective voice. Or maybe not. Demetrius would definitely want to meet Jesus, one healer to another. That didn't make the trip the right choice, though.

He smiled at the thought. The idea of meeting Jesus, even if Jesus couldn't heal Aaron, was worth the trip. He began to feel hope that he might see the new child he and Sapphira were having.

Elam's words about Gideon came back to him. Gideon wouldn't be a good husband to Sapphira, and Caleb didn't like him.

"You look thoughtful this morning. What's going on in that mind of yours?" Sapphira watched him from the other side of the table where she mixed batter to make breakfast.

"What's not to be happy about? I've got my two best girls right here with me."

"Mama's not a girl." Rachelle stood on a chair and moved bowls of flour and water around the table.

"What is she then?" Aaron longed to lift Rachelle up on his shoulder like he used to do before he got too weak to do much more than crawl out of bed in the morning.

"She's a lady."

The front door opened suddenly, and there was Caleb. "Is breakfast ready? I'm hungry."

Aaron looked at his son and frowned. He was nearly a man, and while Aaron hoped for a miracle, he wondered who would be there for Caleb if he didn't live. Demetrius was a fine man, and Aaron had noticed a special look in Demetrius's eyes whenever he'd looked at Sapphira lately. Aaron tried not to be jealous, but he was, although Sapphira had never returned Demetrius's looks or was even aware of them. He would prefer Demetrius to succeed him rather than Gideon.

He felt his family slipping away from him, and he knew there was only one thing he could do to keep his family together. Find Jesus and be healed. Reports of magnificent miracles from all over Bethany, Jerusalem, and the surrounding countryside came via travelers. The blind were able to see; the lame could walk. Jesus had even absolved a prostitute. Aaron didn't care so much for himself, but he cared about his family. He didn't want Sapphira to continue struggling if there was a way for him to live and take care of her. And he didn't want Sapphira to marry Gideon.

Caleb and Rachelle had finished eating and left the house, and Aaron had managed to eat a few bites when someone knocked and then opened the door without waiting for an answer.

Leah walked in with a burlap sack that clunked as she walked. "The children said you were eating breakfast, so I thought I'd come in and get us started." She set the sack on the table. "And while we're working, I can fill you in on the latest gossip in Naraah."

"That sounds exciting." Aaron was surprised. Leah didn't generally gossip.

"You'll want to hear this." She unloaded some figs, olives, and spices from her bag, lining them up on the table. "Someone stole some scrolls from that synagogue the Jewish physician attends. When Philip arrived today, he found them gone."

"How do you know that?" Sapphira asked.

"Esther stopped by and told me."

"Esther visited?" Sapphira opened the bag of spices.

"Do they have any idea who took them?" Aaron asked at the same time.

"They don't know. There was a pregnant woman in the synagogue that night, but they didn't see anyone else during the time the scrolls might have been stolen.

"Those scrolls are priceless. Esther said they would probably bring in a lot of money if someone sold them illegally. They'd have to take the scrolls to Jerusalem, though. No one around here would buy them."

Aaron thought about the bands of ruffians Demetrius had told him were going from town to town, stealing precious religious artifacts. "Have you talked to Demetrius?"

"I haven't seen him today. I know he has a lot of contact with travelers and knows more about the possibilities than I do. He'll be here today, as always. I know he is here quite often."

Aaron caught the knowing glance Leah threw Sapphira's way, and he flushed from jealousy. How dare she? He was not dead yet. "I don't expect him today. He was here only yesterday."

"But I thought…" Her voice trailed away.

"Do they have any idea who the pregnant woman is?" Sapphira brought them back to the original subject.

"No. Philip said that he doubts they'll see the items again."

"That's a shame." She measured out another portion of meal and stirred it into the bowl.

"I heard something else, too." Leah hesitated. "It's about Jesus."

Aaron saw Sapphira open her mouth and then close it again. He wondered if she would tell Leah to keep it to herself. She'd been trying to wait quietly for his decision.

He did believe Jesus had done these miracles. He intended to tell her today that he would make the trip. First, he needed to talk to Demetrius and see how they could get him to wherever Jesus was at the moment. The trip would use up the last of his strength, so this morning spending time with his family was precious to him.

Leah plunked some grapes into a bowl. "There are some more men planning on killing him. I think they are soldiers and guards from the chief priests and Pharisees." She looked directly at Aaron. "We don't have long."

He knew what she meant. It was either now or never. It was unusual for a woman to speak so frankly to a man who wasn't her husband, but he didn't take offense. Leah was looking out for Sapphira, and Sapphira would need her in the days to come.

"I'll talk to Demetrius today." That's all he would say, and he left the women to their cooking.

Sapphira hadn't said anything, he thought, which was unlike her, as he passed by his mat on the floor where he spent most of his time these days. He was tired of it all.

"I think I'll go check on Rachelle," he said, wanting to get away and think about what he'd heard. He could not meditate on it here with the women gossiping in the next room.

"She's in the courtyard with Ruth," Leah told him.

The courtyard was behind their houses, enclosed by a mud-brick wall around the perimeter. The families along their side of the road used the courtyard to take their animals from the back room of the houses around to the road. The younger children also played in the courtyard.

Sapphira and Aaron did not have any animals in their back room at the moment, as Omar was taking care of them until Aaron was well. Or that had been the plan in the beginning.

The courtyard had a large grove of olive trees and grape vines where the children played. Rachelle and Ruth were allowed to play in the courtyard by themselves, so supervision wasn't necessary.

When he slowly got outside, he saw Rachelle at one end of the courtyard handing a kitten to Ruth. He sat on the ground and watched her, not wanting to disturb her play. He enjoyed the chance to watch her play. He wanted to see her become a woman, watch her with her own children. He wanted the chance to become a grandfather.

Jesus of Nazareth was the answer. If he could raise a man from the dead, he could heal Aaron. Couldn't he? If Aaron made the trip, could he somehow get to see Jesus and be healed? There had to be hundreds, if not thousands, of Jesus's followers. Finding the man would not be difficult. Getting through the crowds could be a problem. Demetrius would help. Demetrius would want to go himself. It was a once-in-a-lifetime chance for the experience of seeing a renowned healer at work. Miracles. He could witness, be part of his own miracle.

He started to cough and knew he should lie down. Rachelle looked up and smiled at him. She waved, and he waved back. She went back to her play, and he entered the house and went to his bed. He half lay, half sat as he planned the trip. He'd talk to Demetrius to make sure Demetrius thought it was even possible for him to make the journey before he told Sapphira. He fell asleep. When he woke, he heard Demetrius's voice in the kitchen talking to Leah and Sapphira, as if the trip was ordained.

He sat up, which made him cough. It brought Demetrius to his side, which didn't surprise him. Some things were predictable. Demetrius probably wanted to get away from the women, although he had a close relationship with his sister.

"Aaron." Demetrius leaned over and hugged him warmly.

He returned the hug. "Demetrius, you must have other patients. You cannot neglect them for me."

"They see enough of me. I consider you a friend, and you come first."

Aaron wanted to ask what Demetrius felt for Sapphira, but he stifled the impulse. He did not like these feelings of irritation and jealousy toward Demetrius, but it was hard when he was confined in bed most of the time, and Demetrius was so virile and good-looking and healthy. "Thank you. You are a good friend." And a friend wouldn't take steps to steal away a wife from a man who was dying. "And as a friend, I have a special favor to ask you."

Demetrius knelt on the floor by the mat where Aaron lay. "You know I'll do anything I can to help you, but I don't think there's much I can do."

Aaron waved that away. "I know you've done the best you can, and I thank you. This is something different." He paused and took a deep breath. This was it. "I'd like to take the trip."

"But…"

"Hear me out first. I'd like to go to see Jesus. It's only a half-day trip. I can make it there, Demetrius." He saw the doubt in Demetrius's eyes. "I know I can. It might take us a little time to find Jesus on the road, but I don't believe that will be a problem."

Demetrius sank back on his heels. "Why? It might shorten what time you have left. You know

I'll be happy to go with you and meet this Jesus of Nazareth for myself, but you must know the risk."

"The risk that we won't get there in time? Or that we can't find him? Or that he can't heal me?"

"Yes to all of that."

"Jesus is my only chance. You see that, don't you? And you said you'd like to meet the great healer. This is your chance. And if he can save my life, you'll see a miracle with your own eyes."

Demetrius's excitement shown in his eyes. "I really do want to meet him. I've wanted to ever since I heard of all the miracles he's done. But…"

"But I've been sick." Aaron finished for him. "And you've been a good friend. You haven't left my side."

Demetrius smiled at Aaron. "I'd do the same thing over again."

"I know." Aaron smiled back and held out his hand. "Let's go."

Demetrius took his hand, clasped it, and let it go. "Yes, let's go. We'll need to talk with John. I know my brother-in-law wants to go. He was waiting for you to agree and see the wisdom of this."

"So, you've all been waiting for me?"

"Yes."

"As I've been told the past few days, I don't have much time, so we should start to make plans. Let's talk to the others tomorrow morning. I will let Sapphira know later today. We'll pack tomorrow and leave the next day."

They spent their remaining time together making plans. They hoped to get Elam and Gideon to go with them to help carry Aaron when necessary. Aaron wasn't pleased about including Gideon, but he knew they needed one more man, and it wasn't going to be Omar. Omar would need to stay and run the farm along with Caleb.

CHAPTER 13

Sapphira sensed an underlying excitement in Aaron's mood after Demetrius left. They had spent a lot of time whispering while she and Leah worked in the kitchen.

She barely heard Leah's words as she talked about the happenings in town. What were Aaron and Demetrius talking about? Was it the trip to see Jesus? She heard Aaron laugh. That was good. It reminded her of days not that long ago when Aaron was healthy.

She hadn't realized how unhappy they'd both become. Death hung over every conversation, and fear and confusion were steady companions. They'd forgotten how to laugh with each other. Their only joy came secondhand from Caleb and Rachelle, though Caleb was getting entirely too serious lately. Was that a natural part of growing up or a consequence of Aaron's illness?

"You're not listening." Leah stood at the table, observing her.

"I was thinking."

"Of Aaron and what he and Demetrius are plotting?" Leah smiled at her.

"Yes."

"Maybe Aaron has decided to go."

Sapphira glanced into the sleeping room where Demetrius and Aaron were whispering. "I'm afraid to believe that's what's going on."

Leah nodded. "I would be, too, but I know Demetrius. He's excited. If they were talking about not going, Demetrius would be somber. The atmosphere is different today, isn't it?"

"Yes, you're right." She tried to still the hope that grew stronger with each laugh she heard in the other room. What if Aaron said no after all of her plotting? "What did John say?"

"He'll go if Aaron goes." Leah twirled around to Sapphira's side of the table and hugged her before she went back to her own side of the table. "We're going to see Jesus," she sang.

Sapphira grinned at her friend's antics and felt her spirits rise. "You are so silly. We have a ways to go before we're on the road." She went back to thinking about her own preparations. "But…we should make plenty of bread to take with us, so we'd better get busy."

They grinned at each other and then worked at a steady pace, knowing that if they were to make this trip, they needed to make at least two days' worth of food in case it took them longer to find Jesus than planned.

Sapphira tried to contain her excitement. What if Demetrius and Aaron weren't planning on taking the trip to see Jesus? What if they were talking about what to do when Aaron died? She couldn't think that way. They were laughing. If Jesus could heal Aaron, then she needed to trust that the trip would happen.

CHAPTER 14

Aaron waited until Leah had left before he talked to Sapphira. The way she'd been acting lately bothered him, but he didn't know what to do about it. She'd gone to the Friends of Jesus meeting without telling him and talked to the daughter of a highly regarded Jewish physician. Now he was ready to tell her about agreeing to make the trip see Jesus of Nazareth and hoped she wouldn't get any further ideas in her head. At some point, he also needed to tell her about his family in case he didn't make it home again.

She was convinced Jesus was the answer. After she'd told him about her and Leah's attendance at the Friends of Jesus meeting, he'd seen hope in her eyes for the first time in months.

Aaron was also excited about his trip to see Jesus. He knew Sapphira was right to go to the meeting, even though it had been a dangerous thing to do. She wanted him to get well and believed this was the only way. Demetrius had briefly stopped by again and told Aaron he wasn't sure how Aaron would fare on the trip, but Aaron had decided to take the chance anyway.

They'd always discussed traveling. They'd even talked about leaving the children with Omar and going somewhere. Then he'd become ill, and the topic hadn't come up again. The idea of seeing Jesus and traveling through the hill country should bring some sparkle back to her eyes.

Caleb had gone to help Omar with chores, and Leah had taken Rachelle with her to play with Ruth. Aaron had asked Sapphira to send them away so he could talk to her. She knew he'd come to some decision, but she didn't know if it was yes or no.

He joined Sapphira tidying in the kitchen.

He tugged the dish towel from her hand, and she looked questioningly at him.

"Are you all right?"

"Fine." Aaron let the excitement flow through him and out his voice. The day of repressing his excitement had been long. "Better than fine. How would you like to go on that trip?" He eagerly awaited her response.

She threw her arms around him. "You've decided to go. I'm so glad."

He smiled. This was his Sapphira who he'd been missing for months. Her enthusiasm had kept their lives exciting. "I want to go on a trip with my lovely wife." He put his arms around her and tried to swing her in a circle but ended up coughing instead.

She pulled away from him and pushed him onto a kitchen chair. "Sit. I'll get you a drink."

He didn't let the sternness of her voice depress him. And his cough was a mere annoyance now that there was a spark of hope that he'd have a future with Sapphira. And see Caleb and Rachelle grow up. He took a swallow of water and leaned back against the chair.

"You worried me. I didn't think you were going to come to your senses. Couldn't you have told me earlier today after you and Demetrius made all those plans?"

Her lecture didn't bother him. "Demetrius said John would go. He said he had to force John to stay away until I'd made up my own mind. He was ready to haul me over his shoulder until we reached Jesus."

She sat down across the table from him. "That sounds like John. While you and Demetrius were whispering, Leah assured me that you had finally decided to go. She was dancing around the kitchen."

"Because I'm going to be cured." The smile returned to his face. He could feel it stretching his lips, and it felt good.

"We'll have to tell the children. I hate to leave Rachelle with Naomi, but we don't have any choice. Leah is coming with us."

"I know. Just think. When we come back, I'll be well. That will make up for the time we're away from Rachelle and Caleb. It will only be for a day or two."

"I know. There's no one else to leave her with." She bit her lip.

"Don't worry. She'll be fine. We'll make sure that Caleb keeps an eye on her. He's so protective of his little sister."

"I hope that Omar doesn't work him too hard."

"Just think, when I come back, all of this pain will be gone. I know you've taken on most of the burden of caring for the children while I've been sick, but let's look at the future."

He knew she was worried that the trip would kill him, and he wouldn't come back at all. "I'm going to see Jesus, and he'll heal me. We have to believe that."

She jumped up from the table, black hair swinging. "Fine. We need to get busy, and you need to rest."

"But, Sapphira…"

"You are not getting out of bed until it's time to leave." She folded her arms across her chest.

He felt the need to assert himself. He'd been ailing for too long, and she had to know he was finished with that. "Yes, I am," he said quietly. "There will be a lot to do. I can't expect you to do everything."

She looked ready to argue with him. "Be reasonable," she pleaded.

"I guess you're right. I need to take it easy, but I'm so excited. This is my only chance to become well again. To live a long life with you and the children."

"You can be excited and resting at the same time. Right?" She was standing with her arms folded and her sandaled foot tapping the floor. "Right?"

"Fine. I can still plan while I rest, so don't expect me to keep quiet."

She smiled. "You rest and plan. Leah and I will do what you tell us. I'm sure when Elam and Gideon get here, you can tell them what to do, and they'll be happy to fulfill your orders."

She stopped, biting her lip again. "You'll not overexert yourself. Please." She didn't want to tell him what was gnawing on her mind.

Aaron could tell something was bothering her, and he was scared. More scared of losing her this way than of dying. "Tell me. I can take whatever it is."

"I…" She stopped again. "I don't want you to die on the road," she blurted out. She sat down. "You're a stubborn man. I want as many days as I can get, and if we travel, you'll…be gone sooner. I know it. I'm afraid to hope."

Her dark eyes looked bruised and sad, and he didn't like the suffering he saw there. "I know, but this is my only hope, Sapphira."

She smiled ruefully. "I know that. I pushed the idea, remember? I want you to make it there. I never could resist those eyes of yours."

"Then I have another request." He scooted his chair over to hers. "How about a kiss?" He didn't wait and slid his hand behind her neck and pulled her to him.

He loved the taste of her soft lips and regretted that he could do no more than kiss her. Even that made him so short of breath he had to stop and cough. The mood was shattered.

When he stopped coughing, she said, "We have lots to do. Go rest."

Some of his excitement drained away with the rising fatigue. "Fine. For now. You'll see. A few days from now, I'll once again be the man you married."

"I love you."

He was puzzled by the anger in her eyes.

"I love you as much when you're ill as when you're well. Of course, I want you to get well, but you'd better not die on me during this trip. And

Jesus may not choose to heal you, or we might not find him." She glared at him, then got up and walked away to lay down in the sleeping area.

He stared at her, shocked by the last statement. He understood anger masked her fear. But he didn't understand her sudden, yet brief, disbelief in Jesus. As much as he wanted to argue with her, he let her be. She would accept the idea of the trip and be as excited as him.

He stood up and painstakingly made his way across the room. He was tired from the excitement and Sapphira's outburst. He stood in the doorway. "Demetrius is coming with us. He'll take care of me."

"I can take care of you," Sapphira mumbled into the pillow, as she lay there facedown.

Her voice was husky, and he thought she might have been crying. "He'll help. You'll see. Things will work out."

"I want them to work out. I really do."

He had to strain to hear her muffled words, and his heart ached. "It's going to be all right."

She sniffed. She was crying. He lay down beside her and held her in his arms. "Shhh…it's all right."

CHAPTER 15

Later that afternoon, Sapphira and Leah's walk to Naomi's house passed in a flurry of plans for the coming trip. The day was clear and sunny, but neither woman noticed as they carried supplies that would make up their food during their travel time.

Patches of grass set in the dry hillside waved in the breeze as they walked along. Rachelle had run ahead with Ruth because the girls wanted to watch Caleb and the other men plant the barley in the field they had been preparing all week.

Naomi came to the open door to greet them. "It is good to see you."

Sapphira hugged her sister-in-law.

Naomi greeted Leah, and they entered the house. Naomi had gathered some flowers for the front room, and it looked like summer had arrived.

"It is so good to see you. How is Aaron?" Naomi led them to the corner of the room where they settled on chairs on a woven beige matted rug.

"He's the same. Aaron has decided to see Jesus. He thinks Jesus can heal him, so we've brought a few more supplies to prepare for the trip."

"I've always wanted to meet him," said Leah. "There are so many stories. I'm sure he can heal Aaron."

Sapphira wasn't surprised by Leah's attitude. Leah had always been the one with the sunniest disposition.

"What do you think, Naomi?" Leah asked.

Sapphira remembered their last conversation when Naomi had been dismissive of Jesus, yet had helped them find him.

Naomi shrugged. "Oh, I don't know. They are probably just stories. No man could do all of what they claim Jesus has done."

Sapphira sat back against the cushion. "I agree it seems too good to be true. Making blind men see? Making the lame able to walk? Healing the people with leprosy? It can't be done. Those can only be done by God. And yet, the stories of Jesus are too numerous to be false."

"Well," Leah said, "what if Jesus is the One?"

Sapphira and Naomi drew back in shock.

"Leah, how can you say that?" asked Naomi.

Leah didn't appear offended. "Who else could do what he has done?" she asked gently. She turned to Sapphira. "If I were you, I'd keep an open mind about Jesus. Let's see what happens. He can't make him any worse."

"I'm not worried about that. What if he dies on the road before we can find Jesus?" The words came out of their own volition. Sapphira hadn't meant to say it out loud again. Why couldn't she keep her doubts to herself?

"John and I will be with you," Leah said. "We'll help you take care of Aaron. John is interested in meeting Jesus. Demetrius will be going with us, too. We're all helping." She clasped her own hand over Sapphira's twisting hands.

"Omar and I will take good care of all four of the children." Naomi looked contented at the thought.

Sapphira had meant to ask Naomi if she would watch the children, but thankfully, Naomi had offered to help without Sapphira having to grovel, though Naomi's softer attitude was still a mystery to her. "Thank you both." She hugged them. "You are such good friends. We'll have to see what happens."

She turned to Naomi. "We're leaving the day after tomorrow. We should only be gone for a day or two. I appreciate your help with the children. I know Rachelle's a little shy, but I know you'll be kind to her while I'm gone." She'd never left the children before this, and the thought made her teary-eyed.

"I'll take good care of her, Sapphira." While Naomi could have been defensive, she didn't sound that way. She sounded like she really wanted to help.

"I know how important Aaron is to you, and I know what this trip means. Even though I'm not sure Jesus can help, I do want Aaron to be healed and to come back with you. I care about both of you." She lowered her head to look at her hands, which she twisted in her lap. "I'm not very good at stating my feelings, and I know sometimes I come across as harsh. But I do care."

Sapphira had to strain to hear the last few words. She knew when she and Aaron returned that her relationship with Naomi would be different. All these years after Naomi had married Omar,

Sapphira realized that Naomi had suffered and hadn't told anyone.

Sapphira reached over and gently squeezed Naomi's hands. "I know. Thank you for your help. Rachelle will be fine with you."

She couldn't talk about it any longer, not even to Leah or Naomi, who were her closest friends. "Can we talk about something else for a few minutes before we get busy?"

Naomi patted Sapphira's hand. "Of course." She turned to Leah. "How is Thatcher doing when he's not studying?"

They all knew that Thatcher, at twelve years of age, was fond of studying.

"Thatcher has developed a fondness for his father's line of business and goes with him every day to help with roofs," Leah said.

"I've noticed," Sapphira said. "My Caleb is lost without him, although he's been doing a lot with Elam and Gideon to fill his time."

Naomi's own son Samuel was nine years old. "Samuel has been helping in the fields, too, though I know Caleb merely tolerates him as he is not old enough to work with Caleb."

"That may be, but someday they will be good friends."

All three women nodded knowingly. Their families would stay close and someday the age difference wouldn't matter. Caleb and Samuel would follow in their fathers' footsteps when they grew to adulthood.

CHAPTER 16

The next morning, the day before they were to leave, the knock was loud in the still house. Rachelle and Ruth were playing outside in the courtyard, and Aaron had been dozing, waiting for someone to come and listen to his plans for the trip. He dragged himself upright and stood still for a moment, waiting for the dizziness to pass.

Another knock sounded. "Aaron?" The door opened, and Demetrius came in at once when he saw him standing there. "Do you need help?"

Aaron nodded. "I'm fine. Stood up too fast."

Demetrius smiled and gestured toward the kitchen. "Shall we sit?"

Aaron sank onto the bench beside the table. "What brings you here so early? I thought you were going to see your other patients and make plans for them for the time you're gone."

Demetrius sat across from Aaron. His brows drew together, and he frowned. "I've started doing that already, but I heard some disturbing news that I thought you needed to hear."

"What's happening? Have they already captured and killed Jesus?" Aaron was appalled that such a good man could be hunted.

"No, at least, I've heard nothing new about him. It's about the scrolls that were stolen from the synagogue. There's some talk about the pregnant woman who had visited the synagogue that evening. The guard thought there was something strange about her, but he decided not to approach her. He said she seemed afraid of something."

"Does he think she had something to do with the theft? I can't imagine a pregnant woman would steal the scrolls. He obviously didn't see her carrying anything out, or he would have stopped her."

"No, he didn't see her carrying anything."

Aaron didn't understand how this would affect him. "What does this have to do with us? I mean, yes, I'm concerned about the scrolls. They are important to the synagogue, but what does that have to do with our trip?"

"They'll be searching people on the road. We might be searched. They might not let us leave town."

"That's impossible. We don't belong to that synagogue. I think you're overreacting. You know I haven't done anything wrong. And I trust you and Elam and John. Gideon's questionable, but even he wouldn't steal the scrolls."

At Demetrius's silence, Aaron paused. "Fine. He might. But did he? He's done lots of things wrong, but…" He trailed off into silence. Had Gideon stolen the scrolls? "We're forgetting. The woman. She might be involved. We have to get out of town tomorrow, Demetrius."

Demetrius stood up. "I know. I must finish arranging for my other patients."

Aaron slowly stood up and walked Demetrius to the door. "I can't believe someone from their own synagogue stole the scrolls."

"I'll let the others know what's going on. I'll stop by tonight, and we can make final arrangements. There is one other thing, Aaron. There are those who are making comments about Sapphira attending the Friends of Jesus meeting."

"Who?"

"A lot of people around town. They're wondering why she would be there. Jesus is becoming a contentious subject, and I thought you should know."

"Thank you, Demetrius. Maybe it's a good thing we're getting out of town for a while. Hopefully, when we get back, people will be so excited by my miraculous recovery that Sapphira's indiscretion will be forgotten."

"Let me take your pulse before I leave." Demetrius's strong fingers held his wrist.

"I'm fine." Aaron stared at his physician and friend. "Watch over her for me." He knew Demetrius would know he meant throughout the trip when he was too weak to do it himself—or if Jesus didn't heal him.

"I will. Your pulse is weak."

"I'm weak." He laughed. "I'm not ready to die yet, Demetrius. Take your hand away and help me to my mat so I can rest up for tomorrow, as everyone keeps suggesting. The children are only so patient and will be coming in soon."

Demetrius helped him to his mat. "I'll check on you later."

CHAPTER 17

The morning chill was fast receding as Sapphira took the refreshments out to the men, Caleb, and Samuel, who were all working in the field. The lemonade, biscuits, and slabs of goat cheese would keep them going until mid-afternoon when one of the men would pick up more food or Naomi would take something to them.

Feeding them was the least she could do for their help. When she reached the field, Gideon came to meet her.

"So, we get to see your pretty face again," he said, licking his lips.

She repressed a shudder and handed him the items. "I've brought you and the others some food."

"Thank you." When he took the bags, his hands deliberately touched hers.

"Don't do that," she said sharply, aware of her vulnerability.

"I could tell your husband a thing or two. Perhaps he'd like to know about that meeting you attended and the fun we had at the synagogue." His sneer made him an ugly person.

"He knows about the meeting, and you won't tell him about the other," she said forcefully, though a quake went through her. What if he did tell Aaron? Aaron would only worry about her. Would that make him sicker?

"It would be easy to let it slip. Henrietta saw you there, too."

"Henrietta would never tell anyone. She's part of those meetings. Besides, I told you, Aaron already knows that I went, and he doesn't care." She didn't tell him that Aaron had been furious with her when he'd found out. All had turned out fine in the end, and Aaron was going to see Jesus tomorrow.

"Maybe she wouldn't tell anyone about that," Gideon acknowledged, "But I don't have the same qualms about the synagogue." He winked at her.

She saw Omar, John, and the boys coming toward them, and knew she had to settle this now. "You were in on the theft, too, so you have as much to lose as I do. You've already promised me that you'll help during the trip with Aaron. What else do you want?"

"I want to get those scrolls sold during our trip, and I want you to make sure it happens. If you do that, this all ends."

She didn't trust that he would keep his word. He would certainly blackmail her for a long time over her misdeeds. "You'd better keep your mouth shut." She turned away from him and smiled at Caleb as he came up behind her. "How is it going?"

"We'll finish today or tomorrow," he said with a manly cast to his shoulders.

Beside him, Samuel nodded solemnly. "Weather's good."

She looked up at Omar and John. "Thank you both for all you've done to help us with the fields. We would have been lost without your help."

"You're welcome," John said, sweeping a look between her and Gideon. His brown sable hair looked windblown, but he was handsome and strong. Just like Aaron used to be before his illness. John had promised to help finish as much as they could today before leaving for their trip the next morning. He had finished his thatching jobs as soon as Leah had told him about Sapphira's desire to get Aaron healed by Jesus. "Thank you for bringing the food."

"I'm going back to the house in about an hour," Omar cut in. "I'd like to speak to you."

Her brother's anger cut through her worry about Gideon. "What's the matter?"

"We'll talk then," he said, dismissing her.

She took the hint, bewildered about what he might want to discuss. His brusque manner was not much different than usual. Her brother had always summoned, spoken his opinion, and dismissed her abruptly—as if she were a servant. Usually, she found his arrogant attitude amusing, but with the lack of sleep and Gideon's threats, today, she found him annoying. "Fine."

She turned back to Caleb, Samuel, and John and smiled. "Thank you. Naomi will see you later with more food."

They all smiled back, and she was relieved they had treated her situation with Omar as life as usual. She turned around and strode back to the house to finish packing and check on Aaron.

She had so much to think about. What did Omar want to discuss? How could she get Gideon to stop blackmailing her?

#

103

"You're practically throwing yourself at him. I couldn't believe it when I saw him watching you." Omar stabbed the pitchfork into the odorous soft brown straw, grabbed a gob, and flung another heap of manure on top of the pile he'd already started. Flies buzzed, and the stench became stronger. He was building a pile that they could use in the future for fires when they ran out of wood.

She stood downwind from him to avoid the odor. "Who are you talking about? You know Gideon is repulsive to me."

"I'm talking about Demetrius."

Sapphira had thought she'd hidden her attraction to Demetrius from the others. She'd barely acknowledged it to herself. She loved Aaron. She was sure it was a fleeting thing because of Aaron's illness. She felt guilty about it herself.

"You're imagining things. He's only concerned about me because of Aaron's illness. It means nothing." She didn't tell Omar that she'd noticed Demetrius's increasing attention lately. Demetrius was concerned about her because of Aaron, but she also sensed his feelings carried more than concern for her. She did find him attractive, but she loved Aaron. Nothing would come of Demetrius's feelings for her. She could barely admit to herself that she'd thought of him during some of her more desperate times.

"If you don't want people to talk, you'll be careful." He attached the pitchfork in the wagon with a strap and jumped to the ground. "Especially now that Gideon knows you will be marrying him."

She was furious with him. She wanted to stamp her foot like Rachelle did when she didn't like something. "I don't care what nasty people think. I haven't done anything wrong, and you should know that, too. How dare you treat me as if I've done something wrong?"

"You'll care when Aaron's not around." He continued readying the horse to leave the field as if he wasn't insulting his own sister—and reminding her that Aaron would be gone soon. He did not believe Jesus of Nazareth would heal Aaron.

"How cruel. What would Naomi say if she knew what you were saying to me?"

"Naomi's the one who noticed."

Sapphira didn't know whether she believed him. Naomi had been different lately, and Sapphira doubted she'd said anything to Omar about Demetrius. Omar constantly criticized what Rachelle or Caleb wore and made little digs about Caleb's help. He'd made Rachelle cry and left Caleb hurt and angry. After they returned home from those visits, it always took a day or two to get back to normal. When she and Aaron returned, things were going to change.

"If you do anything with Demetrius, make sure there are others in the room with you at all times. Keep it proper."

"I'll probably marry him the day after the funeral," she said sarcastically. "Of course, Naomi would probably die of embarrassment. How long would you wait to remarry?" She regretted the impulsive words immediately, but it was too late to unsay them. She got into the wagon and waited for him to climb in beside her. She turned her head away from him and felt the wagon sag as he settled his bulk on the seat beside her. The odor of sweat and manure was overpowering.

"That was unnecessarily rude. Naomi and I only want what's best for you, and we're trying to warn you. You'll find it's not so easy to be a widow in this town." He whipped the horse into a walk.

She didn't answer. Everything she wanted to say was ruder than he'd been. She missed her mother. Her mother had listened to her, and she certainly would have understood what Sapphira was going through. Sapphira remembered how her mother had been when her father died after he had fallen from a horse and hit his head. Her mother had been devastated. Omar had taken over the household. Sapphira's mother died a year later from what Sapphira believed was a broken heart.

"You should be grateful that we care for you. Even though you're obviously not," Omar said. "We'll stand by you no matter what happens."

She kept her face turned from him. Because her expression was so openly disgusted, he would have known in an instant how she despised him.

"Thank you." She knew Omar didn't catch the sarcasm in her tone. He took things at face value. He expected her to be grateful, so when she said thank you, he assumed she was grateful.

"You're welcome."

The rest of the fifteen-minute ride passed in silence. As soon as they returned to the stable, she hurried from the wagon, leaving Omar to put it away. She rushed back to her house to reassure herself that she still had Aaron. She hurried inside and slammed the door.

Aaron looked up from where he was sitting on the floor with Rachelle. "Is something wrong?"

"Omar had things to say." She kept it deliberately vague, glad that Rachelle was in the room, making it impossible to go into details. She knew Aaron would understand from past experience that Omar had been insulting, and there was no way she would tell him what Omar had said anyway.

"I see." He nodded understanding.

Rachelle held a wooden block in her hand and looked at Sapphira. "What did Uncle Omar say?"

"Nothing important. What are you and Daddy playing?"

"Blocks." The tone of Rachelle's voice told Sapphira this was obvious.

"It's a lovely tower." Sapphira sat down beside them.

"Thank you. You smell, Mama."

Sapphira felt a load of stress roll from her shoulders, and she laughed. "I took a ride with Uncle Omar to dump some manure."

Rachelle wrinkled her nose. "Ugh."

"I don't suppose you want a hug."

Her daughter moved away from her. "No."

Sapphira pretended to reach for her, and Rachelle squealed and ran to the other side of the room, holding out her hands, palms toward Sapphira. "Stay away."

Sapphira edged in her direction, and Rachelle squealed again. Sapphira laughed and settled back down beside Aaron. "Fine. I won't. I promise." She held out her hand. "Come, sit beside me."

Rachelle ran toward her, but before she could sit down, Sapphira grabbed her and squeezed her in a hug. "Gotcha."

"Mama!" She laughed and squirmed.

Aaron joined in the laughter.

A knock sounded at the door.

"That must be Demetrius," Aaron said. "He was coming back today and discuss the trip."

Sapphira's throat tightened, and the laughter faded. She got to her feet. "I'll see." She opened the door. "Elam, is there something wrong?"

His hair was wild and bushy. His eyebrow stuck out like puffs of straw. "Have you seen Gideon?"

"He was with Omar and John out in the field earlier. What's wrong?"

He caught a glimpse of wide-eyed Rachelle behind her, and his face relaxed into a smile. "Hello, little girl."

She giggled shyly. "Hello, Mr. Elam."

Sapphira had always been amazed by the rapport between Elam and Rachelle. Elam's whole being softened whenever he saw her, and though Rachelle was shy, she always asked where Elam was when he didn't come with Gideon.

"Aaron," Elam said.

"Hello. Can we help you with something?" Aaron rose slowly to his feet.

"No, that's fine." Elam turned back to her. "Can we talk outside?"

"Yes." She turned to Rachelle and Aaron. "I'll only be a moment. Wait here," she said to Rachelle, who was following her.

"Yes, Mama."

Sapphira followed Elam outside. "What's wrong?"

"I want to go with you and Aaron." He was wringing his hands.

She looked at him in amazement. "I thought John had already arranged that you would be helping in the fields while we were gone. But, of course, you are welcome to come. Are you all right, Elam? You're not sick, are you?"

His bushy eyebrows rose. "Not in the way you mean, ma'am. Not like Aaron in there."

She didn't like the pity she saw in his eyes. It made her feel the outcome of the trip might not end how she wanted.

"I want to come and help Aaron meet Jesus." His hands clasped together. "Please let me come and be of service."

"But why?" She hastened to add, "I know you've always helped us, but Aaron might not make it through the journey." She swallowed convulsively before adding, "It's going to take us longer than normal to get there. It'll be a tough journey for him."

"But that's why I want to go. My wife died in childbirth, having Gideon. She had no chance of surviving. I want to go with you and Aaron and see a miracle firsthand. And I want to talk to Jesus."

Sapphira was silent. She didn't think Elam would appreciate hearing about her own lack of faith right now. Elam's reasons for seeing Jesus were his own. Another person on the journey to help them would be welcome. "As I said, you are welcome to come, Elam. We could use your help."

She smiled at him and knew this was the perfect opportunity to bring it up, even though she felt like she was referring to a snake. "I believe Gideon is coming along also." She sensed Elam would disagree. "He's been a big help to us this week in the field."

Elam looked at her for a long time. Somehow, she got the feeling he knew Gideon had some hold over her. Perhaps he'd even guessed that she was the one who had stolen the scrolls for Gideon. He had seen her on the street in her pregnancy clothes when she gave the scrolls to Gideon.

He nodded. "I will talk to him about treating you with respect."

She let out a sigh. "Thank you. And thank you for your help, Elam. We couldn't manage without you."

"You take care." Did his sympathetic look have a hidden meaning? "Aaron will come out of this fine. I won't let anything happen to him."

"I believe you. Thank you." She wouldn't let her doubts of Aaron being able to make the trip all the way to see Jesus show. She'd done what she could. The others coming on the trip had their own reasons for seeing Jesus. The traveling party would be made up of herself, Aaron, Leah, John, Demetrius, Gideon, and Elam. It was going to happen. She could barely contain her swirling emotions of hope and fear.

CHAPTER 18

The sun hadn't risen yet, and Sapphira was packing the final things for their trip.

Caleb was excited for their adventure. "Can I go with you?" he repeated his plea for the hundredth time. He shoved his sister away from Sapphira's traveling bag and peaked inside.

Rachelle pinched him, and he squealed, but Sapphira said nothing. She was tired from caring for Aaron all night and worrying whether Jesus could save him or not. Sleep consisted of two fifteen-minute naps.

"You be good for Naomi and play nice with Samuel."

"We will, Mama," Rachelle said, nodding her head, black curls vibrating against her head.

From the sideways glances Rachelle had sent her all morning, Sapphira could tell her daughter did not want her to leave. Fears from her five-year-old were surfacing. Her own insides were churning with a mixture of dread and anticipation, and the feeling had not abated in the past few hours.

"It's going to be a long few days if you don't relax," Aaron said. His eyes remained closed. "Do you know why Gideon wants to come with us?"

"John wanted us to have as much help as possible, and Gideon and Elam volunteered. Leah thought I should have another woman on the trip, so she's coming, too. I think they all have different reasons for the trip. They all have an interest in seeing you recover. Though why, I can't imagine. You're a lot of trouble." She smiled at him.

His lips turned up at the corners. "In a week, I'm making you take that back. I'll be able to do everything I used to do. We'll be a family again, and you won't have to take care of me. I won't be a helpless invalid."

She couldn't help frowning at him. "Don't you think you might be putting too much hope in him?" she asked.

"Shh." He squeezed her hand. "I'll make it."

She didn't say anything else, knowing that Rachelle and Caleb heard everything she said, and they would certainly have their ears perked for anything out of the ordinary. She tried not to think of the return journey if Aaron wasn't with her. These were her last days with him, and she didn't want to share him with the rest of the people traveling with them.

"Why are you frowning, Mama?"

She looked down to see Rachelle's solemn black eyes on her. She reached down and hugged her to her side. "I was trying to decide if I've packed the right things for the trip." She gave her a reassuring smile and let go. "Why don't you run out to the kitchen and get us some grapes for the trip. Put them into that burlap sack on the table."

Rachelle's expression relaxed into a smile. She threw a triumphant look at Caleb. "I get to help." She stuck out her tongue and ran from the room.

Sapphira looked at Caleb. "Why don't you go check on the men outside? See if they need anything."

Caleb smirked. "You're trying to get rid of Rachelle and me."

"You're too knowing, son," Aaron said. "Now go."

Caleb shrugged and slowly walked from the room.

"What is it?" Aaron asked.

"Do you still want to go? What if…"

He closed his eyes. "I wish I could hand you some of my faith. It would make this so much easier. And you're the one who convinced me to go in the first place."

"I guess we need to trust faith as we go along." She sank down beside him and gripped his hand. "Aaron…this is it."

He patted her hand. "It's going to be fine." He looked up as Rachelle came back to the room. "Did you get the grapes packed?"

Sapphira removed her hand from his and stood up.

"I did." She moved over to Sapphira and grabbed her skirt.

"I guess we're ready then," Sapphira said. There was no turning back now. She felt a shimmer of excitement. "Say goodbye to Daddy, and then we'll go find Naomi."

She watched as Rachelle leaned over Aaron and hugged him.

Aaron tousled her hair and hugged her tight. "I'll miss you. Be good for Naomi and we'll be back before you know it."

Would he be back? She said another prayer.
Let him come back alive for Rachelle and Caleb's
sake, God. And for me. She'd recently started
praying again for the first time since her mother
died, just quick prayers. She didn't know if she
believed in them or not.

"Bye, Daddy." Rachelle released her hug
and stepped away from him.

Sapphira put her arm around Rachelle's
shoulders. Rachelle waved to Aaron, and he waved
back as Sapphira led her out of the room. When
they stepped outside of the house, the cobblestone
road was full of neighbors, all offering advice about
the trip.

Sapphira hugged Rachelle and led her to
where Ruth, Leah, and Naomi stood talking and
watching the men. Ruth and Rachelle were
chattering in an instant, excited at the prospect of
staying overnight at Naomi's house.

CHAPTER 19

Aaron couldn't believe it was happening. He waited impatiently for Sapphira to return so they could go. Although he initially didn't think this would work when Sapphira first suggested it a few days ago, now he wouldn't let a moment's doubt enter his mind. He'd said to her. "It's my only chance. We both know that."

She'd been cleaning the sleeping room as Aaron reclined on a cushion on the floor. "What if you don't make it all the way? We'll be out on the road with…" Here her voice trailed off, and she hid her face behind her hand. She resumed cleaning, her movements vigorous.

"We'll make it in time to see him. I don't believe I'm meant to die yet. There are so many things I need to do with Caleb, Rachelle, and our new baby. So many things I need to share with you as we grow old together."

Aaron struggled up from the floor, distraught that he couldn't move any faster. He pulled her into his arms, and she tried to keep her dirty hands from touching him.

"I'll be all right."

She sighed as she laid her head on his breast. "I know you will. It's just jitters over the trip. You know I'm unsure about leaving Rachelle with Naomi. She's so young, and I've never left the children before."

She stepped away from him and continued with her tidying. She felt restless.

He slid back onto the cushions, his energy depleted. Leaning back, he closed his eyes. What would convince her? "I'll be sitting on a horse, much like I do at home anyway. We'll have Gideon, Elam, John, and Demetrius with us. You know how much they want to go. Especially Demetrius. He wants to meet the great healer."

A slight huff came from Sapphira.

"Leah is looking forward to seeing more of the country. You two will have an adventure."

"With my husband sick? Yes, that's an adventure. I don't have to leave home for that trip."

The words were bitter and surprised Aaron. Up until now, Sapphira hadn't been vocal about her feelings toward his illness. She had cared for him, done what she needed, and never once made him feel less of a man. Her sudden honesty was new.

"Sapphira!" He couldn't help it. His exclamation reprimanded her, and he was immediately sorry. She was a kind, loving wife and mother and deserved a moment of sullenness. "I'm sorry."

"I'm sorry, too. I'm just so tired." She turned away. "I'm going out to the well to wash my hands."

He let her go, regretting his outburst, knowing she needed time. Time. Why was everything about time?

He sat up and leaned against the wall, waiting for Demetrius to tell him it was time to go.

CHAPTER 20

In the midst of the activity outside, Naomi took Sapphira aside.

"I'll take good care of the children. You don't worry about them, do you hear? You take care of Aaron. When you get back, we'll sort everything out."

"What?" Sapphira was surprised to hear Naomi's comforting words. She almost sounded like she would take Sapphira's side against Omar.

"I'm concerned about you." Naomi looked away and over to the activity of the men. "There's something else I need to say to you while I have a moment."

"Oh, Naomi. Can't it wait until my return?"

Naomi met her gaze again, and it was filled with compassion. "No, it can't. Don't throw yourself at Demetrius. It is unseemly. He has that look in his eyes. Try and restrain yourself until a better time."

Sapphira was beside herself with anger. "A better time. A better time! When Aaron dies? When the mourning period is over? Naomi, I forgive you because I will be away for a while, and anything could happen. But I am so angry at you right now I could spit." With a great effort, she hugged Naomi. "Thank you for watching the children."

"I'm sorry if I offended you, Sapphira. Omar told me what to say, and I knew it was wrong." She sighed. "I had to say my piece. I hope

everything goes well, and you and Aaron reach
Jesus of Nazareth in time. When you get back, we
will try and put aside our differences and be better
friends."

Omar told her what to say? Sapphira felt she
shouldn't have been surprised. Sapphira took
Naomi's hand. "Thank you. I'd like to be better
friends. It will be a big help with Elam coming
along. One more man always makes the trip safer."

"Which reminds me. Don't trust Gideon. My
cousin isn't a safe man for you to get too close to,
no matter what Omar's plans are."

"Naomi, you're starting to find something
wrong with everyone." She gave her a quick hug.
"As you said. We'll talk when we get back from our
trip."

Naomi returned the hug. "Stay safe."

"We're ready." The call came from John.

Sapphira saw Caleb talking to John, and she
walked over to them. "Caleb, go say goodbye to
your father, and bring the things from the kitchen on
your way back."

He nodded. She watched him walk into the
house, his back straight and stiff. She'd let him be
alone on purpose. He was at the age when he didn't
want anyone to see his emotions, though she knew
him well and easily read his moods. He was afraid
for his father, and he had no one to turn to at the
moment.

She turned back to John. "Thank you for
coming. I feel much safer having you on this trip
with us."

"Nothing will happen to him on the trip.
You have my word." His steady eyes were kind,

and she relaxed. Between John, Elam, and Demetrius, their trip would be a safe one. She ignored the persistent reminder inside her head that suggested Gideon would be a danger. There were enough others with them that he wouldn't have a chance to be alone with her.

Caleb came out of the house and headed down the street. He didn't have the kitchen things with him. He was headed for the farm, and she understood.

She ran after him. "Caleb."

He turned when she caught up with him but wouldn't look at her. She knew he was crying. She reached down and hugged him, and he gripped her around the waist. "Your father and I will be back."

"I know," he muttered.

She let him go. "Take care of your sister."

"I will."

"Fine. You can go now."

He looked up quickly and then down again. "You'll both come back?"

"Yes," she promised rashly. Dear God, she prayed, let us both come back alive. "You can go. I'll tell Naomi you'll be at the farm."

She watched him trudge away before going back to join Naomi and Leah.

"Caleb is going to the farm."

Naomi nodded, her face kind. "Samuel's the same way."

"I think you should take the girls and go. I'd rather they be at your house, so they don't have to watch us leave," Sapphira said.

Leah nodded. "I agree."

Leah went to get the girls for Naomi.

Sapphira looked around the yard. "Where is Omar?"

"He's at the stable."

Sapphira thought of Omar seeing Caleb in his emotional state and wondered how that would turn out. She got her answer right away.

Omar and Caleb were coming down the road from the direction of Omar's farm leading two horses for the trip. Walking behind them, Gideon and Elam were leading the other two horses.

Omar was talking earnestly, and Caleb was nodding his head, clearly fine with whatever was being said. Sapphira was relieved. She'd been concerned about a clash between the two, but no matter how Omar felt about her, he was treating Caleb well. She was satisfied that it would work out for the short time they'd be gone.

John came up to them and took the horse lead from Caleb.

"Enjoy your time with Naomi and Omar. I'll see you when we get back," Sapphira said to Caleb.

Caleb's tears had disappeared for the moment. "Omar has agreed to show me how to chop wood."

Sapphira ignored the fear that engendered in her and smiled at him. "Don't cut off your foot."

"I won't."

Sapphira hugged Rachelle. "Bye, sweetie."

Rachelle leaned over and hugged her tightly. "Bye, Mama."

She didn't want to let go, but she finally released her.

John and Leah had finished saying goodbye to Thatcher and Ruth.

"Let's go," said Naomi. The children waved goodbye as they followed Naomi. Omar joined them.

Aaron stood in the doorway waving at them, and they waved back. Soon, they were out of sight on their way to Omar and Naomi's house.

Sapphira walked up to Aaron. "Are you ready to go?"

His boyish grin got her heart thumping wildly. He looked at this as an adventure. A little of his excitement transferred to her, and she felt a surge of hope. Maybe…

"Let's go," he said.

Demetrius appeared and helped him onto one of the horses.

The other men had been loading the other three horses with the supplies gathered on the cobblestones.

Sapphira called to Leah. "Come help me get the rest of our things."

Elam joined her and Leah in the house, and they soon had everything loaded onto the horses.

Sapphira and Leah mounted, and so did Demetrius. The other men planned to walk beside Aaron on his horse to make sure he was fine. They would take turns with Demetrius riding the fourth horse. With the roads thronged with people to see Jesus, they didn't think they could take more than the four animals. If they did find Jesus, one of them would have to stay with the animals while the others took Aaron to meet Jesus. They couldn't handle any more.

Once they were mounted and walking down the road, there was cheering from their neighbors. Soon, they were heading east through Naraah on their way to the road between Bethany and Ephraim.

Sapphira rode on Aaron's left while Gideon and Elam walked on the right side of Aaron's horse. Leah rode behind her, and John walked beside Leah. Demetrius brought up the rear.

Aaron coughed, and he pulled out a linen cloth to spit in. The blood-tinged sputum made her shudder. Had he thought she wouldn't notice?

"What's wrong?" he asked. He slumped forward a little on his horse.

How would he ride a horse for a half day when he'd hardly been off his mat the past month? "The dust is bothering you, and we haven't even gotten out of Naraah yet. But I shouldn't complain. It must be much worse for you."

"I like it when you complain. It makes a nice change from hearing my own thoughts and takes my mind off myself." His raspy voice was weak, but she was used to deciphering the words.

"We're only a step away from home. Are you sure you don't want to go back?" Sapphira asked.

"We've been over this so many times. I'm going."

The finality in his voice silenced her. She knew that tone well. He wouldn't discuss it anymore. They were making the trip, come what may. They were only a half day away from possibly finding Jesus. Their travel would be slower than if

Aaron were well, but hopefully, the extra time needed would be minimal.

"Everything fine?" Gideon asked from Aaron's other side.

"Fine." Sapphira nodded. He'd been eyeing her since they'd left, and his constant surveillance made her edgy.

"Let us know if we need to stop or if you need anything." His gaze was on Aaron, but Sapphira knew he was talking to her.

"Fine," she said again, concentrating on staring straight ahead. The morning was going to be long with Gideon's unwelcome attention. At least once they left Naraah, Leah could ride alongside her. Until then, the streets were too narrow.

Her hands twitched on the reins and stilled, but her mind kept on. How far would their journey take them before the end? She thought of their children at Omar and Naomi's home. What would she say to them if she came back without their father? She had been the one to set the plan in motion. What if Jesus couldn't help them?

Aaron started coughing again. She glanced back at Demetrius, and he shook his head. There was nothing he could do. They'd have to keep going and pray that Aaron made it.

Sapphira, used to the children's boisterous spirits first thing in the morning, had no trouble staying alert even though she hadn't slept much during the night.

Leah carried on a soft patter of conversation as soon as the eastern horizon glowed with the first morning light. "The air is so humid. Look at that dew on the fields and the workers turning over the soil."

Two men were working on a small patch of field in the clear morning air.

Demetrius answered, "It's so hot later in the day that the moisture evaporates. They're doing what their ancestors have done for years. They're experienced in the art."

And it was an art. Sapphira watched as families worked together side by side. She had been raised on a sheep farm, and her mother worked hard beside her father. Sapphira and her brother had been taught early on how their livelihood was possible because of all the work her father did. Omar had carried on that tradition.

Demetrius was watching her, and she lowered her lashes. This morning, she was more aware of him. Aware of the vitality he exuded as he sat relaxed in his saddle. From Leah, she knew he had spent a lot of time on the road traveling. This was just another day to him. To her, there was an undercurrent of excitement despite Aaron's illness. Then there were the others in the group, who all expressed a desire to meet Jesus.

This would probably be her only chance to travel. She almost wished she'd allowed Caleb and Rachelle to come with them on their journey. If there had been more than the slightest chance that Aaron would be healed in time, she would have brought the children along. As it was, her shoulders drooped in defeat.

Demetrius turned his attention to Leah. Sapphira listened to them talking.

Leah asked, "How will we find him?"

"That shouldn't be difficult. So many people watch for him and know his movements. We'll ask along the way."

The sun brightened, and a haze appeared on the horizon. Fields looked greener and brighter. Her mood lightened. She felt a moment of hope, squelching it quickly. If only she had something to occupy her mind. Plenty of people were here to help Aaron, and she was unaccustomed to the freedom this gave her to ride and think. She both hated it and welcomed it.

She could not remember ever feeling so conflicted. The exhilaration of new surroundings coupled with her fear for Aaron, and her uneasiness over Demetrius's interest and Gideon's threats caused a tingling in her shoulders and mind.

They traveled for an hour through hill country. Grassy patches covered some of the hills between spots of bare earth. Olive trees occasionally dotted the land. During the first part of their journey, they saw few people. They came across a shepherd tending his sheep and a woman walking along the road close to a small cottage.

The fresh, cool morning air was pleasant, and if it weren't for Aaron's almost constant cough, Sapphira would have enjoyed the ride. As it was, she was increasingly worried about his condition.

When they stopped to take their break, Demetrius and John helped Aaron from his horse. He lay down on the side of the road while Sapphira fetched the sheepskin full of water from the pack on Aaron's horse. She held it for him to drink.

After a few sips, he lay back and closed his eyes. "I'm going to make it, Sapphira." He opened his eyes and grinned at her. "This is exciting."

She thought she loved him the most at that moment. She patted his hand. "My worry is taking the fun away from the experience," she said dryly. "Yes, I know you'll make it. You are one stubborn man."

They climbed further up the hills, and about a half hour later, John stopped them. "Let's take another break. We'll be joining the main road to Ephraim in a little while. There will be lots of people on the road. We should eat something before we continue on."

The others agreed, and they settled in the shade beside a tall cedar. The day was heating up. The sun shone with few clouds to break the brightness.

Dulled by the heat and rhythm of her horse's tread, Sapphira was glad for the break. Her long curly black hair stuck to the nape of her neck. Aaron stayed still beside her, and she knew he'd gone to that place in his head where he went when he had to escape.

Fields turned over for planting covered the landscape along with other patches of uncultivated land. Their passing and current meal break caused no raised heads of interest.

A shout roused her, and she glanced around to see from where the sound came. Gideon and Elam stood beside a small fig bush, each holding the reins of two horses.

Elam gestured wildly with something in his hand, and it looked as if Gideon tried to grab it without success. Elam stuck the object into his tunic pocket, and Gideon made another move toward him. Elam held up his hand, and Gideon stepped back.

Although they both had the same stocky build and short stature, their faces were different. Gideon's was softly jowled with a reddish beard while Elam's chin was a strong firm square, framed in silvery gray hair. They both had the same reddish, bristly hair on their heads. They drifted back to the group.

Sapphira's lids drooped as she tried to put the Gideon problem aside.

"You miss them," Aaron said.

She jerked at the words, so deeply had she been thinking about Gideon. "Yes. I do already. Isn't that silly?"

"No, I miss them, too."

"We haven't spent any time away from them."

"They'll have a good time with Thatcher, Samuel, and Ruth. With luck, we'll be back tonight or tomorrow at the latest."

By tomorrow, the result of the trip would be known. "Caleb and Omar seemed to hit it off today. Omar promised to teach him how to chop wood."

"That was nice of him."

"I don't understand Omar. He's usually so arrogant, and he's reprimanded me all my life. Maybe that's what brothers do. I thought he would be critical of Caleb, but he seems to understand him. At least today, he did."

"Maybe he remembers losing your father and feels for Caleb. They'll be fine. You know

Naomi will take care of the girls, and Ruth and
Rachelle will have a good time together. There's no
need to worry about anything right now." He patted
her hand, which rested on the blanket beside him.

*Except you, Aaron. I'll spend the whole trip
worrying about you.* But she didn't say it out loud.
The subject was closed for now.

Would they make it to Jesus before the
soldiers seized him? Sapphira thought about the
Friends of Jesus meeting. They had mentioned it
would be fourteen days until he was arrested. Five
days had already passed convincing Aaron to
prepare and make the trip. Her mood fluctuated
between hope and fear. What if they missed him, or
what if he was arrested?

Time would tell. It wouldn't be long before
they reached the main road and heard what travelers
were saying. There would be plenty of information
about a man who healed people and brought them
back to life.

Demetrius came over and interrupted, and
Sapphira moved so he could examine Aaron.

Leah walked up to Sapphira. "John has
started taking out some food. We can start up again
when we're finished."

"Thanks, Leah."

"How are you doing?" she asked.

Sapphira shrugged.

Leah hugged her and walked over to John,
who handed her some bread and figs. She took
some over to Sapphira and then settled with the
others a short distance from Aaron where they'd
made a small camp.

Aaron felt too tired to join them, so they left him alone to rest. Sapphira remained by his side. He ate a few bites that she knew he forced down only to keep up what little strength he had, rather than because he was hungry.

Sapphira picked at her food, too. The worry and heat quelled her appetite. She watched Gideon and Elam, who were a distance away in a field discussing something again. Elam's hand reached out, and he pulled something from under Gideon's shirt. A chain with a huge pendant. They were too far away for Sapphira to see what it was.

Gideon grabbed it back and thrust it under his shirt again. Elam turned abruptly and stomped back to the camp area.

This was their second altercation in a brief time, and Sapphira wondered what it was about. Why had Gideon wanted to come to meet Jesus with them? He was not a spiritual man and had no reason to want Aaron to get well. He'd never treated Aaron with ill will, but he wasn't the sort of man to care what happened to Aaron either.

Had Gideon stolen something else other than the scrolls? Was that what this trip was all about for him? Should she warn John or Demetrius to watch Gideon? She blushed as she remembered Naomi's warning about Demetrius. She should stay away from him, or he might think she was throwing herself at him.

CHAPTER 21

They let Aaron rest.

When he woke, it was about ten in the morning, and Sapphira sat beside him looking at the others in their group lazing in the shade of a cedar. The peaceful countryside was a balm, and he was happy to be outside. He had been in the house for so long, he had forgotten what it was like to see the hilly landscape, blue sky, and green trees. He struggled to sit up, and Sapphira turned to help him.

"How are you feeling?"

"Tired of jostling around, but with any luck, I will be healed soon." He smiled, then started coughing. He had felt the tickle in the back of his throat and tried to hold it in.

Aaron watched Sapphira between slit eyes. Her color was good, and she didn't look as wan as she had at the house. The trip, the fresh air, and the company were doing her good. Many times, he'd wanted her to spend more time with other people, but she'd been determined to stay at his bedside.

From the moment he'd first seen her years before, he'd loved her. When he had moved to the countryside by Naraah, he'd gone into town to pick up some spices, and he'd seen her at the market. She'd been picking out a length of cloth to make a tunic for her brother's wedding. She'd been running her fingers through all the bolts of linen. He smiled. Sapphira was a handful, but she'd been the only woman for him. He'd waited until he felt Omar would approve his suit before approaching him.

He thought they'd been happy. Up until he got sick. She wasn't one to sit idly by when something needed to be done, so she'd done everything she could to make him well. However, it was beyond her ability. That had been hard for her to accept. Usually, no matter what she'd wanted, if she worked hard enough, she got it. Realizing his illness was beyond her control was tough.

"What did you see in me?"

She scrunched up her face as if in deep thought, but her eyes sparkled. "You were taller than me."

"That I was. There are a lot of shorter men out there. Demetrius, for example."

Her eyes lost the sparkle. And then she laughed. "Yes, he is much shorter than you." She twined her fingers with his.

He was surprised at how often she touched him these days. She'd never been clingy, but lately, she was always holding his hand or patting his covers in place. She was afraid of him dying and afraid to discuss it. Whenever he tried to reassure her that she would be fine if he died, she changed the subject. "What do you want most?" he asked her.

"For you..."

"Besides that?"

She looked bewildered and lost. "I haven't thought about it. I suppose for Caleb and Rachelle to grow up strong and healthy."

"But for you?" He knew the question threw her. They didn't talk about such things. The harvest and what needed to be done, the measures to make the farm prosperous. Those were their usual topics of conversation. They didn't discuss feelings or wants. Life was a focus on needs. But he had this day on the road with her, and they couldn't spend it on anything practical. He wanted to know more about his wife.

She shook her head. "I don't know. What do you want?"

He'd been waiting for her to ask. Would she want to know? As much as he believed in God and Jesus, this might be his last chance to talk to her about this. Praying to God to live longer was one thing. God's answer, another. "I'd like you to believe in God again."

"I believe in God."

"Not like you used to believe, before I became ill. And before your mother died." He looked at her steadily. "Why are you so angry at Him?"

"Because you're sick. No God would make a kind man like you sick. And because my mother's death and my father's death changed my life. I don't want to talk about it."

"What if that's all I want to talk about? Are you going to ignore me for the rest of the trip?" It was a cruel thing to say and do. He knew her lack of control in making him well again was difficult for her to live with already. "I'm sorry, Sapphira. I just want to know someone will take care of you."

"Omar will watch over me." She turned her gaze downward, staring unseeing at her hands.

"I'm talking about your soul."

"I believe my soul is just fine, thank you. Leave it. I don't want to argue with you. The day's too beautiful."

Even as she said it, clouds were gathering in the north. They were likely to get wet if they had to go north, and Aaron didn't know how that would affect his illness. He'd taken care to stay out of the open air for months now. Would he make it to Jesus in time? He felt weaker than ever, or maybe he noticed it more because he knew he had to get help soon. Jesus could heal him, but would he make it in time?

"I have other family, Sapphira. They will take care of you." He gripped her hand tightly. "You won't be dependent on Omar if something happens to me."

"You've never mentioned other family. I thought you were an only child, and your parents were no longer living?"

"I have three brothers named Daniel, Levi, and Noah, and my sister Keziah. My parents are alive as far as I know. I haven't been back to Jericho since I came here to Naraah. I'm closest to Noah. I had Elam send a note to Noah about how sick I am. If he hasn't changed, he will come to see how I am, and I've asked him to help you and the children with anything you need." He watched her take in this information.

"Why haven't they ever come to Naraah? Why didn't you tell me about them? I don't understand how you could have kept this secret for so long."

"I didn't think I'd ever see them again, so I didn't think it was necessary."

"Necessary? Your children might have cousins they could get to know. I would have loved to have aunts and uncles."

Aaron realized she was probably thinking that she'd like to have more than Omar, Naomi, and Samuel in her life.

"There was a reason I couldn't go back to Jericho."

"Why? What possible reason could you have for not seeing your family for over ten years?"

Their conversation was cut short when Demetrius came up beside them. "Let me check on him, Sapphira, and then we'll get back on the road."

Aaron watched Sapphira help the others gather their belongings and repack the bags for the horses to carry. "We're getting there, Demetrius."

Demetrius had his hand on Aaron's wrist, checking his pulse. "We'll get there. You keep hanging onto that horse. Your pulse is a little higher than normal."

"I'm excited." He could feel the tremble in Demetrius's hand. "You are, too."

They grinned at each other like boys. "I can't wait to see a miracle in person, instead of hearing about one. The fact that it will be you who is healed is even better."

Sapphira appeared at their side, leading her horse, and John brought Aaron's. John passed the sheepskin with water to Aaron. He took a drink and spluttered between sips, getting wet in the process.

"Are you all right?"

"You know how it is." He stopped to cough again. "Just a little while." He handed the sheepskin back to John. "Let's get on the road."

The others in their party were pretending to fuss with the horses, but Aaron knew they were waiting for him to gain his strength so they could continue. He held on to the hope that he would be healed soon, and they could make the return journey in a few hours instead of this leisurely pace. He remembered when he was strong and quick. It wouldn't be long now.

The rest of the day passed in a slow and monotonous film of dust and heat. He coughed, willing himself to stop, but was unable to. Sapphira never left his side, and while there was not much she could do, he appreciated her support.

He needed to tell her more about his brother Noah, but that would have to wait until they had a free moment. He should have told Sapphira years ago about his family instead of keeping them a secret.

CHAPTER 22

John had been right. Shortly after their break, they reached the well-traveled road between Bethany and Ephraim. A constant stream of travelers flowed in both directions. They could see many people ahead of them and behind them.

They took a moment to decide which direction to travel. Should they head toward Bethany or Ephraim? Which way were they likely to meet up with Jesus? After a few conversations with some travelers, they were rewarded with the information that Jesus had not reached Ephraim yet. They chose the direction most likely to cross paths with him and continued their journey.

The sun was high in the sky. Leah rode beside her, and Sapphira began to find the constant movement jarring. She was aware of Aaron's cough and that he slumped over his horse, barely able to hang on. Demetrius walked beside him, and Gideon rode the extra horse. Elam and John followed behind them. Neither looked as weary as Sapphira felt.

She could feel the tension in the group as Aaron's strength dwindled. According to the last traveler they had spoken with, Jesus was only an hour's ride away.

"How are you doing, Sapphira?" Leah asked.

She glanced at Leah as the horse plodded at a gentle pace. "My rear is sore."

Leah laughed. "Mine, too. I didn't want to say anything."

"I think he's going to make it." Leah gestured toward Aaron. She spoke quietly so no one else heard.

Sapphira looked at Aaron, slumped over the horse's neck. "He's determined, but I don't think he has much strength left. I hope those people who told us where Jesus is are right." Her voice broke, and she took a deep breath. Just a little longer. That was all the time they needed.

They continued talking quietly, pointing out travelers as they progressed along the road.

The road sloped up and down as they traveled. Less vegetation was near the road because of all the animals that had traveled along the packed dirt. Many travelers had allowed their horses to nibble the green near the road. Grapevines grew along the route in the distance, and acres of tilled land waited for planting that would happen in the next few weeks.

Sheep and goats roamed, guided by their herders.

As Leah and Sapphira talked, Demetrius glanced at them, then motioned to Aaron. Aaron no longer directed the horse's steps. Demetrius was leading it.

"John," Sapphira called to him. "Please help Demetrius." She stopped her own horse, and the group stopped.

"Let's get off the road," Elam said, steering them toward an area off the road and out of the way of the travelers.

When they pulled over to the side of the road, Sapphira slid off her horse and handed the reins to Leah. Demetrius and John lifted Aaron to the ground. Sapphira grabbed his hand, but he didn't move.

Demetrius leaned over Aaron, checking him. "He's unconscious but still breathing."

Sapphira took a deep breath. They were so close. Aaron couldn't die now.

John stood over Demetrius and Aaron.

"It's getting hotter. Maybe a drink will revive him," Demetrius suggested.

They couldn't revive Aaron enough to get him to take a sip. He moaned once, then fell back into his stupor. He was no longer coughing.

Sapphira had thought the coughing worried her. The silence was worse.

While Sapphira watched, the men struggled to get Aaron back on his horse, and then they continued on. Demetrius walked on one side of the horse and John on the other side to keep Aaron from sliding off. Sapphira kept to the side and slightly behind to keep an eye on him. They rode this way for a while, and then Elam and Gideon took turns watching over Aaron.

John asked another traveler if he knew Jesus's whereabouts.

The man scratched the top of his head and looked at the other man traveling with him. "I think he must be a little east of Ramah, don't you think?"

"Ah, yes. I believe that's about where he is."

Another traveler overheard their conversation and stopped walking. "I think he's closer to the north of here. You've probably gone too far south," he said to John.

John thanked the travelers, and the men continued on their journey.

John stopped the group. "I think we'll need to send someone ahead to find out exactly where Jesus is. We're getting conflicting reports, and that isn't good. I hope we didn't miss him."

Sapphira looked around at the country beside the road, looking for a place for them to rest. There was a little hillside with no tilling or other work done to indicate someone needed the area for their crop, and she suggested they rest there and wait.

"Who should we send?" John asked.

"I'd be willing to go." Gideon spoke for the first time since Aaron had fallen into his stupor.

The men looked at each other. "Do we send him alone? Is it safe?"

The morning had been peaceful on the road, but they had heard stories of people being set upon by ruffians. As a big group, they weren't concerned, but should they send Gideon alone?

"I'll go with him," John said. "I don't think we should let anyone travel alone. Besides, if there are two of us, we can talk to more people."

Gideon looked disappointed but went along with the plan.

Sapphira wondered if he had the scrolls with him and was trying to find a way to sell them. They were trying to save Aaron, and Gideon was here for his own purpose.

After Gideon and John had left on two of the horses with supplies they might need, the others settled at the bottom of a hill in the shade of a sycamore tree. A stream flowed on the other side of the tree, and Sapphira sighed in the cool shade.

Aaron lay beside her, still and quiet, his breathing shallow. She wanted to cry, stomp her feet, and yell. Instead, she sat listening to the birds and Aaron's breathing. Was this the end? She reached out and held his hand.

Leah sat quietly beside her, and Demetrius sat on the other side of Aaron.

Elam took care of the two remaining horses.

"Why did Gideon want to go alone?" Demetrius asked.

Sapphira shrugged and kept her suspicions to herself. "I wondered the same thing. He and Elam were fighting earlier. Did you notice?"

"No."

"You were probably helping Aaron at the time."

"I'm sorry, Sapphira. There's not much I can do for him anymore. We just need to keep him comfortable until we can get to Jesus. We have to have faith."

She saw regret in his eyes that he couldn't help her or his friend. "I know. I'm clinging as hard as I can. I have to believe God wants us to get to Jesus in time."

Leah glanced at Sapphira. "What do you think he will be like?" she asked. "I heard he's handsome and strong."

Demetrius's face reddened, and he got up. "Excuse me." He walked over to join Elam by the horses.

Sapphira shook her head, but her frown was only slightly disapproving and her words mild. "Leah, you're married."

"I know. That's just what I heard." Leah's smile was not penitent. "You know this is our only chance of ever getting out of Naraah and seeing part of the world. And to see Jesus. No one in the history of the world after us will have the opportunity."

Sapphira's discomfort over their journey grew. They pinned their hopes on a man who was simply that. A man. Aaron's life hung on the possibilities of one man saving him. What if Jesus was killed before they arrived, or what if Aaron died here on this hillside?

Leah's voice shook when she said, "Tarad was scary when he talked about their plans to kill Jesus of Nazareth. Jesus has made himself unpopular with his teachings and healings, especially on the Sabbath."

"I know, and I can't help but fear that we'll be too late. Either Aaron won't make it before we meet Jesus, or we won't be able to find him." She spoke softly to keep Aaron from hearing them. She didn't add that she had some doubt that Jesus could heal Aaron. She kept that doubt to herself. She was losing hope that this trip had been the right thing to do.

Everyone else had been so positive. What did they think about Jesus? They all wanted to see him, meet him, and watch him preach and heal people. Even Gideon, whom she thought of as an unscrupulous thug, had several of his own questions and requests of Jesus. The trip had started out with Aaron's desperate plight, but the others were as committed to reaching out to Jesus and finding their own answers.

"I think you will feel much better if you'd show a little faith. It seems to me that you go out of your way to find the most difficult path."

Sapphira fought the retort that sprang to her lips. Leah's husband wasn't the one dying. John was in perfect health.

His dark hair and thick beard bespoke of excellent health. His body strong from climbing on roofs and thatching. "It's easy to show faith when you don't need something as badly as I do. If your husband were dying, I think you'd feel differently."

Leah drew away from Sapphira, and her lip quivered.

Sapphira drew breath to apologize, but Leah spoke first. "That's not fair. Aaron's my friend, too. Do you think it's been easy for John or me to watch him as he became sicker and sicker? We know the result of consumption just as you do. We know this is his only chance."

Sapphira's knuckles whitened as she gripped them in her lap. Shame joined resentment. Had she turned into a bitter old woman at twenty-eight? She glanced at Aaron, hoping he hadn't heard. He seemed to still be unaware of his surroundings.

"I'm sorry, Leah. Ever since Aaron's been sick, I've been afraid. And I know it's no excuse to treat you shabbily when you've been such a good friend. The past few days since we've decided to take this trip have been stressful. I know you're as worried as I am."

Leah patted her clenched hands. "It's fine. I know how hard it is. It's just that you don't seem to be aware the rest of us are suffering, too." She raised her hand to stop Sapphira. "I know it's harder for you, but we love Aaron. He's like a second brother to me." She glanced back over at Demetrius, who was preoccupied with his own thoughts. "I can't imagine losing Demetrius or Aaron. As for John…" She shuddered. "I'm sorry, but I can't even imagine."

"I try not to either, but I feel so helpless. Let's talk about something else. I appreciate Demetrius coming with us. He's been a tremendous help."

"He wouldn't miss it for the world—not only to help Aaron, but he's fascinated with Jesus and has wanted to meet him ever since stories emerged about his healing and teaching. To him, it's like finding the source of healing."

"As a physician, is there something Demetrius wants to ask about?"

"I don't know. He hasn't said, and you know how close-mouthed my brother can be."

"I can't imagine Demetrius with a secret. He seems so open and honest."

"Secrets don't have to be bad. They're just things others don't know about us."

"True." The sun was in its zenith, and Sapphira relaxed under the shade tree as she thought about secrets. Aaron's and hers. Aaron would never know because if she told him about the scrolls, it would kill him. She recommitted every line and angle of his face to memory, longing for more time with him. A tiny bead of hope caught her by surprise. She had begun to believe it might be too late for Jesus to heal him. But, while Aaron was still alive, there was still hope.

"I bet Gideon has tons of secrets. He looks like a man who hides a new secret every day," Leah said.

Sapphira laughed, albeit a tiny one, keeping her own secret about Gideon. "You make such stories of other people."

Leah laughed, too. "And you find it entertaining. Admit it."

Sapphira caught sight of John and Gideon in the distance and hoped that meant good news. "They're coming back already."

Leah's gaze followed hers to where the men were returning. She leaned over to whisper in Sapphira's ear. "Demetrius has been watching you."

"Leah." Her shocked gasp went ignored in the arrival of the men. Why had Leah said that to her, especially now?

Demetrius rejoined them beside Aaron and asked, "What have you found out?"

John looked down at Aaron's unconscious form. "We missed him."

Sapphira gasped. "No, don't say that."

"Jesus took a route off the main road and went around to Ephraim. We don't know exactly where he is, but we'll have to turn around and go north to Ephraim. We should be able to catch up with him there."

"This is not good." Demetrius eyed John meaningfully.

Sapphira refused to give in to their fear. "We need to continue on then. We've been resting for a while, so we should get going right away."

Leah held up her hand to stop her. "Maybe John and Gideon need a few moments to rest before we start?"

John shook his head. "Let's get Aaron loaded on the horse and go. If Gideon and I need a break, we can stop and let you go ahead of us. We can easily catch up once we've rested. I don't think we'll have to stop, though. Ephraim is only an hour away."

They quickly got ready, mostly in silence with only a few words of direction to get Aaron mounted and the supplies repacked and placed on the horses. Leah rode on one of the horses that John and Gideon had used because she weighed the least. Aaron and Sapphira each rode the two rested horses, and they left the last horse riderless.

"We'll get Aaron to an inn in Ephraim," Demetrius said. "I'll sit with him while the rest of you search for Jesus."

"No," said Sapphira. "You go look with the other men. Leah and I will keep watch over Aaron. There's nothing you can do anyway, and I'd prefer we have as many people looking for Jesus as possible."

They all knew the urgency and silently trudged back along the road they had taken. When they reached the point where they had entered the main road, they had walked about thirty minutes.

They stopped when they heard a scream from somewhere ahead on the road.

John ran past them. "I'll check it out. You stay here with the women."

They waited impatiently, but soon, John was back and said it was only a family dispute, and they could continue on their way. Demetrius held Aaron firmly on the horse as they walked along.

When Sapphira and Leah reached the top of the hill, they saw a young boy around the age of six sitting on a horse ahead of them. A young man was trying to lift him off the horse, and a woman and little girl watched from the side of the road. As they came closer, Sapphira heard the scream again.

"I don't want to get off." The little boy's legs clung to the saddle, and the man shrugged at the woman.

Sapphira couldn't hear what the man said. They were still too far away. "I don't understand why they let that boy do what he wants," she said to Leah.

"What would you have them do?" Leah asked. "His legs are clinging to the horse."

Sapphira thought the parents should forcibly lift the boy off the horse. They were bigger than him.

John had reached the little group and was talking to the man. The boy had quit screaming and was fascinated by Elam, staring at his gray beard. He reached out as if to touch it, but after a quick look at his father, his hand dropped.

"What's going on?" Aaron asked.

Sapphira jerked around on her horse at Aaron's words. "You're awake. Thank goodness! There's a family in front of us, and their little boy's upset. Elam and John are talking to them."

They came abreast of the family, and Elam stepped away. The little boy continued to stare at Elam but backed away when Aaron coughed.

John nodded at them, and the family started their horses moving again. Sapphira waved at the family as she urged her horse on.

Demetrius talked quietly to Aaron, and then Aaron slumped forward again. She felt Demetrius's gaze on her. "He said he'd make it to Ephraim."

She nodded. There was nothing else they could do but keep walking. At least Aaron was awake and wanted to continue.

Leah spoke. "I'd like another little boy. Do you want more children, Sapphira?" Then she slapped her hand over her mouth as she looked at Sapphira.

Sapphira didn't know what to say. She hadn't told anyone other than Leah and Aaron of her pregnancy. If Aaron didn't get well, there was no way she wanted more children with another man. She shuddered at the reminder of Omar's edict, that she would marry Gideon. Please, God, not Gideon. Aaron had to get well. He had at least woken for those few minutes. Surely, that was a good sign. He would endure until they reached Jesus. "It's fine," she said wearily.

The long day was getting to her. The heat and dust stirred up on the road clogged her nose and dried her throat. Would they ever get there?

"We're almost there," John said.

She could see the town in the distance and felt her spirits briefly uplifted. They were so close.

The silence lengthened until Demetrius spoke. "We're making good time. We should get to Ephraim soon. We're lucky it hasn't rained. These roads would be difficult to travel."

He caught her gaze over Aaron's back, and she lowered her head. Leah had made her self-conscious about Demetrius's feelings for her. When she thought he would no longer be looking at her, and she had her expression under control, she raised her head.

Demetrius was still watching her. "We'll make it," he said softly.

She dropped her gaze again, holding back the tears. She had cried when she first found out how sick Aaron was and then again just this week. Now Demetrius's compassion was almost her undoing. He might have feelings for her, but he knew she loved Aaron.

Leah continued talking. "I hope Naomi is doing fine with the children."

Sapphira was grateful for the distraction. "The children are very well behaved. They'll be fine. I'm afraid Omar will have worked Caleb too hard by the time we get home."

Sapphira tried not to think about what would happen if Aaron was gone. How would she provide for the children? Who would do all the things the man of the house does? How would Omar treat the children? Her head bowed and tears blurred her vision. What she wouldn't give for a few moments of privacy.

CHAPTER 23

Gideon had been watching her slyly all day. His sideways glances and knowing looks were getting to her. Would he keep quiet about the scrolls? She knew he planned to sell them in the first big town he could find. Now that they were going to Ephraim, he would have his chance. Maybe he would leave her alone once he had his money.

Without realizing it, she had fallen behind the group the closer they got to Ephraim. Elam and Demetrius were holding Aaron on the horse, and she wasn't needed except to watch Aaron. Gideon slowed down, and soon, he was walking beside her.

She tried to move ahead of him to join the others, but he put his hand out and slowed her horse to match his pace. Elam looked back at them, but Gideon shook his head. When Elam looked at Sapphira, she shook her head also. She was safe, and everyone could see them. Gideon wouldn't try anything, and she had to hear what he was planning.

"All alone?" he asked.

She ignored his comment, waiting for him to get to the point.

"Too good to talk to me now, huh? It wasn't always that way." He threw her another of his suggestive glances. "Remember the synagogue."

"What do you want?" she asked, tired of his games.

"Since we don't have much time before someone interrupts, I'll get right to the point. I want to sell the scrolls at Ephraim."

So, she had been right.

"You can make sure I have the time to do that."

"You forget. Everyone will be out searching for Jesus. You can do it then. Although I'd appreciate it if you'd find Jesus first before you take off and follow through on your plans. You know how sick Aaron is. We don't have a lot of time."

"If you don't give me the opportunity, I'll talk to Aaron. As sick as he is, it could be the end of him, if you know what I mean."

"Would you really do that, Gideon?" she asked. "Are you that mean?"

"You have a lot of faith in Jesus."

She noticed his tone had become thoughtful rather than his usual sarcastic twist. "I do. It's Aaron's only chance."

"We have a deal then. You'll help me get away to sell the scrolls, and I'll make sure Aaron gets to see Jesus."

Elam rode toward them.

"We have a deal." A deal with the devil. Why would God help her get Aaron to see Jesus when she was plotting with a man to sell sacred scrolls? Because Aaron had done nothing wrong. That's why. And she'd gotten herself in this mess by helping Gideon in the first place. All to get money to have the Jewish physician Tobias, the son of Uri, see Aaron. Which had been a waste of time because he hadn't required money to examine Aaron anyway.

Gideon grabbed her hand where it lay on the reins. "Keep this information to yourself, or you'll be dead before your husband. My father doesn't need to know any of this. Understand?"

She nodded, trying to get her shallow breaths under control. Gideon let go of her hand, leaving a red imprint where he'd squeezed it. She flexed it as an ugly grin returned to his face, and he slowly rode back to the others.

Her heartbeat slowed, and she shrugged off Gideon's fearful threats. She couldn't believe he'd threatened to kill her. She shuddered, then jumped when she heard Elam's voice beside her.

"Are you fine?"

"I'm fine."

"He's someone you should stay away from," Elam continued.

Too late, she thought. "I know. Unfortunately, they're going to marry me off to him when Aaron's gone."

"I know. You don't want that, do you?"

What should she say to Elam? He was Gideon's father, and yet he was warning her to stay away from Gideon. "That's what Omar wants. Let's not talk about it today. Let's wait and see what happens with Aaron." If only Jesus could heal Aaron.

"Are you sure you're fine?"

She nodded again. "I just need a few moments. Thank you."

He looked at her. "Aaron made plans for you if he doesn't make it. I thought you should know. We'll make sure you don't end up with Gideon, even if it's your brother's wish."

He joined the others, and it wasn't long before she moved back into place beside Aaron, satisfied that Elam had followed through on Aaron's request to contact Noah. Elam's comment also rekindled her curiosity about Aaron's family. Aaron's recent revelation to her about his family was abruptly interrupted earlier when Demetrius wanted to check on Aaron. She needed to get Aaron alone and alert and have him finish his story.

CHAPTER 24

Elam pulled Gideon aside a few miles outside of Ephraim. They trailed the others, watching for any danger on the road. "What was that all about with Sapphira?" He watched his son's face, recognizing the usual shiftiness and secretive behavior. Elam suspected it had something to do with the night he had interrupted Gideon and Sapphira.

"Nothing. We were talking about the scenery. She hasn't traveled much."

Gideon's smile was cruel.

"I don't think so. She's a woman in mourning. It's best if you leave her be."

"She started it. She wanted to talk to me." Again, the knowing smile.

Elam knew that wasn't true. He had seen Gideon deliberately slow his pace so he could talk to Sapphira. "We've known her for a long time. You've always been a little smitten with her, ever since we moved in with Omar and Naomi."

"Are you asking or telling me?"

"She's not going to love you back, son. You know that. I'm sorry."

"It's not your business."

"It's my business to protect her. Right now, she's married to Aaron, and it's our duty to help Aaron get to see Jesus. Whatever business you've come to conduct on your own behalf should wait until we're done with Aaron." Elam didn't know why he was pushing it now. Maybe because it was time to get it out into the open, and Gideon needed the cover of arriving with a sick man to do his business if he wanted to remain undetected in his thievery.

"I'll be able to do both. Sapphira has agreed to help me."

"Because you forced her. I don't know what hold you have over her, but it's not right when she has so much to deal with already," Elam said. "Going against God's word. I have an idea what you and Sapphira were doing in Naraah that night. I saw her dress."

At the surprised look on Gideon's face, Elam laughed, a humorless grunt. "And do you think I don't know about the subversive meetings you had going on? The times that you fomented strife and uprising against Jesus's teaching? Do you think I don't know how you and Tarad plot against Jesus? He has only done good, and you plot to kill him," Elam said.

A look of righteous indignation crossed Gideon's face, as if he'd been slighted by his father's words. "Sapphira had her own ideas. She was against God because of Aaron's sickness. If it hadn't been at my meeting, she'd have gone elsewhere to find answers. I led that woman nowhere."

Sadly, he wasn't mistaken about his only son. He left the subject of Sapphira. "And you've stolen religious artifacts and plan to sell them when we get to Ephraim."

Gideon smiled. "There will be plenty of takers. Lots of believers who will want something holy to hang onto and pray over."

"That's blasphemous."

"You can't stop me. That would prolong this trip, and you know we need to get Aaron to Jesus as fast as we can."

"So, you don't plan to see Jesus for yourself?" Elam asked, sure that Gideon's answer would be a scornful agreement.

There was a pause. Then Gideon laughed his scornful laugh again, although Elam detected some hidden fear as well. "I will. I'll ask him about Mama and why she had to die." He laughed again. "Just to see what he says." He rode away from Elam.

Elam watched him go, surprised by the moment of tenderness he felt for Gideon. He understood the fear. Was Jesus the Son of God? Or was he only a teacher of God's word? Would they get answers to their lifelong questions? He didn't know if Gideon's fear was that Jesus was real or that he wasn't. For himself, he was afraid of the answer about why his wife had to die. Elam wasn't even sure why he knew Jesus had come from God, but he did believe that.

CHAPTER 25

"He's worse," Sapphira said to Leah. They rode side by side down the road several paces in front of the others. The men made the women ride in front of them, so they could see them and any potential trouble. The roads were full of travelers the closer they came to Ephraim.

Sapphira kept turning around to check on Aaron and tried to keep her fear to herself but had been unable to keep from telling Leah. "I think the journey is a mistake."

Leah shook her head. "Demetrius said it's his only chance."

Her hands clenched the reins. "He has an ulterior motive." She knew the scathing tone was a mistake, and Leah's face confirmed it.

Leah frowned. "I thought you liked Demetrius. You were certainly standing rather close to him when he helped you onto your horse."

"Of course, I stood close. How else could he help me?" She felt heat rising to her face and ducked so her hair hid her blush. "I love Aaron. You know that."

"I thought you loved Aaron, but your behavior lately has led me to wonder if that's true."

Sapphira lifted her head to see Leah's expression. There'd been a note of slyness when she said the word behavior. "What are you talking about?"

"You and Gideon. Do you think I don't know?" Her expression was definitely one of accusation.

What did Leah know? She certainly couldn't have any idea that Gideon had blackmailed Sapphira to help him steal the scrolls.

"What are you talking about? You know I despise Gideon. He's the one chasing after me."

"He forced you to do something, didn't he? That's why he wanted to come on this trip. He's been arguing with Elam, too. What's going on, Sapphira?"

"Has anyone else noticed?" Was Aaron more aware of her actions than she'd given him credit for? The thought caused her heart to flutter. Was she causing his illness to progress so rapidly?

"If you mean Aaron, I doubt it. No one would tell him. It would break his heart and his spirit."

The hint of derision was evident to Sapphira. "I can't help that. I did what I thought was best."

"You mean you did what you felt like. Your hurt and anger at God came out in a way that will surely hurt Aaron when he finds out. You know that."

"Aaron will never find out." She glared at Leah. "You will not tell him whatever you think you know, and you know why not. You do not want to hurt him. He will not live much longer."

"But if Jesus heals him—"

Sapphira threw up her hand, scaring her horse. "If we don't find Jesus in time, Jesus cannot heal him. Aaron is as good as dead. You can see that, can't you?" All her pent-up anger and fear poured out. "Why does everyone insist he will live? He gets worse with each step we take. We will never reach Ephraim in time, and Jesus cannot heal him. I could be holding him in comfort at home, and instead, we're on this never-ending journey. It's too late. Jesus cannot heal him."

"You are tired, Sapphira. We are almost there. Look!"

They were about a mile outside of Ephraim. The others were far enough behind to let her and Leah talk in private, but close enough to keep them in sight if there was danger. They were so close to getting Aaron to Jesus. She prayed that everything would be all right.

"I'm sorry I scolded you about Gideon. I know it's not your fault."

Was Leah just saying that? Or did she believe Sapphira was innocent of wrongdoing? "I think we're all getting tired. You're right. This is hard on everyone. I'm sorry, too."

John separated himself from the others and came to walk between her horse and Leah's horse. He had a purpose. Would no one leave her alone?

"What's going on?" he asked Sapphira, keeping pace with them.

Leah watched from her seat on the horse.

"Nothing. What do you mean?"

"It looked like you and Gideon were fighting about something earlier."

First Leah, now John. "Nothing to worry about. He was going a little too fast, and I wanted him to keep Aaron in mind when he set the pace, so I slowed down."

"It looked like more than that to me. I saw him grasp the reins of your horse."

She cursed that her friends kept such a close watch on her. Sometimes she felt like they actively looked for things that she did wrong. She knew John only had her best interests at heart, but he considered her headstrong. Which was silly because his wife Leah, though quiet, often did things without thinking and got herself into trouble. "It was nothing."

"It looked like something."

"Leave it alone. Please, John. Leah and I were having our own little argument and have agreed that we're all getting tired. We're almost there."

"Then maybe you can tell me what's going on with Demetrius?"

Not John, too. Why did they keep asking her? She turned away from John and patted her horse. "He seems fine to me."

"That's what I mean. He's doing an excellent job with Aaron. I only hope we reach Ephraim in time. I know you've spent a lot of time with Demetrius since Aaron became sick."

She ignored any underlying meaning and stared at John, who had shown nothing but kindness since Aaron's illness. He was Aaron's close friend and had always looked out for him.

"John, I'm tired. We're almost to Ephraim, and we need to focus on Aaron."

"You're right."

She looked back at Aaron and slowed her horse until she was even with his horse. He was still unconscious. He had not woken up once since the child had screamed an hour ago.

CHAPTER 26

Elam and Demetrius called a halt to the journey right outside of Ephraim.

"We need to find a place for Aaron to rest while we search for Jesus," Demetrius said.

John stood beside Demetrius where they were still holding Aaron on the horse. "Let's stop at the first inn we can find, and then we'll go out and search for Jesus while the women take care of Aaron."

"We can't stop," Aaron said. Beads of perspiration stood out on his forehead, and what was left of his hair stuck to it. His eyes were dim and filmy.

Sapphira looked at him, noting the change in his appearance since he'd been slumped over his horse. She'd become so used to how sallow his skin looked, she wasn't conscious of the huge change that one day had made. Fear swept through her. This was it. Not sometime, not next week, not tomorrow. Probably within a few hours. A hope she hadn't realized existed was extinguished in that instant. Despite her words to others and her conscious thoughts that Jesus could heal Aaron, she had, in some tiny corner of her heart, feared the inevitable, that they wouldn't reach Jesus in time to heal Aaron.

She took his hand, holding it gently between her own. "We have to, darling. I'm sorry."

161

He shook his head. "It isn't over yet. I'll feel better after a little rest, and we can continue on."

"Let's get you into the inn for that rest. We can talk later."

His hand turned over so their palms were together. He squeezed hers with a grip firmer than she expected. "Thank you."

She knew he meant for everything they'd been to each other. It was as close to a goodbye as he would give. She knew he still held hope that he would be well enough to meet with Jesus.

She was certainly going to do everything she could so it could happen. Even if she had to drag Jesus of Nazareth to the inn where they were staying.

"I love you," she said, leaning over him and placing trembling lips on his. She didn't care about the display she was putting on for the others. In that moment, Gideon and Demetrius didn't exist. Only Aaron, whose lips returned her kiss softly and gently as they held hands.

"I love you, too. It'll be fine, Sapphira," he said against her lips before he started coughing again. Slumping forward on his horse, he let them lead the way into Ephraim.

They found an inn in Ephraim where they could stay. The innkeeper said they could have two rooms for the night, so they moved Aaron into one of the rooms. Demetrius stayed with Aaron and Sapphira. Leah, John, and the others took the other room.

Aaron roused somewhat as they settled him in the bed at the inn. His cough was low and full of phlegm. There was seldom a time when he wasn't coughing. The men carried him into the inn where the room was ready.

Her tears flowed freely now. Leah put her arm around Sapphira, and they followed the men. "Do you want me to stay with you?" Leah asked.

"No, thank you. I'd like time alone with Aaron." She looked apologetically at Leah, but Leah understood.

"I'll be in the room next door. Call if you need something."

Sapphira watched her walk away, then looked down at Aaron who lay on the bed. He wasn't coughing, but his breath was wheezy and shallow. She said to Demetrius, "I can take care of him now."

She was grateful when he didn't object, but it was another indicator of how bad the situation was.

"Can I get you anything?" he asked, getting up from the small wooden chair that had been placed by Aaron's bed.

"No." She shook her head. "Thank you for your help. I know you want to meet Jesus as much as Aaron does. I'm sorry for the delay."

"No apology necessary." He turned to Aaron, who lay with his eyes closed. Demetrius touched him gently on the shoulder. "Get some rest."

"Thank you," Aaron croaked, opening dim eyes and smiling weakly at Demetrius before closing them again.

Once Demetrius had left to talk to the other men about searching for Jesus, Sapphira took the chair beside Aaron's bed and held his hand.

The silence of being alone with Aaron and being still comforted Sapphira. She was not used to being on a horse for so long, and her rear was sore. She was tired from lack of sleep and constant worry.

She couldn't have her associations with Gideon be known and be Aaron's last memory of her. What was she going to do about him? Hopefully, he would get rid of the scrolls and not involve her in any way.

"I may die."

She was startled. She'd been thinking so hard about Gideon, and Aaron hadn't spoken for a while. He hadn't fallen back into his stupor, but she could tell he was barely functioning.

"Don't say that. You'll make it, and we'll get to Jesus in time." She suppressed her tears. "Don't give up now. You're almost there." She squeezed his hand.

"I'm tired, Sapphira."

"I know, dear. Close your eyes. Get some rest and you'll soon be well enough to travel the short distance we'll need to go. The other men have gone to find Jesus. Just hang on for a little while." She watched his eyes droop and hoped he'd fall asleep. They were so close, and even if Jesus couldn't heal him, Aaron deserved to see him before he died.

There was a quiet knock on the door, and she reluctantly let go of Aaron's hand. "I'll be right back."

She opened the door and was surprised to see Gideon. "What do you want?"

"Is he going to be all right? Will he make it to see Jesus?" He twisted his fingers in his beard, twirling it around his fingers.

She'd never seen Gideon so nervous and anxious. "I don't know. What's wrong?"

"Come with me."

"I can't come now. I can't leave Aaron alone."

"Who is it?" Aaron asked from the bed.

"Gideon. He wanted to tell me they were going downstairs to get some food. I'll have him bring some broth up for you." She turned back to Gideon. "Go. I'll come to see you in about fifteen minutes at the stable."

Some of Gideon's confidence returned. "You do that, or I'll have a story to tell your husband." He winked.

The good-for-nothing. She closed the door behind her and went to sit by Aaron again. "He'll bring us some food."

Aaron stared at her. "You never were a good liar, Sapphira." He closed his eyes and missed her mouth dropping open.

She clamped it shut again and didn't say anything. Hopefully, he'd sleep soon, and she could find out what Gideon wanted.

CHAPTER 27

When Aaron fell asleep, she slipped out of the room and went to get Demetrius from the room next door. He would know what to do to keep Gideon in line until they could get Aaron to Jesus. When she knocked, Demetrius opened the door. It was only him and Leah in the room.

She looked at Leah. "Do you mind if Demetrius checks on Aaron? I'm sorry to leave you alone."

"That's fine. I'll make sure the door is locked."

"Thank you." She turned to Demetrius. "Can you please bring your bag with you? He might need something to help him sleep."

"Yes, I'll do that." He picked up his bag of physician supplies and joined her in the hallway.

When they closed the door to Leah's room and had nearly reached her and Aaron's room, she stopped Demetrius. "Demetrius, I need your help."

She found herself pouring out the whole story about Gideon and the scrolls. "He's blackmailing me. He'll tell Aaron, and that'll kill Aaron. I know it will. We're so close to getting Aaron healed by Jesus. What am I going to do?" She looked at Demetrius in desperation.

"Let me think." He stood still in the hallway. "Calm down for a minute and let me think."

While he stood there, she could hear sounds of activity on the second floor of the inn. Footsteps were above them. They had been lucky to get rooms on the first floor as far away from the taproom as possible. The taproom was close to the entry of the inn, and they were on the far side. Occasionally, she could hear loud laughter and more footsteps, but her attention was on Demetrius as he paced the hallway.

She watched him anxiously. What could he do? There was nothing anyone could do. Gideon had all the power. If only she hadn't agreed to steal the scrolls. Gideon had promised to help Aaron meet Jesus, which he was doing, although he had ulterior motives. She hadn't thought Gideon would blackmail her during the trip. She'd thought he'd have the decency to leave her alone until after they returned home. She'd been so focused on Aaron and not Gideon that she didn't think of the consequences of stealing the scrolls.

But now here she was, and Aaron's last thoughts would be of her desertion and disloyalty because Gideon couldn't keep his mouth shut. The greedy… She sighed and looked down at her twisting fingers. She'd been twirling her gold marriage band around her finger. Somehow, Demetrius would help her. He'd know what to do.

Demetrius stopped in front of her. "I don't know what we can do."

Her heart sank at the words. A stone sinking to the bottom of her stomach and settling there, solid and heavy. Some fighting part of her still hoped. "There has to be something. We can't let him kill Aaron by telling him the truth. Not when Aaron has so little time left."

Demetrius stared at her, his mind working. "Perhaps there is one thing we could do."

She looked at him hopefully. "What?"

"Keep him from seeing Aaron. If you remain by Aaron's side, and I watch Gideon, we can keep the two apart." He looked satisfied. "That would work."

She felt the heavy mass in her chest breaking up, and she felt lighter. "That could work. Do you think the others could help do that? We don't need to tell them why. Just let them know Gideon shouldn't be left alone with Aaron?"

"Yes, I'll talk to them."

"Can you check on Aaron now? I need to see Gideon. I said I'd meet with him, and I need to pacify him, so he won't bother Aaron." She started walking to her and Aaron's room. "We have to get back to Aaron. He'll be waking up soon."

He touched her on her arm to stop her, and she felt the burn of his fingers and cursed herself for it.

"I don't think it's a good idea for you to meet with him alone."

"There will be plenty of people in the stable." At Demetrius's doubtful look, she said, "I'll be careful. I'll only be gone a few minutes."

When he started to object, she interrupted, "I'm going, Demetrius. You can't stop me. Please watch Aaron. Now, we have to hurry and not leave Aaron alone any longer."

She opened the door. "Thank you, Demetrius. For everything."

He came and stood close. "You're welcome."

She blushed and stepped inside. Aaron was sleeping. While Demetrius checked him out, she left the room to talk to Gideon.

CHAPTER 28

When Sapphira returned to the room, Aaron was listening to Demetrius, who sat in the chair beside his bed. Demetrius had a mesmerizing voice. She shook her head to dispel her thoughts. She needed Jesus to heal Aaron fast for a few reasons now.

Demetrius noted her arrival and stood up. At his questioning look, she nodded. Gideon was taken care of. For now.

She came over and sat beside Aaron on the chair beside the bed that Demetrius had vacated and took his hand. "How are you doing?"

"I'm fine." His voice was a bare whisper.

"You're looking a little better." Although, in truth, he didn't look much better. His eyes had puffy bags beneath them and were sunken in his bruised face. He looked small lying in the big bed.

"That's because I'm not clinging to a horse." He smiled.

Demetrius walked to the door. "I'll go and check if there's been any progress with the search for Jesus."

"Thank you for sitting with Aaron," Sapphira said.

"You're welcome." He left.

Aaron squeezed her hand gently. "Tell me what you've done." His eyes focused on hers.

Mesmerized, she couldn't look away. He knew. *Everything*. He'd always been good at reading her expressions most of the time, and she'd been so tired from this trip that she couldn't hide her feelings any longer. "I…" She couldn't continue. Did he want a full confession? What did he want from her?

"Tell me," he commanded.

And she found herself telling him some of it. "Gideon has been blackmailing me. I don't want to marry him, and he promised if I did one thing for him, he wouldn't force me to marry him. I knew that if we could get you to see Jesus, you'd live, then it wouldn't matter. But he's been bothering me during this trip. I think Elam knows something about it, but he hasn't said anything to me. Gideon threatened to tell you, and I was afraid that would kill you, and then your death would be my fault." She started sobbing and felt his hand smoothing the hair on her bowed head.

"Oh, Sapphira, I wish you'd come to me and told me sooner. I would have understood." He spoke in a raspy hushed tone.

"But if you had known what I'd done, you might have gotten sicker from worry, and it would be all my fault."

"I'm not going to die, Sapphira."

The zeal in his eyes frightened her. His pale face heightened the effect.

She stared at him through the tears blurring her vision. "You don't know that."

"Oh, Sapphira, come here." He held out his arms.

She laid her head on his chest.

He stroked her back and felt her shaking from her tears. "It's fine. I'm fine."

She held herself stiff, trying to keep her weight off of him.

"Relax. See? I'm not coughing."

And he wasn't. She rested against him. "I'm glad you know the truth." But he didn't know she'd gone and talked to Gideon again. That Gideon had threatened to tell Aaron about the scrolls. It didn't matter anymore. It was too late. Aaron knew what had happened.

"How did you find out?" she asked.

"I had someone watching over you."

She pulled away. "What do you mean, watching me?"

"I didn't say watching you. I said watching over you. Making sure you were safe."

"Why wouldn't I be safe?"

"People aren't always kind to those they view as vulnerable. I didn't want anything to happen to you."

"Why didn't you tell me what you were doing?"

"I knew you'd object. You're upset now over the idea."

"So, if I hadn't told you about the Friends of Jesus meeting, you would have found out?" She noticed he hadn't mentioned the scrolls.

"Yes, someone told me a few days ago. I'd asked him to look out for you, and he did. He didn't want to tell me what you were doing because he knew what those meetings were about. He was concerned about you, and he wanted me to know that time was limited—that we only have a few days before they'd arrest Jesus."

She had almost forgotten that Jesus was to be arrested. When Aaron had fallen into his stupor, she had only thought they wouldn't get to Jesus in time. The reminder of Jesus's enemies concerned her. Would John and Elam find Jesus in time? Had Demetrius gone to look for them?

Sapphira felt stuck in this inn. She wished someone would come tell her what was happening. At least Aaron was gathering strength for the final trip to see Jesus, which couldn't be very far now. Would he be well enough to travel? He'd at least been conscious most of the time since they reached the inn, which was a good sign. "I thought we'd get there in time. That it didn't matter," she said.

She burst into tears again, thinking she'd cried so much in the past week, she was sick of herself.

When he didn't comfort her, a bigger fear intruded. He didn't love her anymore. She cried for that, too, along with everything else. Finally, the tears subsided. She waited for Aaron to speak, but he didn't say anything. She looked up to find him watching her with understanding. She felt a flicker of hope.

"Do you feel better?" he asked.

She nodded, suddenly shy. He knew of her fear, her disloyalty. She felt open and exposed. She cleared her throat and wiped her nose with one of the clean rags he always had by his side these days.

"Good. Soon we'll find Jesus, and the trip back will be quick. We'll see the children again and be a family and have our new baby."

As if they had all the time in the world. Perhaps they did. "Do you still love me, or have I been too much trouble? You had to have someone watch over me." She held her breath.

"More than I've ever loved you before. Come and lay beside me."

She took a deep breath and slid in beside him. "I love you, too. I'd do anything for you."

He could have said something about her activities in the past month, but he didn't. He pulled her against him, and she relaxed. She enjoyed feeling the heat of his body next to hers and wished they could make love.

"What are you thinking about?"

"That there's still hope." And there was. She didn't know where the tiny kernel came from, but she did hope they would make it to see Jesus, and despite all her doubts, he could heal Aaron.

"There's always hope."

She fell asleep.

CHAPTER 29

Aaron woke to find himself alone. It was an odd feeling after the day's travel and everyone taking turns sitting with him. Where was Sapphira? She must be checking with Demetrius and Leah to see if the men had found Jesus. Gideon was blackmailing her. Aaron remembered Sapphira's confession that Gideon was blackmailing her but not what Gideon's hold was over her.

God, forgive her. She doesn't understand. Help her to understand. I'll do anything to save her soul. Even if I need to die now to save her, take me. But, please, help me live so I can lead her on the right path. She doesn't know You like I do. I want my children to grow up with their father there to guide them. I want to lead them to You. Please don't let me die here in this inn. Please let Jesus save my life to show Sapphira the truth. Whatever I need to do, I will do it.

He felt hot and cold by turns. One minute, he was throwing off his blanket, the next, pulling it to him and huddling beneath it for warmth. The coughing continued until finally he nodded off, only to wake up when the door opened.

He didn't recognize the man standing in the doorway. Aaron jerked to a sitting position. He didn't know what to think. "Who are you? What do you want?"

The man entered the room. "My name is Jesus. I've come to help you."

Aaron rubbed his eyes. Was he dreaming?

"No, you're not dreaming." Jesus smiled.

A radiant warmth spread throughout Aaron's whole body, and he relaxed. If the man truly was Jesus of Nazareth, he had nothing to fear. He didn't feel any threat from this man who called himself Jesus. "Come in."

Jesus walked further into the room and closed the door.

Aaron struggled to rise from the bed. To offer hospitality.

Jesus waved him back down. "Stay where you are."

He looked at the chair beside his bed. "You can sit if you'd like."

"I'm not going to be here long. My faithful disciples are probably looking for me." He walked closer and stood at the foot of Aaron's bed.

"What are you doing here? Did my friends find you?" Aaron asked.

"I was traveling, and we stopped here for a meal before going out to preach. I have not seen your friends, but I know you've been looking for me."

"I see." Although Aaron didn't understand. Was he dreaming?

"You are not dreaming. I came to heal you."

"I haven't coughed since you entered my room," Aaron said in wonder.

The man named Jesus smiled again and touched Aaron on his shoulder. "You won't cough from consumption again. You are healed."

Aaron stared at him, uncomprehending. "I'm well?"

"You're well."

"Why? Why me? You came for a special visit. Directly to me. Thousands have asked for your healing, and you've come to me. Why?"

"Because you are special to me, Aaron. As is your wife, Sapphira. She has done some terrible things, and she thinks she can't be forgiven. She's wrong. Sapphira has been forgiven. I could have healed you from a distance. One word to our Father, and you would have been healed. But I wanted to talk to you. I want you to talk to Sapphira when the time is right."

Aaron was confused by what he was hearing. "What has Sapphira done?"

"She'll have to talk to you about it, and you can assure her of the Father's forgiveness. That's why I needed to talk to you. Some things you already know, but she has done other things you do not know. Tell her she is forgiven."

Aaron heard someone calling outside his doorway in the hallway.

"Jesus! Jesus! Where are you?"

Jesus remained focused on Aaron. "You will tell her she is forgiven?"

"Yes, I will tell her." But Aaron was confused. He had no idea what Jesus was talking about. He had talked to Sapphira this afternoon and thought she had told him everything.

Jesus walked toward the door and stopped before opening it. "Don't worry. You will understand. And you are forgiven, too, Aaron. You can go home again. Noah will be with you soon. All will become clear to you. I must go."

As Jesus put his hand on the door handle, Aaron jumped from the bed. This man knew what he'd done in the past. How could he? He must be God. He ran to Jesus and got down on his knees. "Thank you. Thank you for everything. For healing me. For taking care of Sapphira."

Jesus touched Aaron on the head.

The same vibrant warmth spread through Aaron again.

"There are men plotting to kill you." Aaron hadn't meant to blurt out the words, but he wasn't fully alert yet.

"There is many plotting to kill me. I know what I need to do. The men outside the door looking for me are my friends. Get some rest. I must go." Jesus slipped out of the room.

Aaron heard someone talk to Jesus in the hallway.

"Where did you go?" the man asked.

"I had business, but I'm here now," Jesus replied to the man.

Aaron heard their sandaled footsteps recede. He was suddenly exhausted, as if he hadn't slept in weeks, which he hadn't. He climbed back into bed, determined to think about everything Jesus had told him.

God forgive her. She didn't realize what You can do, who You are. Please, let me live to help her. I forgive her for Gideon, and the Friends of Jesus, and Demetrius. She has sinned against You by going to that meeting, but please, forgive her. I will do anything You ask, just please, give her time and forgive her like I have. Only You know the true state of her heart, but I believe she's just afraid and ignorant of the extent of Your love. Please, God, I beg You, save her soul. Jesus said he loves Sapphira, and I believe Jesus is part of You. I trust You to take care of her.

He was overcome with fatigue. His last thought before sleep was a resolve to talk to Sapphira and share his incredible experience with Jesus. And find out what she'd done that she hadn't told him.

CHAPTER 30

Sapphira had finally dozed for a time beside Aaron, and her neck was cricked from her position in the chair. Aaron was in a deep, almost natural sleep, and he did not wake. When she'd returned from talking to Leah and Demetrius, who had heard nothing from John or Elam, she'd sat by Aaron's side and tried to relax. Her fatigue must have overcome her, or she wouldn't have fallen asleep.

She hurried from the chair when she realized the sound of people running in the hallway had awakened her. She went to the door, peeked out, and saw Demetrius and John going into their room. Glancing back at Aaron, she saw he was still asleep, so she slipped from their room and followed Demetrius and John.

They had left the door slightly ajar, and she opened it slowly, knocking as she entered, looking for Leah. John and Demetrius were leaning over Gideon, who lay on the bed. Leah was sitting on the room's chair, facing away from the bed, watching Sapphira enter the room.

Leah's face was white, and her lips were pinched together. They all heard the heavy boots of the innkeeper along the outside passageway, and Demetrius and John exchanged glances. Immediately, they pulled the covers up to Gideon's chin and turned to the door as it swung open.

"What's going on here?" the innkeeper asked, taking in the scene at a glance. "My guests expect quiet. I demand to know what the disturbance is." He looked down at Gideon, who hadn't moved since Sapphira had entered the room.

John stepped up to the innkeeper. "We're sorry, sir." He glanced back at the bed. "Our friend got a little out of hand. I'm afraid we've had to take care of the matter, and he's a little worse for wear." He looked the innkeeper in the eye. "If you know what I mean."

The innkeeper nodded, and Sapphira realized John was implying he'd knocked out Gideon because he'd been unruly in some way. "See that he doesn't cause any trouble."

"We'll take care of the matter quietly. Your guests won't hear anything the rest of the night. I guarantee you."

"You'd better, or I'll call the constable." He looked at Leah. "Are you fine? You look a little peaked." he asked in a kindly voice, unlike his prior roughness.

She nodded.

"You can come to me if there's a problem," he said. He looked at the men with a warning glance. "See that nothing happens to her or to any of the other women in your party." He glanced at Sapphira, whose mouth was open in shock. She snapped it shut. "Ma'am, I hope your husband is better soon. I hear you're looking for Jesus. He came here earlier. I told him about your husband."

"Thank you," she said.

He nodded and left.

When he was gone, they all looked at each other until the innkeeper's boots could no longer be heard clattering along the floorboards. Then John locked the door behind him.

The innkeeper had told Jesus about Aaron? Aaron hadn't told her anything, but he'd been asleep ever since she'd returned from talking to Gideon. She itched to get back to Aaron and see if he'd spoken to Jesus, but first, she needed to find out what had happened here. "What's going on?" she asked John. He seemed to be in charge.

So many other thoughts were running through her head, she had trouble focusing on John.

"Gideon's dead." He pulled the sheet over Gideon's head.

Sapphira stared at him, avoiding Demetrius's gaze. "What? What happened?"

He hesitated.

"What's going on, John?" Her voice rose at his name, and she pinched her lips together. No wonder Leah sat frozen on the chair, not looking toward the bed where Gideon lay.

"He's been murdered," Demetrius said. He ignored John's hushing motion. "They need to know. We have to make a plan, and everyone must be involved. I'm not keeping this from Leah."

"I'd prefer to know what's going on, though I don't want to see him," Leah said to John.

John looked unsure but didn't object to Leah staying. Demetrius nodded.

Sapphira took one more look at the motionless figure of Gideon, then turned back to John. "What about Elam? He'll want to know what happened. Where is he? He'll prevent us from seeing Jesus. He'll want to know what happened to Gideon."

"No one's going to stop us," John said. "If Jesus was at the inn, then we're very close. We might need to leave Gideon here until we've taken care of Aaron. I know it sounds cruel, but we can't do anything for Gideon right now."

Relief coursed through Sapphira. Aaron was resting quietly now, but how much longer did he have? She needed the men to talk to the innkeeper. "Leah, do you want to come to my room? We'll let the men take care of this situation. Maybe when they are finished, one of them will come with us to talk to the innkeeper?" She sent John a questioning look.

"I don't think there's much more we can do here, so I think we should talk to him."

She nodded. "What happened to Gideon?" She tried to keep the impatience out of her voice but didn't think she succeeded. She needed to get back to Aaron. "How did he die?"

"Looks like a knife wound," John said. "I found him in the stable when I returned. I came here to get Demetrius. He said Gideon was dead, and there was nothing we could do for him. We were lucky to find him and bring him here before anyone else saw him. We can't let this stop us from getting Aaron the help he needs."

Demetrius nodded in agreement.

Although Gideon had not treated her well, Sapphira was sorry that Gideon's death brought so little sadness to any of them. He, at least, deserved some mourning. Elam might be the only one to mourn Gideon.

"On second thought, we can't let the innkeeper know. He'll keep us here for a murder investigation. That may delay the meeting between Jesus and Aaron." Sapphira looked beseechingly at John. "Please. What are we going to do?"

"We don't tell the innkeeper he was murdered. We take him with us back home," Demetrius announced.

Leah shuddered, keeping her gaze fixed on Sapphira.

"There's no other way," John said. "We load him on a horse. Clean up the room and go on our way."

Sapphira looked at the blood on the sheets. "We'll have to exchange these bloody sheets with Aaron's and pretend that's Aaron's blood. We'll have to pay for the sheets."

"Leave it to us," John said. "Take Leah to your room and check on Aaron. I'll be with you shortly."

She looked at Leah, who jumped to her feet at John's words and wavered a little before she settled solidly on her feet.

John reached out to steady her, and she leaned on him for a second. "I'm fine," she mumbled.

"John's right, Leah. Let's check on Aaron. You can stay in our room until John's ready to talk to the innkeeper."

She followed Sapphira out of the room and closed the door firmly behind her. The women heard the lock click behind them.

CHAPTER 31

Aaron was still in a deep sleep when they entered the room. Sapphira frowned at the steady rise and fall of his chest.

"Is something wrong?" Leah asked. "He looks like he's better."

"I don't know. He seems to be breathing normally."

"Isn't that good?" Leah stood there, shifting from one foot to the other.

Sapphira edged nearer, looking closely at his cheeks. They had a hint of color. She touched his forehead, and it was cool to the touch. She frowned and shook her head. "I don't understand."

She was puzzled by Aaron's condition. "We might have to get Demetrius, though I don't want to go back to that room any more than you do."

"What is it?" Leah stared at Aaron's peaceful face. "What's wrong?"

"I don't know," Sapphira whispered. "He seems fine. He hasn't slept this well since he's been sick. He should be coughing and restless. But, he's peaceful."

Leah looked at her as if she'd gone crazy. "So why are you so concerned? Isn't that good? If he's fine now, we have more time to search for Jesus and take Aaron to him."

"I mean fine." Sapphira shook her head. "Like healthy fine. Like there's nothing wrong with him. He's been in this deep sleep for at least a half hour. Probably longer. I don't know. I fell asleep. And then I came to your room, and all that took time. I don't know how long it's been, but he's breathing normally. He's not wheezing, and you know he coughs constantly. He hasn't coughed at all."

Leah looked at Aaron. He still hadn't woken. His breathing was steady. Sapphira was right. He hadn't coughed once since they had come into the room a few minutes ago. She started smiling. "Maybe he's been healed."

"He wasn't healed by Jesus," she said sarcastically.

"What if he was healed by Jesus?" Leah asked quietly. "The innkeeper said Jesus was here and was looking for Aaron."

"I think you've taken a knock across the head." Sapphira stared at Aaron, wondering if Leah was right. She was tired and on edge. She wanted badly to believe that Leah was right, and Aaron was better, but what if he wasn't? Maybe this is how it is right before the end.

"I'll get Demetrius," Leah said, walking toward the door.

"Don't go in that room." She noticed the look of scorn that Leah threw her way.

"I know what's in that room. I'll knock and wait for Demetrius or John to answer the door. I won't go in."

When Leah left, Sapphira stayed beside Aaron's bed. She gazed down at him, and except for his breathing, he didn't move. She hadn't seen him rest so well in months. What had happened?

The door opened, and Demetrius went straight to Aaron's side. He did a brief exam and turned with an exultant look to Sapphira. "He's well. No fever."

"He hasn't coughed either," Sapphira said, unable to believe that Aaron was truly well.

Aaron stirred, and she brushed Demetrius aside. "Aaron, talk to me."

He stared at her in bewilderment.

CHAPTER 32

He didn't understand her urgency, and it took him a minute or two to fully come awake. His sleep had been dreamless and deep. Demetrius, Sapphira, and Leah all stood around his bed, staring at him. Their presence finally sunk in, and he sat up and slid his legs over the side of the bed. "What time is it?"

"Around six in the evening," Demetrius said.

"Why are you all staring at me?" He looked at them, surprised by their scrutiny. They had all been hovering around him for months, but now they had a look of disbelief on their faces.

"You're well." Sapphira shook his arm. "Look. You're not coughing. You're sitting up and talking like normal. You're not wheezing."

Aaron held up his hand. "Fine. I get it." But he didn't. He tried to make sense of it all. He didn't feel like he needed to cough. He'd actually sat up without starting to wheeze. What had happened? He remembered the man who called himself Jesus coming into his room, and then he'd fallen asleep. Had he been healed? Had he witnessed his own miracle? He grinned at Demetrius and turned to Sapphira.

"I'm healed. I saw him!"

Sapphira stared at him.

He could tell she didn't understand. "Jesus of Nazareth. He was here. He came to my room and talked to me."

They looked at each other in surprise.

"We missed him," Demetrius said, disappointed, but he grinned at Aaron. "You'll have to tell us all about it."

"He knocked on my door and came in." He looked at Sapphira, but she averted her eyes. "You must have gone to talk to Leah because I was alone when he came."

Demetrius turned to Leah. "I'll go let John know, so he doesn't hurry to speak to the innkeeper about Jesus. I think this changes our plans. We'll sort out the other situation, and I'll be back. I don't want Elam to come back from his search and find Gideon alone with John. We'll come back to talk when we're finished."

He clasped Aaron's hand. "I'm so happy for you. Save the story about Jesus for when I return."

Demetrius turned to Sapphira. "Explain to Aaron. I'll talk to John about our plans. Even though Aaron is well, we may need to stay overnight. It's getting late. Or maybe John will want to travel under the cover of darkness."

Bewildered by Demetrius's words, Aaron watched him leave. What were John and Demetrius doing? Why would Elam be upset if John was alone with Gideon?

Sapphira pointed to the chair beside the bed. "Have a seat, Leah. I'll sit by Aaron on the bed, and we'll discuss this."

Leah pulled the chair away from the bed and sat down.

Sapphira hugged Aaron. "I'm so glad you're well. I can't believe Jesus was here, and I missed him."

Aaron hugged her back and got up from the bed. He walked slowly around the room, testing himself. "I'm almost as puzzled as you are."

Sapphira and Leah watched him.

He didn't cough. His chest didn't feel all squeezed together any longer. He was well. The thought settled in, though he still couldn't comprehend it. "Why did Demetrius need to talk to John? It can't just be that I'm well. Tell me what's going on."

Sapphira frowned. "Gideon has been murdered. John came back from searching for Jesus and found Gideon stabbed to death in the stable."

She looked at him in wonder. "I can't believe you're well."

Aaron couldn't believe it either. What miracle had happened to him? Why for him? "Tell me more about Gideon."

"John and Demetrius moved Gideon's body from the stable to the other room. No one knows Gideon is dead except us. Leah screamed when she saw him, and the innkeeper threatened to throw us out of the inn. I think the only reason he hasn't is because he knows how ill you are. Or how ill you were. He doesn't want us to cause any more trouble."

"I think we'll have to stay one more night."

Leah shuddered.

Sapphira patted Leah's arm. "I don't think we can go back to Naraah this late. It's been a long day. You can stay in our room."

"Maybe the innkeeper would have another room for us."

Aaron didn't think the innkeeper would be so accommodating if they'd already caused problems, though Aaron might be able to convince him. Maybe the innkeeper would be happy to say that Jesus had been in his inn and healed someone.

Sapphira was smiling. "You're well."

"How many more times are you going to say that?" But he smiled, too, feeling guilty that he was so happy when Gideon was dead. A feeling of dread settled in the pit of his stomach. Someone had killed the man.

"What's wrong?" Sapphira asked. "You look ill again."

"I was thinking of Gideon."

Sapphira nodded. "I can't believe it. Who could have killed him?"

"It had to be one of us."

She looked at him in horror. "It can't be true. You don't believe that?"

"I do." He watched the understanding take root. "One of us, Sapphira." He emphasized her name.

"Don't," she said. "Don't ruin this moment. You're well. We've been waiting for this moment. Please."

"The truth will come out, sooner or later."

"Later. Let's savor this moment. Please, Aaron. Hold me." Sapphira's dark eyes were huge in her pale face. Her hair wild from resting on the bed beside him. "I love you, Aaron."

He strode over and held her. "I love you, too, Sapphira. How I love you." He stroked her back. "For this moment, nothing can come between us."

"Nothing will ever come between us." She reached up and touched his cheek. "Promise me."

"I promise." He hoped he could keep that promise. He wanted to kiss her, but Leah was in the room with them.

There was a knock on the door, and John entered without waiting for a response.

"We've decided to stay the night. It's too dangerous to travel at night. I've talked to the innkeeper, and he has another room available."

"If the innkeeper told Jesus about me, he probably already knows I've been healed. Men were looking for Jesus earlier. I think they were some of Jesus's followers. He knew them. He probably told them what happened, too."

"I doubt if he told them. He's not one to brag about what he's done. He heals people and moves on," John said. "I'm glad you're well, Aaron. I'm sorry our focus must be on Gideon, but we'll celebrate your return to health when we get back to Naraah."

"Thank you. You think it's due to Jesus that we are able to stay in another room?"

"He has a lot of influence. The innkeeper seems to know him. I wouldn't doubt that Jesus told the innkeeper to give us what we need. He came to us for some reason. Why would he do that?"

"Maybe the innkeeper sent out word with someone to find Jesus for us," Sapphira said impatiently. "I don't care how or why, only that Aaron is healed."

"Has Elam returned?" Aaron asked.

John shook his head. "Demetrius is standing outside the door waiting. When Elam returns, John will talk to him."

"I should be there, too." Aaron walked toward the door, but Sapphira stepped in front of him.

Sapphira glared at Aaron. "You may be well now, but you've been sick for a long time."

"I'm perfectly fine. God has healed me totally. I'm as strong as I ever was." He put his hands on her arms and gently moved her aside. "It's my turn to help. I need to go with John."

Sapphira stood as if stuck to the floor. "Help the others? You've just gotten up from your sick bed."

"I know. Isn't it great?" He grinned at her. He felt well. His chest didn't feel tight, making breathing easy again. His arms were strong. His legs no longer shook. His mind was clear. And he knew one thing. He wanted to see Jesus and thank him. For it could only have been by a miracle from God that Aaron was healed in a mere few hours. And he had another request of God.

Sapphira frowned at him. "I guess you're right, though I don't want to let you out of my sight. Leah and I will stay here. Let me know if you need help packing Leah's bag to move to the new room. I don't think she wants to go back into her old room." She looked at Leah.

Leah shook her head.

"We'll come back and let you know." It would take her a while to get used to him being himself again. He knew that. He exulted in the fact that he was well. He smiled again. He couldn't help

it. He'd have to remember the minute he stepped
out the door, though, that Elam was a grieving man,
and the others had their own battles to fight yet.
Sapphira had her own battle to fight. He took a deep
breath, opened the door, and waited for John to step
out ahead of him.

CHAPTER 33

Sapphira settled on the end of the bed and looked down at her hands, where she gripped them together in her lap. Aaron had been healed. She couldn't comprehend the suddenness of it at all. She'd worked so hard to find a solution, and just like that, he was healed.

"Are you all right?" Leah got up from the chair and settled beside Sapphira. She put her hand on Sapphira's clenched hands.

"I don't know. It's so sudden, and I wasn't here to see it happen." She was surprised at the bitterness she felt over that thought. She should be happy Aaron was well.

"It's hard to understand, isn't it? That Jesus really did heal Aaron." Leah patted Sapphira's hands again and stood up. "It will take a while for the truth to sink in. You need to give yourself time. You've been through a lot this past year."

Sapphira thought of all the things she'd done to get Aaron well. The things she regretted doing hurt the most, and had those actions been necessary? Aaron was well. She couldn't go back and undo them.

"You're overthinking everything," Leah said gently. "Maybe you need a nap while the men are doing whatever they're doing."

Sapphira looked fully at Leah. "You've had a shock. I'm so sorry. Here I've been thinking only of myself. Would you like to lie down?"

She shrugged and swallowed hard. "I'm fine."

Sapphira got up and hugged her. "Thank you for being such a good friend. Now that Aaron is well, perhaps I can be a better friend to you."

"You don't have to change anything. I would do it all over again for you and Aaron. If it weren't for what happened to Gideon, this would be a much happier moment."

"Who do you suppose murdered him?"

"Probably one of the men he associated with. Those men at the Friends of Jesus meeting were the sort who might murder him. Maybe someone followed us."

"You could be right." If only it were that simple. Sapphira sat down again. "Let's be happy for Aaron for the moment, and let the men sort out what to do about Gideon."

CHAPTER 34

When John and Aaron knocked, Demetrius came out of the room where Gideon lay.

"Where's Elam?" Aaron asked.

"Elam wanted a few minutes alone with Gideon. I'm afraid Gideon's taken your spot, Aaron. You'll have to walk back, and we'll put Gideon on your horse."

Aaron shuddered. Gideon, who was dead, had taken his place. He tried not to think of it in some symbolic way, but it was difficult. He nodded. "I think I'm healthy enough again and can walk. I feel fine." His miraculous healing was overridden by the reality of Gideon's death.

Elam came out of the room. His eyes were red, and his face sagged. He looked Aaron over. "I'm glad you're healed."

Aaron bowed his head to Elam. "I'm sorry about Gideon. I know you loved your son."

Elam's brow furrowed. "He did some things wrong, but I did love him. No matter what our children do, we can't help how we feel about them."

Aaron agreed.

"I'd like to talk with you alone for a minute, Aaron."

John broke into their conversation. "We haven't settled into the new room yet, but it's next door." He pointed to a room across the hall from Aaron and Sapphira's room. "Why don't you two talk in there? Demetrius and I can wait for you here."

"Thank you for not leaving him alone." Elam shook John's hand.

Aaron walked to the door John indicated and opened it. Elam followed him inside. The room was the same layout as his. There was a bed, a chair, and a small table. That was it for furnishings. "Why don't you take the chair, Elam? You've been walking all day, and I've gotten to ride on the horse."

Elam sat down on the chair, eyes fixed solidly on Aaron.

Aaron perched on the end of the bed. "What did you need from me? You know I'll help any way I can after what you've done for Sapphira and me." Aaron's thoughts centered on who killed Gideon and why. If they didn't leave before Gideon's death was discovered, an official investigation would start. He was afraid that one of their own group killed Gideon, and he didn't want the authorities involved. They would put to death whoever killed Gideon, and Aaron knew that wasn't the punishment he'd want to see one of his friends get, no matter what their motive had been. They might have had a good reason to kill Gideon.

"Are you feeling fine, Aaron?"

"I'm fine. Totally well, it seems. Jesus did come to my room and heal me. It's a miracle." He was still having trouble believing it, but his health was so good that he couldn't doubt Jesus. "I'm sorry about Gideon."

"Thank you. He was not always honorable, but he didn't deserve to die this way."

"We'll find the answer."

"Would you?" Elam stopped and pointed at Aaron.

"Would I what?"

"Will you find out who killed my son?"

"Why me? John or Demetrius could probably do a much better job of it," Aaron said. They had been involved with community events of Naraah the past few months, much more so than him. He didn't know anything about Gideon's life except what he occasionally heard. Someone else would be much better at discovering the truth.

"Because you were sick. I know you couldn't have killed my son, so I want you to find out who did. You'll be fair about it, too, and I know you'll seek justice as much as I would."

"I'll try, Elam, but I make you no promises."

"That's good enough for me." He held out his hand.

Aaron reluctantly shook it. They walked to the door. "I'll start as soon as I can. I'll make inquiries and see what I can find out. With everyone wanting to meet with Jesus, we'll still be in town tomorrow. That will give me time to ask questions before we return to Naraah." He said nothing of the possibility that the murderer was returning with them on the trip back.

"Thank you. I'll owe you a debt when this is over."

"No debt. I owe you for the time you've spent helping me and Sapphira while I was ill. Time spent by you and Gideon."

"He was at the Friends of Jesus meeting, too." The words came out painfully slow.

"So, he might have had enemies from that group? One of them might have followed us to the inn and killed him."

"That is a possibility. I had to tell you."

"I already knew, Elam, but thank you for being honest with me. That's the only way we'll find Gideon's killer."

When they entered the hallway of the inn, Leah and Sapphira were talking to John.

After Leah and Sapphira offered their condolences, the group went down to the main room to eat.

Before they entered the room, Sapphira pulled Aaron aside. "Are you fine? What did Elam want?"

Her words were rushed, and he didn't know which of her questions meant more to her. He thought it might be the one about Elam. "I'm fine. You can quit asking."

She clung to his arm. "I'm sorry, but I have to know if you get sick again."

He clasped the hand she had on his arm. "I'm fully healed, and everything is all right now. You can quit worrying about me. I'll tell you if there's a change."

"Promise?"

"Promise."

"Fine. What did Elam want?"

"He wants me to find out who killed Gideon." He heard her sharp intake of breath.

"That could be dangerous. Can't someone else do it?"

"Elam thinks I'm innocent because I was too sick to be able to kill Gideon. But I am well now, so I could have killed him."

Sapphira laughed, and the sound was high and strained. Leah and Elam turned to look at her, and she snapped her mouth closed. "I have to agree with Elam. You are the perfect one to find out the truth."

"But you don't like it that he asked me."

She shook her head. "Anybody but you."

He was unaccountably hurt. "Don't you believe I can find out the truth?"

"I have no doubt you'll find out the truth. But then what? As you said, it could be someone in our party. One of our friends. And you've just recovered from being ill. I don't want you to spend time on this. Gideon had enemies. He wasn't a nice man."

"Then we need to know which enemy killed him. We can start with the Friends of Jesus meetings. You and Leah can tell me who was there, and we can check them out."

"Yes. Gideon and Tarad were there. It was at Henrietta's house. We'll have to ask her who the other men were because I didn't know many of them. Since they were plotting to kill Jesus, it's quite possible that they killed Gideon." She was cheered by the prospect.

Aaron wasn't convinced that it wasn't one of their friends. He suspected Demetrius because of Gideon's hold over Sapphira. He knew how Demetrius felt about Sapphira. Maybe Demetrius had killed Gideon in a moment of anger. Demetrius probably had something sharp in his physician bag he carried with him.

"I still can't believe you sent someone to follow me."

"I thought we were past that. That you forgave me."

"I have, but it still bothers me. I can't get over it in only a few minutes, though I am trying. I'll need time, Aaron. Everything's changed, and I can't tell you how tired I am. I'm glad you're well," she hastened to say. "Please believe me. But part of me is still afraid I'm going to lose you."

"I'll try to be patient, but I feel so well physically right now. I keep forgetting what it must have been like for you."

"This will all be over soon. Do you think one of those people, like Tarad, might have killed Gideon?"

"It's possible." He didn't want to scare her and tell her he suspected it was someone they knew.

"I know it can't be Henrietta. Tarad runs the meetings. He's a mean, angry man. I can see him killing someone. But I haven't seen him on the road."

"Were you looking?"

"No, I was concentrating on you."

"While being blackmailed by Gideon. I think you had enough to think about without looking around for people you knew on the roads."

She didn't disagree. "It's possible. Wait. I do remember something. When we were in Gideon's room, I saw some religious artifacts in a corner of the room. They were spilling out of a bag."

"The stolen items from the synagogue in Naraah, and some other things he had stolen elsewhere. Elam told me in confidence."

Sapphira gasped and clutched his hand.

"What's wrong?"

She didn't answer.

"Sapphira?"

She shook her head. "Nothing important."

What wasn't she telling him? Her silence concerned him. "Maybe his death had something to do with those scrolls." He didn't imagine her hand tightening on his. She was concerned about the scrolls. Which made him concerned.

"That makes sense."

"I think so, too." He was eyeing her closely now. "I remembered wondering why he wanted to come to Ephraim with us. He was insistent, and I didn't think it was because he wanted to see Jesus."

"He wanted to sell those items in the biggest town we came to where there was a market for stolen goods."

"Exactly." And what did all that have to do with Sapphira?

They joined the others in the common room.

CHAPTER 35

They'd settled into the common room to eat.

Sapphira watched Aaron as he talked to Demetrius. Aaron sat straight in his chair. His voice was strong. There was no hesitation. No stopping to cough as he waved one arm, gesturing as he spoke. The only leftover from his illness that she could see was a paleness in his face that would be gone after a few days spent outside. He was lean now but would be muscular again as soon as he was back tending the animals and working in the fields. There was wisdom in his eyes that hadn't been there before. And gratitude for his life being spared and God's gift of health.

Her gaze swiveled to where Leah sat beside John. She felt a moment of unreasonable anger toward them. They were so happy at Aaron's recovery, and the journey had become an exciting adventure for them in spite of Gideon's death. Her own feelings were muddled.

Gideon's death had to be resolved. Elam would not rest until he knew the truth about his son's murder.

Aaron and John ate quickly and then left to find news of Jesus's travel plans from the innkeeper. Aaron wanted to thank Jesus, and the rest of their group wanted to see Jesus for themselves.

After they were gone, the talk at the table was sporadic. No one wanted to mention Gideon's death in front of Elam. They talked a little about Aaron's recovery, but it seemed in bad taste to exalt over that when Elam had lost his son.

John rejoined them, and they waited to see what news he brought. "I've found where Jesus will be speaking this afternoon."

"Us and those hundreds of people on the road that we passed and who passed us on the way here," Leah said.

They all nodded. The numbers of people traveling had been more than they expected.

"We'll need to get back on the road home as soon as we've seen him. Omar can't be expected to do all the work for any longer than that."

John agreed. "Aaron is back in his room. He has called a meeting. There is a meeting room where we can gather and discuss things as soon as we're finished eating."

The innkeeper brought John some ale, and he thanked him.

"What does Aaron want?" Elam asked, soaking up the last of the gravy from the stew with his bread.

"He didn't say. If you asked, I was to tell you he has a plan." John picked up his ale and took a long drink.

"Plan for what?" Leah asked the question for all of them.

Sapphira let the talk swirl around her, not wanting any attention to focus on her or her fatigue and fear. She was scared to see Jesus. Scared of what Aaron would find while looking for Gideon's killer. And she was tired. Tired of people and illness and death. She longed to return home to Caleb and

Rachelle. To Omar's scolding and Naomi's gruff kindness. They seemed so far away.

"To see Jesus before he's arrested."

Silence descended on the table. Sapphira knew they were all wondering if they'd get a chance. Elam was the first to speak. "We'll see him. We didn't come all this way and go through what we've gone through only to miss him. It'll happen."

They all agreed, and Sapphira didn't know if it was to prop up Elam, or if they truly believed it would happen. Now that Aaron was well, she didn't know what she thought. That Aaron wanted to see Jesus and thank him, she understood. She wondered why Aaron attributed his wellness to God through Jesus. Perhaps Aaron's innate strength had finally fought the consumption, and he got well.

She remembered Demetrius's words when she had said to him a month ago that Aaron could still recover.

"It's not going to happen. No one who has come down with consumption has ever lived," Demetrius said.

"No one?" She remembered pleading for some assurance.

"Not one. If there were, I'd have heard about it. It would be a miracle."

Now here they were. Witness to a miracle. Aaron believed it was a miracle from God in the form of Jesus. She didn't know what to believe. She wanted to ask Demetrius, but she hadn't spoken to him since Aaron recovered. She was ashamed of her attraction to him.

What did he think of Aaron's miracle? She looked over at him. He looked up, caught her eye, and smiled. He had such a nice smile. She smiled back. They were fine. Demetrius understood she belonged to Aaron.

The other problem was her own relationship with Gideon. Aaron had known more than she thought he did. Did he know about her part in stealing the scrolls? Either Elam had told him of his suspicions, since he had seen her after she gave the scrolls to Gideon that night, or he had kept the knowledge to himself. She couldn't be sure. If she could work up the courage to tell Aaron the truth, he would probably understand and forgive her. Considering the circumstances of his illness and how desperate she had been, he wouldn't hold it against her. She hoped.

It seemed like Aaron's return to health had created more problems. She was irritated that she couldn't be as happy about Aaron's recovery as she should have been. Why did it have to be so complicated? Even if he had gotten well a day ago, things would have worked out. But now…she sighed and kept her emotions in check. She wanted to run back home to her children, take Aaron with her, and start their new life with him as a healthy man. But she had to sit here and listen to the plan to see Jesus. She did want to thank him for healing her husband, and secretly she was fascinated by the stories she had heard about him.

She focused on how the children's faces would beam once they saw their father was healthy again.

There had been no time for her and Aaron to speak alone. Aaron had risen from the bed and joined the other men in Gideon's room. What had gone on between the men, she didn't know. When they'd finished their male conference and returned, they'd told her and Leah their intention to see Jesus as planned and return to Naraah immediately after seeing him.

There'd been that brief time for Aaron to tell her Elam had asked him to solve the mystery of Gideon's death. How they'd convinced the innkeeper of all of this, she had no idea.

Between Aaron's conversations with the others in their party and Leah's deep conversation with John, she felt left out.

CHAPTER 36

They were settled in a circle in a room the innkeeper kept for meetings, looking at Aaron expectantly. He held Sapphira's hand gently in his, and she could feel the strength in it. It surprised her that his grip remained firm despite his recent illness. The group was quiet in deference to Elam, but eagerly waited for Aaron to speak.

Sapphira moved her hand from Aaron's and let it drop to her side. She couldn't allow Aaron to feel her reaction to whatever he had to say. She nodded at him to start, unable to bear the suspense any longer.

Aaron looked around the room. "Elam has asked me to look into the death of Gideon. He feels that since I was so ill, I was unable to harm Gideon. Is there anyone here who disagrees?" He looked at them all. "Please, feel free to speak up if you do. Now is the time before I begin asking questions."

Demetrius said, "I believe you were too ill to get out of bed, much less kill someone. We all saw you slumped over the horse by the end of the trip. I feel it's only fair for you to be the one to look into this matter."

"I agree," Leah said, and the others all nodded.

"Thank you for your regard. I want to start by saying that I'll be asking intrusive questions. I mean no harm, nor do I plan to tell anyone what you tell me in confidence. We all have secrets we'd like to keep secret. They're safe with me. Not even Sapphira will know what you tell me."

She nodded in agreement. She didn't want to know their secrets. "Aaron's judgment is sound. I don't need to know what you tell him." She felt their sympathy and at the same time felt like a fraud. Aaron was fine now. She'd gotten him back. There was no need for their sympathy. She thought of the things she'd done to keep Aaron's love and nearly groaned out loud. The memory of the Friends of Jesus meeting made her squirm. How would she look Jesus in the eye when she'd been to a meeting where they'd discussed killing him? She had to warn him. It was the only way for her to atone for what she'd done and thank him for healing Aaron.

She missed what Aaron said, but they all nodded again in perfect unison.

"I'll start with Demetrius. Anybody have any questions?"

"When do we see Jesus?" Leah asked.

"I believe we have a few hours. As soon as I'm finished speaking with Demetrius, he and Elam will be on the lookout for him and let us know the details. The innkeeper has inside knowledge, and I think he will help us. I can see Jesus last, as I have my answer and am well. That way I can continue asking questions until the end of our time here. Hopefully, I'll figure out what happened before we leave Ephraim. Any other questions?"

"What will happen to the person who murdered Gideon? Isn't death by sword the usual punishment?" Elam asked.

Sapphira wasn't surprised that Elam was thinking of vengeance.

"It's your decision." Aaron looked at him. "When I have the answer, you can decide. Until then," he looked at everyone else, "I think we need to wait and see."

He stood up from his chair. "Consider getting some rest in the next hour while I take turns talking to each of you. It's been a long few days for everyone."

They agreed and dispersed.

CHAPTER 37

That evening, Aaron smiled when Demetrius walked into Aaron and Sapphira's room. Sapphira had left to take a walk with Leah in the inn's garden. They had discovered the innkeeper was a garden enthusiast.

"It's good to see you looking so well," Demetrius said.

"I am."

"And so you should be. I'm only sorry that your recovery has to be relegated to the bottom of the list because of Gideon's death. But I am so happy for you, my friend." He clasped Aaron's hand in a firm shake.

"Thank you. You kept me going long enough for recovery to happen."

"And as your physician, I want to know all the details and how you managed to recover." Demetrius shook his head and cleared his throat. "I've never seen someone so close to death's door escape and look so well so fast. It is indeed a miracle."

"That's what it is, Demetrius, a miracle. To you, I can tell the whole story, and you'll understand." And suddenly, Aaron was relieved to have a friend, someone close to talk to. Sapphira was pushing him away in her mistaken belief that she didn't deserve him, or some such nonsense. But Demetrius was acting his normal self. He pushed away the thought of Demetrius's attraction to Sapphira. He had understood and forgiven them.

"I want to hear it, first as a friend, second as a physician." Demetrius leaned forward eagerly, hands clasped between his knees as he sat in the chair beside the bed.

Aaron sat on the end of the bed facing Demetrius.

"You know how Sapphira has been lately?" Aaron asked.

Demetrius nodded.

"Nervous and distracted. Depressed and rebellious. I had Elam follow her to keep her safe."

Demetrius whistled. "I bet she didn't like that."

"She didn't know until I told her yesterday. We had a bit of a fight, but she forgave me. You know how she went to the Friends of Jesus meeting, and so did Gideon. Elam told me yesterday that he suspected Gideon had stolen the scrolls and some other antiquities from other synagogues."

Demetrius nodded understanding.

"There were other things." Aaron refused to go into details. "Anyway, I had a talk with God and asked him to spare me so I could be here and save Sapphira. I guess he decided to listen to my prayer. And here I am. Healthy and whole."

Demetrius considered Aaron. "Do you really think God listened? All this time you've been sick, you never brought God into the conversation. I don't understand this sudden belief you have in Him."

"I grew up Jewish. I have never told anyone in Naraah because I quit practicing the Jewish faith years ago. Even though I didn't follow the Jewish rules, deep down, a part of me still believed in God."

"Did Sapphira know?"

"No, we talked briefly a few days ago. I learned she also had a Jewish upbringing until her parents died. Then Omar stopped following the faith practices. Neither of us knew about the other."

Demetrius started pacing. "Do you think that was why Jesus healed you? He grew up Jewish."

"I don't think that has anything to do with it. He didn't ask me my faith when he was here. He certainly can't have time on the road to question people, as he's constantly in demand. I don't know why he came to me specifically." Aaron remembered what Jesus had told him about Sapphira being forgiven for what she had done. It almost seemed like Sapphira was the one Jesus had come to save, not Aaron. Why? Aaron would probably never know the answer.

"You can ask him when you see him this afternoon."

"I will if I get the chance. At least I've seen you recover. That's a miracle. I'll probably never see another miracle like it in my life."

"You never know. You're a physician. I bet you'll see plenty more."

"None as miraculous as this. But you and Sapphira deserve it." He looked sheepish, his face flushed. "I'm sorry, Aaron. You probably don't want to call me friend any longer."

"Why?"

Demetrius looked him straight in the eye. "I liked Sapphira. I still do. I don't hide it very well, and I'm sorry. Forgive me, Aaron, although I don't deserve it."

Aaron returned the look, pleased that he could respond honestly. "I did feel betrayed. By both of you. But God has been good to me, and Sapphira obviously needed a friend, and for some reason, she couldn't turn to me. She's a lovely woman. I've seen you look at her."

Demetrius's face flushed even darker red, but he continued to face Aaron respectfully.

"I made my peace with it. I thought I'd be dead today, and you'd be her next husband. It wasn't to be. But you're forgiven, and I hope you'll continue to visit Sapphira and me, even though I'm well now. Friends?" He held out his hand to Demetrius.

Demetrius shook hands vigorously. "I don't deserve your friendship, but I'll take it, Aaron. My apologies to you and to Sapphira."

Aaron let go. "Apology accepted. It's over and done with."

"I plan to leave Naraah once we get back, and I've had time to take care of my patients. I have heard that Jesus has a follower—Luke is his name. He's a physician, too. I might follow him."

"You don't have to do that, Demetrius, but if you do, I'll miss you."

"Thank you."

"Let's move to another subject."

"Gideon."

"Gideon," Aaron agreed. "It's been suggested that a Friends of Jesus cohort might have followed us and murdered Gideon."

"What's your perspective?"

"Possible. I like that alternative a lot better than the one where someone from our group killed him."

"Me, too. But we must be realistic. It isn't necessarily so just because we want it to be." Demetrius shook his head.

"After we reached the inn today, what did you do?"

"I helped John unload some of the supplies. Gideon stayed with the horses. I ate something in the common room. Then I went up to your room and checked on you. When I realized there was nothing I could do, I left you in Sapphira's care." He stopped and looked down at the floor.

"Then Sapphira came to talk to you." It was a guess, and he kept his expression neutral. Sapphira had gone somewhere, and Demetrius would have been the obvious person. Leah couldn't have helped her with Gideon.

Demetrius's head jerked up. "She told you?"

"No." He let the word hang there.

After a few seconds, Demetrius started talking. "She came to tell me that she loved you. That whatever had happened between us was a mistake and that she regretted it. I understood. Gideon was blackmailing her, but she didn't want to tell you because she was afraid it would jeopardize your health."

Aaron waited. Although he'd forgiven Demetrius and Sapphira, he found he could still be jealous. He wanted to lash out at Demetrius, but he kept his mouth shut.

"That's all. She left, and I took a nap, knowing I might be needed later to help you. It had been a long day on the road, and it didn't take long to fall asleep. The next thing I knew, John was knocking at my door. We went to the stables, and he showed me Gideon. I checked and knew he was dead. So did John before he even came to get me. I did a brief exam and found he was stabbed. We moved him to the room."

"Any idea how long he'd been dead?"

Demetrius thought for a few minutes. "I'd say about an hour, given the state of the blood that had congealed on the stable floor."

"So, as soon as we left Gideon in the stables, someone killed him. It's almost as if someone was waiting for him to be alone."

"It seems like it." He stared at Aaron. "Did someone follow us from Naraah and wait for an opportunity? It wouldn't have been hard to follow us without any of us knowing. We weren't paying attention to anyone other than you and those we asked about where to find Jesus."

"It seems maybe someone from that subversive group might have followed us." Aaron didn't mention that he was still considering someone from their group might have killed Gideon. Demetrius could have gone down to the stables as soon as Sapphira left him. He might have wanted to talk Gideon out of blackmailing Sapphira and ended up killing him instead. He didn't want to think that about Demetrius.

Demetrius leaned back in his chair, unaware of Aaron's suspicions. "I wonder what else he's done besides attend the Friends of Jesus meetings." He paused and then spoke again. "I saw some religious artifacts in his bags when we were packing up his things. I think they were the stolen scrolls from the synagogue in Naraah."

"I had hoped this would be easy, and we could get back to Naraah after seeing Jesus. I'm not sure how I'll figure out who killed Gideon. We have a possible suspect among our traveling group, stolen items from the synagogue, and a possible follower of the Friends of Jesus group."

"We don't know who is involved in the Friends of Jesus group except those people Leah and Sapphira saw at the meeting. There are probably more. Do you want to question Tarad? I wouldn't." Demetrius looked intrigued at the idea. "When I first heard they were against Jesus, I was astonished. I had thought they were devoted followers, only to discover they were plotting against him."

"No, they're not for Jesus. I wonder how close Jesus is to being arrested. I wish there was something we could do. Gideon had been at the last meeting, and they were plotting to turn Jesus over to be arrested. He's supposed to be arrested some time this week. We need to talk to Jesus as soon as possible. I tried to warn him yesterday when he came to heal me. I have to admit that I was so surprised, and he was with me for such a brief time, that I don't know if I got the message across or not."

Demetrius leaned forward. "What did he say when you told him?"

Aaron scratched his head, puzzled. "He told me that lots of people were plotting against him. He didn't seem concerned."

"That's odd. I guess if a lot of people wanted to kill me, I'd be concerned."

"Some of his followers look pretty rough. He probably thinks they will save him."

"Not if soldiers are after Jesus. They will get their way."

Aaron shook his head. "Jesus's followers think he has a way to escape. We will need to consider the Friends of Jesus members as suspects in Gideon's death."

Demetrius shrugged. "There's no way to check the Friends of Jesus out until we get back to Naraah. They can only be eliminated as potential killers if they stayed in Naraah. I don't know how we'll know if they came to Ephraim unless we see them, or someone tells us they were in Ephraim."

Aaron shook his head. "I can ask when we return to Naraah. Keep in mind, we traveled at a slow pace. Gideon was killed at a time when most people were not at home. They were out working. Anyone could have traveled faster than us, killed him, and got back to Naraah, and no one would have been the wiser."

"They couldn't have traveled faster than us because we didn't know where to find Jesus. They couldn't have known we'd end up in Ephraim because we didn't know where we'd end up finding Jesus. I don't envy you the task of finding Gideon's killer, but I'm willing to help in any way I can. All you have to do is ask."

Aaron nodded and wished him goodnight as Demetrius left. He wondered about Demetrius. If Demetrius wanted to protect Sapphira, would he have gone to warn Gideon and killed him instead?

Was his surprise at Gideon's death genuine? Aaron thought it was real. He sighed. He was well, and now he was spending time questioning and suspecting friends of killing Gideon. He had thought it had to be one of them who killed Gideon because only their group knew where Gideon was. Now he wasn't sure. Maybe it was a Friends of Jesus devotee.

Was it possible that Gideon had worked with another person to steal the relics and then left town without telling that person? Had that person found out and followed them? He didn't like the idea of someone like that in their vicinity. He would have to warn the others that it wasn't safe to be on their own in the city, especially since they now had the relics. Maybe the person who had killed Gideon would come looking for them.

A tiny voice inside asked how safe they were if the person who had killed Gideon was one of their own traveling party. Which of the men couldn't he trust? John? Demetrius? Elam? It couldn't be one of them, so it must have been one of Gideon's unsavory friends.

CHAPTER 38

Sapphira joined Aaron in their room. They hadn't been alone since Aaron had gotten well. He wished his relationship with Sapphira had eased with his recovery, but she seemed more distant and nervous than ever. But then he had to remember that none of them in their group had gotten much sleep in the past few days, getting ready for the trip and today—only he had gotten any rest. The others had been awake throughout their travels and had gotten up early this morning to leave. He wished Elam had put Demetrius or John in charge of Gideon's death investigation so he could spend time with Sapphira and talk. He realized there was no hurry. He wasn't dying.

How would he solve Gideon's death? Something had to break for him. For now, he didn't need to think about it. He was well and with Sapphira. His face broke out into a smile, and he savored the feeling of being alone with her.

"Why the big smile?" she asked.

"I've just realized we're finally alone together, and I feel well."

"You haven't told me the story about Jesus yet."

"We'll talk about what he said." He didn't miss the uneasy expression that flitted across her face. He stepped to her and pulled her into his embrace. Her eager gaze searched his face. "You don't know how long I've waited to feel well and come to you again."

She smiled slowly. "As long as I've been waiting?" She tugged him over to the edge of the bed and tried to pull him down beside her. "Come sit beside me."

"You're luring me in." He stood there, hesitating. They needed to talk.

"As if you need to be lured," she said knowingly.

He sat down beside her on the bed and hugged her to his side. "I've missed you so much."

"We've been together every day and night. More than we used to be." Her fingers stroked his back.

"Not the way I wanted it to be." He pulled away to look into her face. "Not this way." He kissed her thoroughly, reveling in the feel of her soft lips and hungry mouth. He pulled away. "Not now. When we're home."

She sighed and snuggled against him. "Home. With you. I was so lost without you."

He pulled away and held her so he could look into her eyes. "You are strong, Sapphira. You helped me to this place to get well. Without you, I wouldn't have had any chance of living. Remember that. My illness made you a stronger person."

"I didn't want to be the strong one." Her eyes dropped. "I wanted you back the way you were."

He pulled her close again, her face pressed to his chest. "We can't go back. Life doesn't work that way. We're both stronger than before this happened. Jesus said something about you."

Sapphira drew in a deep breath, waiting for Aaron's next words. How did Jesus know about her? "Did you tell him about me?"

"No, he knew all about you. And about me." Aaron frowned. "It's all so hazy and yet clear in my mind. I remember everything he said, but it was so strange. I felt this surge of warmth, like a warm fire on a cold day. Cozy." His voice trailed away.

A warm, cozy fire didn't sound pleasant to her right then. She was burning with impatience to hear what Jesus had said.

"He said you were forgiven, Sapphira." His gaze was no longer focused inward but on her.

She read the gentleness in his eyes and wondered if she should tell him the truth about the scrolls. If he forgave her for that, maybe he could forgive her final desperate act.

"He said you could tell me, and everything would be okay."

She moved away from him to think. "How could he know what I'd done?"

"He seemed sure. And he told me something about my own family that I hadn't told him. He knew." He waited.

She was tired of secrets, and this would be one less on her conscience. "I helped Gideon steal the scrolls." What would he do now? She shouldn't have told him while they were away from home. What if he left her here in Ephraim? But she didn't see any condemnation on his face. Only sorrow.

"I'm sorry."

She circled the room. "Why are you sorry? I'm sorry. I did it to get money for the Jewish physician. But it didn't accomplish anything except

223

to give Gideon something to threaten me with. He threatened to tell you. And I thought if he told you, you would get sicker and die. And it would be all my fault." She started crying.

"Do you know that whenever you're with child, you cry all the time?" he asked tenderly.

She looked at him in wonder. He was right. Being pregnant did make her more teary-eyed. "You aren't mad at me?"

"I love you, Sapphira. I had guessed Gideon had some hold over you, and the scrolls make perfect sense. Your decision not to tell me about what you'd done, or about Gideon's threats, was meant to protect me. I appreciate that. If you had been the one who was sick, I would have done anything to protect you."

"You would?" She couldn't believe she had finally told him, and he wasn't the least bit angry. She felt the weight drop from her shoulders.

"I would do anything for you and the children. Without you, I am nothing."

She hugged him fiercely. "You are everything, with or without us." She thought about Jesus saying she was forgiven. She'd have to think about that when she had a free moment. She remembered that Jesus had also spoken about Aaron's family. "What did he say about your family?"

"Jesus said I'd see Noah again soon. I haven't seen him in about fifteen years. I didn't think I'd ever see him again. Something happened that made me leave the town where they live, and I can't return. We can talk about this later."

So, she wasn't the only one with secrets.

"How would Jesus know about them?" She was having trouble believing some of the things Aaron was telling her about Jesus. He knew everything about her and Aaron. She didn't understand.

"I don't know. But I think he was sent by God." Aaron paused. "I know he was sent by God. It's the only explanation."

Sapphira didn't know what to think about his belief.

CHAPTER 39

The next morning, Sapphira and Leah walked in the gardens behind the inn while Aaron continued questioning the men about Gideon's death. The birds sang, and the air was fresh with the smell of cedar and greenery. She smiled, and something in her heart lifted.

"…and then he said Gideon had several items in his room. I had my eyes closed most of the time, so I didn't notice."

"What?" Sapphira asked, catching the name Gideon. "What did he have?"

Leah looked at her reproachfully. "Weren't you listening to what I said?"

"Yes, but then I started thinking of Aaron, and I drifted off."

Leah smiled. "That is so great that he's well. I can't believe we traveled all this way, and Jesus came to him. What healed him do you suppose?"

Sapphira shivered. Aaron believed God had delivered him from certain death. And that meant God knew what she'd done. She looked around furtively, even though Aaron said Jesus had said she was forgiven.

"What's wrong? You look scared." Leah also looked around.

"Gideon's death has made me uneasy." Sapphira shrugged it off. She couldn't let anyone know what she'd done. Aaron had forgiven her for the things he knew she'd done—or not done. She never really had a relationship with Demetrius. Only a few feelings that were wrong because she was married. She couldn't talk to Leah about her brother. "What did you say was in Gideon's room?"

"John thinks they are the missing relics from the synagogue," she said. "He's sure Gideon stole them or knew the person who stole them. He thinks he came with us to Ephraim to sell them."

She hadn't told Leah that Gideon had forced himself on the trip for that reason. She'd confessed enough to Aaron. She wasn't about to tell anyone else what she'd done. She didn't tell Leah that Gideon had forced her to help him steal the scrolls and then blackmailed her to help him sell them. She hoped her secrets could stay hidden from everyone except Aaron. No one else had known her secrets except Gideon, and he was dead. Elam might have guessed, but since he had never confronted her, she didn't think he'd ever bring it up. Besides, he was grieving Gideon's death, and bringing up Gideon's deceit would do no good at this point. "I see. He didn't really want to help Aaron? He wanted to use our trip as an opportunity for himself?"

"Yes." Leah agreed. "But most people love Aaron and would help him. In spite of Gideon's ulterior motive, I'm sure he liked Aaron."

"Right. Now you're giving Gideon the benefit of doubt for being nice. He stole from a synagogue." She could barely stand her own hypocrisy. If Leah knew she had helped Gideon and was just as culpable in stealing the relics, her respectability would disappear. Omar would disown and disinherit her. Aaron would probably stay with her, considering their latest conversation, but would they have to move and start all over somewhere else? She was getting a headache, and there was no end in sight. Sapphira sighed.

"You're still so sad at times. I would think you'd be happy because Aaron is well." Leah peered closely at her. "Are you all right?"

"I think I'm just tired."

"It's probably the baby."

"Yes, I keep forgetting Aaron is well. I keep thinking he's sick, and then it hits me that he's healed. It's hard at times to remember that he's well because I've seen so little of him since he has gotten better. I'm at a loss as to what to do with my time. For the past months, I've been mothering the children and Aaron. Now I'm with nothing to do here in Ephraim because Aaron's busy solving Gideon's murder and the children are still in Naraah. It's scary." Scared. That's how she felt. She'd done so many questionable things to save Aaron and help her family. When would the truth all come tumbling out, and who would find out?

"What's to be scared about? Soon, we'll see Jesus and then head back to Naraah where you and Aaron will have another little baby to care for and love."

Leah made everything sound so easy, but there were still some secrets that Sapphira hadn't told her. "Aaron has a family he had never told me about before he was sick. His brother Noah will probably be coming to visit. There's also the new baby. I'm also concerned about Naomi. She always wanted another child, and it didn't happen."

"I wouldn't worry about Naomi. Lately, I've noticed Naomi has more say in the marriage with

Omar. Maybe she noticed you were more assertive when Aaron was sick, and that attitude worked for you. I can't decide what has changed with her, but something has."

"Maybe." Again, Leah made it sound so easy. Like throwing out the old bread to the chickens. Sapphira couldn't forget her past fear of Omar so easily when he'd had control over her life. Naomi probably felt much the same, though she was finally coming to terms with him. Feelings didn't just disappear because they were in the past. Fear over Gideon's death and fear of Gideon's actions before he died. Fear about everything she'd done. Jumbled in there was a longing for the simple days before Aaron's illness when he was well, and the children were innocent and not afraid of losing their father. And she was innocent, too.

She had never talked to the children about Aaron's illness, and now she regretted it. Then she remembered he was well now, and she could still talk to them about it and how lucky they were Aaron had survived. Why had Jesus come to Aaron, and Aaron hadn't had to seek him out?

When would they have more time to really talk? Probably not until they returned home. Maybe that was for the best. Her head was muddled.

"…and you're still not paying attention to what I'm saying."

Sapphira had been staring at the ground for a long time while she was thinking. She looked up as she realized Leah was watching her. She shrugged ruefully. "I'm sorry. There's just so much I have to think of, and I can't seem to concentrate."

"Do you think we're in any danger?" Leah asked, glancing around the gardens.

"No," Sapphira said. "If Gideon's thugs murdered him, they would have taken the bag of stolen goods. They didn't. Therefore, he wasn't killed by other stealing cohorts." Oh, why had she said that?

Leah looked at her in admiration. "That was incredibly clever thinking."

Sapphira smiled at the praise, glad she'd said something intelligent for a change. "Thank you. I surprised myself. Unfortunately, Gideon didn't have the scrolls with him when he was at the stables, so we've still got a problem."

"What are you ladies looking so pleased about?"

They turned to see John striding up the path toward them. He stopped by Leah.

"You're smiling, too," Leah said to him.

"I've been successful in getting information about Jesus from the inn across town. They know where he will be and when we can see him."

Sapphira longed to fling herself at John, beg him to convince Aaron to return to Naraah now, and forget seeing Jesus. But that was selfish. John and Elam still wanted to see Jesus. As did Demetrius, who wanted to discuss healing with another great physician. She was stuck in this town, as she had been stuck with Aaron's illness, only now for another reason.

Aaron had received his miracle. Would she get hers? To escape back to Naraah and resume life with Aaron and keep his love? That would be a miracle because he would certainly someday learn the truth about her. Would he then forgive her and still love her? That would, indeed, be a miracle.

"Where will he be?" Leah asked.

"On the other side of town, off in the countryside in a few hours. We can see him and then leave for Naraah."

"Thank goodness. I want to get back to Naraah and see the children. I miss Ruth and Thatcher, but it's also been nice to get away." Leah suddenly looked self-conscious. "I'm sorry, Sapphira. I know this was a journey that you would have preferred not to take. But it has turned out well," she finished.

Sapphira smiled wryly. "Yes, it has. I understood what you meant."

Leah looked relieved. "I just wish we knew what happened to Gideon. Who do you think killed him, John?"

Sapphira watched him with concern. What would he say? The sun beat down on her back, and she felt faint. Her heart beat fast.

John shook his head. "I don't know. I'm wondering about that Friends of Jesus group, but I'm afraid it's one of us."

Sapphira thought they were the top choice in everyone's mind.

"Who do you think killed him?" John asked Leah.

Sapphira held her breath and waited for the answer.

"I think it was someone who followed us and hated Gideon. He was a rough character."

Sapphira nodded. "That's probably the most likely thing to have happened."

John shook his head. "I don't think so."

"If you think it's one of us, who would do it?"

He looked at Leah. "I don't know."

He was lying. Sapphira realized he thought it was Demetrius, but he didn't want to say that to Leah. She would be protective of her brother, and John obviously didn't want to point the finger at him without proof.

He shrugged helplessly. "It's a difficult problem."

He looked at Sapphira. "Aaron will have a difficult time of it."

Sapphira agreed. Aaron should be resting, not entangled in a murder investigation. What would the end result be?

John left Leah and Sapphira to walk in the garden for a bit longer. The shade from the sycamores and cedar trees was welcome. Birds chirped, and flowers bloomed. The innkeeper had done a fine job with the garden. There were even wooden benches to sit on and enjoy the day. The garden was peaceful, unlike Sapphira.

CHAPTER 40

Sapphira had not yet returned from the garden with Leah, and Aaron had decided to go find them when there was a knock on the door to their room. When he opened it, Elam stood on the other side. Aaron invited him in. "Have a chair."

Elam looked at Aaron. "I'll stand, thank you. This won't take very long. You seem fine today. Looks like Jesus really did heal you."

Aaron nodded, happily taking a deep breath and relieved to note that it didn't make him cough. "I feel well."

"Gideon was our first and only child. My wife died in childbed. I still miss her even though it's been twenty-one years."

Aaron murmured his sympathy.

"Some marriages are made for convenience. Rebekah and I married for love. It did help that our parents wanted us to wed, but it was love at first sight. For both of us."

"Sapphira and I married for love, too. Sometimes, lately, I wonder if she still loves me."

"I'm guessing that every marriage goes through that stage. Rebekah and I weren't married long enough to reach it, though. She died young." He swallowed hard. "Let things be. They'll work out for the best."

Aaron wasn't reassured by Elam's advice.

"You're not even tired."

At the note of accusation, Aaron studied Elam.

Elam frowned, and if Aaron hadn't known him so well, he might think a sneer marred Elam's mouth.

"No, I don't feel tired at all. I'm amazed at how well I feel. There doesn't seem to be any lasting effect at all. It's almost as if I was never sick, except those months in bed were very real. Sapphira will tell you how real." He smiled, but Elam glared back. "Is something wrong?"

Elam pulled at his scraggly beard. "It seems to me that you're well at an opportune time. Like when my son is suddenly murdered. If you know what I mean?"

At the suggestion behind the words, Aaron pulled back. He saw Elam's hand close into a fist at his side. His straight back was unyielding, his stare hostile.

"How hard are you working at finding my son's killer, Aaron?"

Aaron measured his words before speaking. "I will find out who killed Gideon. It's important for you to know. And it's important for all of us to know."

"What if you murdered Gideon? Are you going to share that information?" Elam spoke through clenched teeth.

"You don't believe that I killed your son. Don't talk nonsense." He would have spoken more harshly except he couldn't imagine what Elam was going through, losing his only child.

"I think you've recovered at an opportune moment, as I've already said, that's all. And we all know what Gideon and your wife were doing."

Aaron froze. He couldn't mean…Sapphira would never…not with Gideon. He struggled to clear his throat. "Sapphira? You're not making sense."

Elam's gaze never wavered. Whatever he was about to say, he believed it to be true. "Gideon and Sapphira were conspiring in a subversive group. The Friends of Jesus."

"You told me that, Elam, back in Naraah. Why are you bringing it up again?"

"There's more that I didn't tell you. You were so sick. Sapphira stole artifacts with Gideon. So, will you tell me the whole truth about what you find?"

Aaron was glad Sapphira had admitted to stealing the scrolls before Elam told him. "Sapphira told me what happened with Gideon and about the scrolls and how he almost attacked her, but you saved her. Whatever I find out that pertains to your son's murder but has nothing to do with innocent people, I will tell you."

"You've put a lot of stipulations on what you'll tell me. And as much as I care for Sapphira, she's not an innocent person."

"I understand you're hurt, Elam. When I've found the answer, I'll make sure you're satisfied." His gaze didn't waver.

Elam's hand straightened out, and he flexed his fingers. He nodded. "See that I am. I won't rest until my son's murder has been avenged."

"I know Gideon was your only child," Aaron said. He held out his hand. "I'll find the answer."

Elam hesitated, and then shook Aaron's hand. "I'm trusting you to be honest."

After Elam had left, Aaron sat down. He hesitated to go find Sapphira.

Elam didn't know all the things she'd done, though he knew things Aaron hadn't known until this trip, such as stealing the scrolls. What was done could not be undone. He would always know she'd had feelings for Demetrius. Had he truly forgiven her?

Most of him was happy to have been healed. The other part was wondering what happened to his life while he was so sick. Elam suspected Aaron might have murdered Gideon. He couldn't believe Elam really thought Aaron had something to do with Gideon's death and replayed the conversation over in his head. It helped him to keep his mind off Sapphira. Sapphira, who suddenly was anywhere but near him. Now that he was well, she had decided she didn't want to speak with him. Her reticence was unnatural. What else hadn't she trusted him enough to tell him? How could anything be worse than stealing the scrolls?

CHAPTER 41

Mid-morning, Aaron watched John come into the taproom at the inn and sit down across the table from him.

"I talked with Sapphira and Leah in the garden. You've got your work cut out for you solving Gideon's death. What can I do to help?" John gave his order to the barmaid, and she left.

Aaron had decided to avoid Sapphira for the time being and let her come to terms with her feelings. "What do you know about Gideon's death? This investigation seems like it should be easy, but there are too many variables and too many possibilities. I'll never get to the bottom of this."

Aaron liked talking to John, who was always so calm and full of common sense. John thought things out, took them slow, and never jumped to conclusions. Perhaps Elam should have suggested John solve Gideon's murder. Aaron should have suggested it when Elam accused him of murder, but he knew the responsibility of this search couldn't go to anyone other than him. He had been idle too long and owed Elam for helping out his family while he was ill.

John took a sip of the ale the barmaid had brought him and thoughtfully turned the mug on the rough table. "Someone followed us. They killed Gideon when they had the opportunity. They probably wanted the relics he had. Unfortunately, he didn't have them in the stable with him. That's what the women think."

Aaron shook his head, unsatisfied with that conclusion. He didn't know why, but he didn't think anyone had followed them. Who else had helped Gideon steal artifacts? That was probably the guilty party. The obvious solution was probably the right one. How did he convince Elam?

Aaron hadn't paid any attention to anyone else on the road. At the end of the trip, he had been so unwell that he wasn't aware of anything. How would he find this person who had killed Gideon?

He set his empty mug at the end of the table, and the barmaid came back to their table. He smiled at her and held out his hand. "Nothing more for me, thanks."

She took the mug and left them alone.

John watched him rub his chin. "A cohort of Gideon's seems like the right answer to me. When I look at the people in our traveling party, I can't think of any of us who would gain by Gideon's death. Do you think any of us could have killed Gideon?"

"No, I don't." When he considered Elam, Leah, Sapphira, Demetrius, and John, the only one with a motive was Demetrius. He didn't think Demetrius had killed Gideon, and the others seemed unlikely murderers.

"You don't want to consider it's a woman." John grinned at him.

Aaron returned the look ruefully. "Do you think it was Leah or Sapphira?"

"No, but let's consider them one by one. Demetrius?"

Aaron didn't want it to be Demetrius. He'd forgiven Sapphira, forgiven Demetrius, but he couldn't quite quell the jealousy that filled him when he thought of Demetrius. Thank goodness Demetrius planned to leave Naraah when they returned. He felt guilty because he knew Leah would miss her brother. If only he'd been able to spend more time with Sapphira today, he'd feel a lot better about the situation. He may have forgiven them both, but he was having a hard time forgetting.

"You must be considering him because you've been quiet for a full minute." John looked inquiringly at him.

He shrugged. "Just giving it some thought, but I simply don't see what Demetrius has to gain." He refused to bring Sapphira into the equation. "I can't think how he would have anything to do with stolen goods."

He conveniently ignored the thought that Sapphira had something to do with the stolen goods. But he couldn't see Sapphira and Demetrius working together. Then again, he never thought Sapphira would be stealing artifacts with Gideon. What had she been thinking?

"He wanted to come on this trip to meet Jesus and discuss healing with him. Demetrius has some notion of the state of the soul influencing the mind and making the body sick or well."

John looked bewildered. "I'm a simple man, and I don't understand that at all. Demetrius is an intelligent man and makes a good physician. But even though I don't understand him sometimes, I feel he's an honorable man and wouldn't kill

Gideon. In fact, I can't even see Demetrius having a knife on him."

"Not even a knife to use for medical reasons?" Aaron asked. Was that what had happened to the knife that had stabbed Gideon? Was it in Demetrius's bag? He had not thought to search it. Even if Demetrius had used a knife from his bag, he wouldn't return it bloody to the bag. He would have cleaned it off before bringing it back to his room. It was too late to check.

"What are you thinking?"

"I'm giving your suggestion a little too much weight, I think. I am starting to seriously suspect Demetrius, but I hate to admit it."

"Isn't that good? Until you consider everyone thoroughly, you won't come to the correct answer. Although I disagree with you that it was Demetrius. I've known him for so long because of Leah, and he's never been brutal."

His calm words settled Aaron's thoughts. "You're right. I hadn't thought of it like that. I'd been feeling guilty for even considering my friends. But I must put that aside and think about this until I discover the true answer."

John stood up and slapped him on the back. "That's the spirit. If there's anything I can do to help, let me know."

Aaron also stood up. "You've already helped me. Now I must meet with Leah."

They walked into the hallway and toward the stairs where their rooms were.

"Leah should be in our room by now. I think she and Sapphira must be done with their walk."

"It's a warm one out there. I've spent way too much time indoors for the past few months. If she's not in your room, I'll be quite happy to find her outside. Do you want to be in the room with us when I ask her questions? As her husband, you have a right to be there." Aaron stopped outside of John's room and waited.

"We'll see what Leah wants to do." John raised his hand and knocked on the door.

"Come in." Leah's voice was muffled.

John walked in, and Aaron waited outside.

"Aaron would like to talk to you about Gideon."

"Why are we wasting so much time on that odious man?"

"Leah."

The reproof was mild, and Aaron nearly smiled. That was Leah.

"Do you want me here with you when you talk to Aaron?"

"Whatever. You decide."

John opened the door wide and let Aaron into the room.

Aaron stood by the door and looked at Leah, sitting at the writing desk.

"Since I have no place else to go, I'll stand here quietly if you don't mind?" John said.

Aaron shook his head. "I don't mind. I doubt if I'll take much of your time." He looked at Leah. "Unless you have a lot to tell me."

She smiled at him. "I'd love to confess and tell you I did it, and we could move on with more important things."

"Leah!" This time John's voice was shocked.

"I didn't." She got up from the chair, took his hand, and patted it. "Sit down, dear. You're looming over me."

John sat on the edge of the bed, and Leah returned to the chair by the writing desk. "Do you want to sit on the bed by John, or would you like to use the other chair?"

"I'll take the chair. John will sit quietly and only interrupt if I accuse you."

Leah laughed. "Obviously he won't be interrupting you. And I don't have much that I can tell you." Her face became serious. "I didn't know Gideon at all. I knew he was at your place frequently helping, along with Elam and John. He was always helping, and whenever I'd visit Sapphira, he was around."

Aaron ignored the comment about Sapphira and Gideon. "Did you know about Gideon's activities with the Friends of Jesus group?"

Leah shook her head. "Not until Sapphira and I went to that one meeting. I'm sorry I went, though. It did help us find Jesus, and you're healed now." She smiled at him.

He nodded.

"That's good then, isn't it? I think his death had something to do with those stolen scrolls. He must have come with us to sell them and the other things he stole. He talked about seeing Jesus, just like the rest of us, but when I found out about the stolen goods, I assumed that's why he came with us."

Aaron considered her for a moment. She didn't know Sapphira had helped Gideon steal the scrolls. Sapphira had kept that secret from Leah, too, which made him feel a little better. He wasn't the only one who had been left in the dark. "That's what we think happened." He looked at John. "Do you want to tell her about the Friends of Jesus?"

"We're starting to agree with you that someone from that group might have followed Gideon. Now that I think about it, maybe one of Jesus's friends found out and stopped Gideon. They might have wanted to protect Jesus."

Leah looked horrified. "But that's awful. I think Jesus's group is peaceful. Some of the men may be rough, but I don't think they would follow Jesus and purposely kill someone. Jesus preaches healing."

"You're probably right. I'm looking at everyone as a suspect." Aaron was beginning to dislike this part of the search. He was suspecting friends and now the good people of Jesus. "Who do you think killed Gideon?"

"I still think it's someone who followed him. Probably a friend of Gideon's who helped him steal artifacts. This probably wasn't the first time he's done something like this. It must break Elam's heart."

It was breaking Aaron's heart to have Sapphira involved in stealing with Gideon. He wondered how much it broke Elam's heart to know that his son had been part of a subversive group and a thief. Enough to make him angry and kill his own son? It didn't seem like Elam would do that. But he remembered Elam's anger at himself and his probing stare as he tried to decide if Aaron had pretended to be ill. He couldn't rule out Elam. He did rule out Leah. "Do you know of anyone in our party who was angry at Gideon?"

She looked down at the writing desk and pushed the quill away from her. Then she twisted the ring on her finger before clasping her hands in her lap. She looked up at Aaron. "The only ones who I saw angry with Gideon were Sapphira and Elam."

A shock wave traveled down Aaron's spine. "Sapphira?"

She looked contrite. "I shouldn't have said that. It's not that I think Sapphira killed him. It's just that she's the only one I saw who had angry words with Gideon besides Elam."

He'd been waiting for this moment. For someone to mention their names together. He pushed down his fear and tried to look at the situation objectively. He needed to look at everyone and rule them out. Each one. All of them. That's what he had decided to do in the barroom with John, whose expression he couldn't read at the moment. "That's fine, Leah. Someone had to say it, and I guess it's best if it comes from you since I know you're her friend and don't believe she killed Gideon." He thought how his expression must be a sickly combination of annoyance and frustration.

She sighed. "I'm sorry. I know this must be difficult for you, but others saw Sapphira and Gideon arguing. And you probably know Omar wanted Sapphira to marry Gideon when something happened to you." She looked at John, who had sat quietly through the exchange. "What was I supposed to say?"

"You did fine," he said, as calm as ever. "Aaron knows that."

Aaron stood. He might know it needed to be said, but he needed to get some air. "Do you have anything else to add?"

"No." Her voice was even softer than normal. "I'm sorry, Aaron."

He tried to smile at her but knew he had failed. "Don't worry. I'm not angry at you. You did the right thing. Someone had to say something." He opened the door. "Thank you both." He escaped before either could say anything. Their faces lingered in his mind. Leah's a mixture of hurt and sympathy. John's a mask of pity.

They felt sorry for him. Sorry that he had to look at his own wife as a suspect. He walked down the stairs and outside, wanting to get some perspective before talking to anyone else. Sapphira was a suspect. He'd known that. Now, he realized she was a suspect in everyone else's mind. He'd briefly forgotten that Elam told him that Omar planned to have Gideon marry Sapphira.

The shock of it still lingered. How could he think of her as a killer? He thought of her gentle ways with the children and how she cared for him during his illness. He shuddered at the idea of her plunging a knife into Gideon's side. Impossible. Had any of this come to Elam's mind? Probably not, or he would never have asked Aaron to help him find out who killed Gideon. His mind slowed down at that thought.

Elam knew better than anyone how much time Sapphira had spent with Gideon. He also knew the things Gideon had done. And he knew Aaron knew what Gideon had done. And what Sapphira had done with Gideon.

Now what was he to do? He couldn't question his own wife. How could he cross her off the list after Leah had brought up her name? Why had Sapphira fought with Gideon in front of the others? She hadn't had a choice. Gideon was blackmailing her.

What a mess. He let the sound of the birds chirping relax him. The sweet smell of the yew trees and the scent of flowers drifted on the slight breeze. He drew in a deep breath and blew it out. The gardens were beautiful. The rains he'd heard in the night had obviously left their mark here. The greens were a bright hue, and the leaves sparkled as the light reflected off the fluttering silver olive trees.

He'd missed this. The activity around him filtered through a haze of gratitude. He could walk and not get tired. Not cough. He laughed for the sheer joy of it and startled a blue jay pecking at the ground. Two women, who had been walking toward him on the path, veered in the opposite direction, and he smothered another laugh. He hadn't meant to frighten them. He only wanted to enjoy the moment. His walk took on a jaunty step. He was free again. Free to take care of Sapphira and the children. No longer dependent upon Elam, John, Gideon, and Omar.

Sapphira could return to her regular activities and not treat him like a child. He thought of the night ahead. Could they mend the distance between them? Sapphira had done a lot of things in the past few months that he didn't approve of, but she had done the best she could. He missed her by his side today. He had become used to spending a lot of the day with her or, at least, hearing her nearby as she worked.

His steps slowed, and he stopped. Where were he and Sapphira in relation to each other? He needed to ask her. To straighten out the situation. To fix it any way he could. She had shouldered a burden for months. It was time he took on his share. While he'd been thinking and walking, he hadn't found her in the garden. She must be back in their room. He strode toward the inn, ready to end the distance between them. He smiled at the thought of the coming night and their reunion with the children at home. For today, he would forget that his wife was a suspect in a murder investigation.

CHAPTER 42

Sapphira shifted uneasily on the chair in her room at the inn and waited for Aaron to return. She'd heard him talking to John in the hallway and then go into John's room. She knew Leah was in there because they had parted only moments before in the hallway.

When Aaron didn't come back out immediately, she knew he was questioning Leah, and her hands clenched. What would be the outcome of Aaron's questioning? Leah blamed fellow thieves for Gideon's murder. Would Aaron learn the truth?

She wished it were over, and they could return to Naraah. If she thought Aaron would agree, she would have already asked him to leave the city and return to Naraah and the children. But she knew he would refuse. Not only was he determined to solve Gideon's murder, but he would never leave his friends at this time. They had all come on a pilgrimage, and Aaron would stay until every last one of them had talked with Jesus.

The thought caused her despair and a deep love at the same time, and she nearly wept in frustration. She lay on the bed, determined to rest. Perhaps if she got some sleep, she would be able to better deal with the situation. The past few months of little sleep and much worry had caused her to do a lot of things she would never have done in ordinary circumstances.

She recalled seeing Gideon lying dead in the inn bed. Of the innkeeper telling them to be quiet or leave. Of the shock of Aaron's recovery. His lack of cough and virile body. She shuddered in a kind of fear and longing. Would he try to make love with her tonight? She wanted him with a fierce longing that she had denied herself for so long. A feeling that she'd buried when Demetrius had told her Aaron was not going to live.

She thought of those days of despair that she'd tried to hide from the children and herself. The other life she'd lived for four months. A life where she'd changed from a simple wife and mother to an angry woman. A woman mad at God, and still angry with God in spite of Aaron's healing.

Why? Why had he made Aaron well now? She'd gone to the Friends of Jesus meeting. She'd been attracted to Demetrius. Had even briefly considered him as a possible husband when Aaron died. Could she forget how it had felt to flirt with him, only a little? Forget how he'd made her feel like a woman again? A young woman who still had a life ahead of her.

She felt ill and was trying not to throw up. She'd stolen from the synagogue where her parents had worshipped. How had she been able to do that? Could she ever wipe these images from her mind? Or would they keep whirling around inside her head, a constant swirl of everything she'd done in the past few months? Reminding her of the woman she'd become. And forever changing her into someone she wasn't sure if she was comfortable being. She knew she'd never change back. Never be a simple wife again. Would Aaron care? Would he

still love her as this new woman? He'd made her
that way. Made her stronger by leaning on her and
depending on her. She found herself angry with
him, too, even knowing it wasn't his fault.

The emotions twisted and turned inside her
until she thought she'd go mad. She finally got up
from the bed, gave up on resting, and decided to go
for another walk. Surely, the grounds would be safe
enough for her to go by herself. She didn't want
company right now, but she couldn't sit here in this
room as it closed in around her.

She passed no one on the stairs and stepped
out into the inn yard. The sun burned her eyes, and
she blinked and looked around to see if any of the
others were around. She saw no one she knew, and
she walked along the path at the side of the inn to
return toward the back where the grounds were full
of gardens and walking paths. She and Leah had
explored only part of the grounds before they had
met up with John.

As she turned the corner around the
building, she ran into Aaron. She squealed. She
hadn't heard him come up the walk.

He smiled at her as his arms closed around
her. "Sorry to surprise you. I quite like having you
in my arms again."

She quite liked being in his arms, too. The
warmth felt soothing and comforting, and she
suddenly knew why she'd been so restless in the inn
room by herself. She needed Aaron. She leaned
against his chest and inhaled his warm male scent.

He laughed warmly, his hand tangled in her
hair at the small of her back. "We are in a public
place."

"No one is back here, and I don't care," she muttered against his chest.

"Me either. I've missed you, Sapphira." He tugged gently at her hair.

She lifted her mouth toward his, closing her eyes in delight as his mouth met hers, his warm breath melding with hers. She savored the closeness, and her fears about the night vanished. This was Aaron. The man she loved. The man who'd been in her bed for thirteen loving years.

Because of everything they'd gone through, there was a feeling of newness to his kisses. She didn't know if it was her perception or the depth of near loss she felt.

The kiss ended. He stared at her with dazed eyes. The same look she must have had on her face.

"We have so much to talk about. So much catching up to do."

"Let's go home." She regretted the words instantly as she felt his arms stiffen and drop. At least, he didn't step away.

"I can't."

She could see the regret in his eyes.

"I'd like to, but the others want to see Jesus, and I do, too."

"But you're well now. You don't need to see him." She could sense a widening gap as he took in her words. She stepped away before he could. Even though the day was warm, she felt a chill as she stood alone again.

"Sapphira," he chided, "I want to see him and thank him now that I've been healed. I want to meet the man who can do all these wondrous things. Heal people with leprosy, make the blind see, bring dead men back to life. Don't you want to meet him?"

She had to smile at the passion in his eyes and voice. And what was so wrong about it? Even though she was curious about Jesus, she didn't want to meet a man who knew her actions without having her tell him.

She couldn't begrudge Aaron or the others the opportunity. She could stay back in the crowd while he and the others talked to Jesus. She'd see him from afar.

Aaron was well again. In two more days, they'd be home in Naraah. Everything would return to normal, except better. She had him back. It would work out. She loved him; he loved her. She should look on this time as a holiday before they returned to Naraah that evening. Her smile brightened, and she suddenly felt free. She twirled away from him and then back, looking up into his face and fluttering her eyelashes at him. "I love you, Aaron. I'm glad to have you back, and whatever you want to do is fine with me."

The smile that had at first brightened his face at her antics, dimmed a little, but she thought she might have imagined it because he pulled her to him and kissed her breathless. "We'll see him this afternoon and then go home," he said as he linked arms with her, and they walked back to the inn.

CHAPTER 43

Elam stopped them as they entered the inn. "What have you found out?" he asked Aaron. "Who killed my son?"

Sapphira withdrew from Aaron's arm. "I'll go back to the room and wait for you."

Aaron watched her walk away before he turned his attention to Elam. The bustling hallway was no place for this conversation. "How about we go to the taproom and discuss this?"

Elam shook his head. "Outside." He jerked his head toward the front entrance.

They walked outside. The front of the inn was bustling with travelers, horses, and wagons. Aaron led them to the side of the building and down a short path that took them behind the stables. He stopped and stood in front of Elam. "I have not discovered who killed your son yet. I'm sorry." And he was. He wanted the matter settled.

"What have you done so far? Or are you spending time with that wife of yours?" Elam's anger radiated from his pores, and the heated sweat spoke of long hours of disquiet.

Aaron hesitated. How much did Elam really want to know? "I've found out some things. I'm close, but I can't tell you yet. You must trust me."

"I know my son wasn't the nicest or the most honest man, but he deserves to have his death avenged."

"I didn't know you planned vengeance. What if it is one of our party? John? Demetrius? Then what?"

Elam's face transformed into a mourning mask. His sunken cheekbones no longer looked healthy the way they had at the beginning of their trip. It seemed to Aaron that as he had been healed, others around him had aged or become fretful. Elam's mouth trembled. "I just want to know the truth."

Aaron softened his tone. "I don't know the truth yet. I'm working on the fact that Gideon stole the relics from the synagogue before we left Naraah."

Elam nodded. "I fought with him about that on the way to Naraah."

Light dawned. "That was the fight you had with him?"

Elam nodded again. "Almost the last words I spoke to him were that he would burn in hell for his sins." Tears came to his eyes. "He was all I had left in this world. I loved him in spite of his bad ways."

"We'll find out what happened, but if it had to do with the scrolls, it might take a while."

"I know. If it's someone from our group, they're all returning to Naraah with us anyway. If it's one of Gideon's friends, they've already returned to Naraah. Thank you for your help. I know my ways are gruff, but I want to know the answer."

"No apology necessary. He's your son, and you loved him. I'll get answers, and if it turns out to be one of our party, we'll decide what to do then."

Elam nodded. "If it was one of the women," he said painfully, "they probably had good reason."

"Don't worry about it. We'll make it right."

"Thank you." He shook hands again. "I'm staying here for a little while."

Aaron left him, wondering how he could figure out the answer. He'd spoken to everyone in their group and had a hard time believing any of them could be the killer. His stomach churned as he treated his wife like a suspect for murder. But Leah had brought up her name, and he couldn't very well leave her off the list.

How could he find out about Gideon's friends? There was really no way until they returned to Naraah. He would explain that to Elam.

John and Demetrius had no reason to benefit from his death. Except that Demetrius had known Gideon was blackmailing Sapphira. Could he have killed Gideon to protect her?

Would that take away some of Sapphira's allure for him? He was ashamed of the thought. He thought he'd forgiven the two of them, but there were still twinges of jealousy.

CHAPTER 44

Inside their room at the inn, Sapphira stood by the tiny window, holding the curtain back and looking out at the back garden. After trying to rest, she'd finally come to the conclusion that there was no sense in hiding the truth from Aaron. She couldn't live with the secret between them any longer. Whatever happened, happened.

Jesus had told Aaron that Sapphira was forgiven. Somehow, even though she'd never met him, she knew he wouldn't have said that to Aaron if it hadn't been true. Aaron was healed, and if Jesus could perform that miracle, he could forgive her of the sins he knew she had committed.

She needed to throw herself on Aaron's mercy and hope it turned out for the best. He would not want their children to be motherless. Or at least she was counting on his compassion, if not his love.

She heard him enter the room and turned.

"You didn't sleep? Why not?" Aaron asked.

"I don't know, except I'm not used to a lot of sleep anymore." She turned to look out the window again, postponing the inevitable. "It's a beautiful day."

He stood watching until finally she turned back to him. They stood there for a long time, looking at each other. She was taking in the sight of him, memorizing his face in case she saw disgust once she told him.

She let out a huge sigh and dropped the curtain back over the window. She walked over to the writing desk and sank into the chair beside it.

"What is it?"

"I'm sorry, Aaron. I never wanted it to come to this." Her eyes welled with those stupid tears again, already missing him.

"You know I love you. I know there's more for you to say, but I want you to know that whatever it is, whatever you've done, I'll still love you." He stood there, waiting.

A faint smile appeared at the corners of her mouth. "Yes," she said softly, "and I love you."

"But?"

"Will you still love me after what I tell you?" She didn't wait for an answer but continued. "I killed Gideon." She stopped him before he could interrupt. "I have more to say. Please don't interrupt because I don't think I can finish if you do."

She knew he wanted to interrupt. He'd opened his mouth to speak, but she raised her hand to stop him.

"You were dying, and Gideon wanted to tell you that I helped him steal the scrolls. I knew it would shorten whatever time we had left together. I didn't want him to tell you before we had found Jesus. I wanted every minute with you that I could get. Gideon grabbed me, and I stabbed him. I had taken Demetrius's knife from his physician bag. Gideon attacked me right after we stole the scrolls, and Elam had stopped him. No one was in the stables, and I was desperate." Her mouth twisted into a bitter grimace. "I think from the moment you became sick, I've felt desperate. It's become a familiar feeling for me, unfortunately.

"When I returned to the room, you were breathing better, and I knew I had done the right thing in stopping Gideon from telling you about the scrolls." She frowned. "But it really wasn't right because I'd killed a man, even though I didn't mean to kill him. Just stop him from attacking me."

"Are you finished?"

He didn't look like he hated her, but she couldn't know for sure until she asked. She didn't want to ask.

She stood up and paced, agitated. "Then you recovered." She swung around and stopped in front of him. "You recovered totally."

Some part of her still believed she'd lose him. That he'd get sick again or leave her. "I couldn't believe it. If I had waited two hours, I wouldn't have had to kill him. In the end, it didn't matter. And now I will have that man's death on my conscience forever."

"I don't blame you. He attacked you."

She took a quick breath and pushed down a brief hope that nothing would change. "What am I going to do, Aaron?" She knelt in front of him. "What am I going to do?" She laid her head on his knees like a weary child.

He smoothed her hair and uttered soothing phrases. "You did it to save me. I'm as much to blame. I should have protected you from Gideon. I should have sent for Noah sooner, but I didn't realize how fast I would get sick. Perhaps if Noah had been summoned, he could have watched over you when I couldn't."

She stood up quickly and grabbed his hands. "You will not blame yourself for the things I have done." She refused to have Aaron take the blame for her and absolve her for what she'd done. Her eyes were red from crying again. "Can you forgive me? That's all I want. Your love."

"Of course, I love you." He hugged her. "We'll get through this together."

She drew away from him. "I'm asking too much." She moved away and stumbled to her feet.

Before he could move, she was out the door, hearing him call after her. "Wait!"

Maybe he did still love her, but she was so ashamed. She needed some time to think, and so did he. She needed to be sure that after he thought about it, he would still love and want her.

CHAPTER 45

She hurried out into the inn yard where the bustle of oxen and carts and people shouting matched her mood. Her eyes stung from the dirt and grit and from Aaron's parting expression as she ran. The dumbfounded look on his face broke her heart. She didn't know what she'd expected, but she'd hoped he'd follow her when she left the room. Which was stupid since she was the one who had fled, even though he assured her that he loved her. She looked back toward the inn door longing to see him. He didn't appear.

She turned and walked along the path to the gardens, wondering what would happen now. The dark overhanging trees soothed her, and she sat on a bench in the shade deep in the gardens where the sounds of the inn yard were muffled and distant.

Would Aaron cast her out? It was no less than she deserved, but she loved him. Should she have kept her mouth shut? But she found she loved him too much to keep that lie between them for the rest of their lives.

The tears began again as she wondered why the happiest moment of her life, Aaron being healed, had turned into the loneliest, saddest moment. What could she do to mend it? Could it be patched over? Did Aaron really still love her? Or would he look at her in horror and revulsion? She didn't know. He'd been bewildered and shocked. She could tell, but he had stood by her.

Someone sat beside her, and she instinctively started to stand up to get away.

"Stay, please."

The gentle voice belonged to a man a little older than herself. His weathered tan face held kind eyes. She debated.

"Please. I didn't mean to send you away." He waited patiently.

She hesitated. Why, she didn't know. Something about his soft voice held her.

"Perhaps I could help." His voice remained calm, as if soothing a skittish horse.

She didn't know why, but she settled back on the bench, not quite sure what to say. A feeling of warmth flowed through her.

He looked away from her, out at the yew trees. "You are in trouble? I can listen."

She, too, looked out at the trees, their twisted branches resembling something inside her, too mangled to be beautiful. "I did something terrible. Something I can't undo." She stopped. Why was she telling this stranger, kind though he may be? She couldn't tell him everything because he could turn her into the authorities.

He did nothing but sit there, nodding his head, as if she'd said the weather was beautiful. He didn't even appear surprised.

She found herself mesmerized, continuing her story. "My husband must hate me. I just told him about a terrible thing I've done." She hated the tremble in her lips.

He turned to her. "I doubt that he hates you. Perhaps he needs time to adjust. I'm sure it was a surprise to him."

She laughed bitterly. "It was a surprise. And he's been ill. He's finally well, I just got him back, and now he's leaving. This time, it's my fault."

"Did he tell you he would leave?"

"No, he actually told me he loves me, but he didn't have time to think about it. When he does, he'll hate me."

"You don't know you've lost him yet. You must talk to him. See what he really thinks once he processes everything." The words were calm, again as if nothing surprised him.

Her hunched shoulders loosened, and she sighed. "You're right. I'm much too impatient." She felt hope stir. Perhaps she hadn't lost Aaron after all.

He stood. "You'll see. It will turn out well. Aaron loves you. Death is not the end. I must go now."

He was a few steps away before she realized he was nearly gone. "Thank you," she called after him.

"You're welcome."

And he was gone. She hadn't asked his name. Her face flushed at her temerity. She'd told a complete stranger the intimate details of her deeds. How could she? And he had known Aaron's name. How had he known? She looked frantically around, but the stranger was gone.

Her thoughts had barely settled when she heard someone approaching. She looked eagerly, hoping it was the man again, so she could ask his name and thank him. Instead, it was Aaron.

She searched his face and felt some of the hope the stranger had engendered grow. Aaron looked serious, but not angry. "Hello," she said tentatively.

"Hello." He sat down beside her on the bench. "I thought we might talk some more."

"I'm sorry I told you so abruptly. It must have been a shock to you to find out that I..."

He took her hand in his and looked her in the eye. "It was, although I suspected it may have been you. But, I still love you, Sapphira. Love doesn't go away because the other person isn't perfect. If I only loved you when you did the right things, what kind of love would that be?"

She couldn't believe what she was hearing. He really loved her. Her heart glowed inside her, and a warmth that had been missing for months expanded from her chest into her mind. She'd told him everything. There were no more secrets, and he was still with her.

"There will be problems with this. Somehow, Elam needs to know. What he'll say or do, I don't know."

"I want to go with you when you tell him. Or I will tell him myself." She had to at least do that much. Whatever Elam did, she would deal with it. He had saved her from Gideon at one time. Perhaps he would understand. But if he didn't, at least Aaron loved her. She was still amazed at that. The stranger was right. She spared a moment to think of who he might be. Certainly wise. And where had he come from, and why at that moment?

"We'll go together. But let's wait until the end of the day. The others want to go see Jesus. We should find them and tell them we're ready to go."

She had forgotten. Aaron was well, and the reason they were all still in Ephraim was so the others could meet Jesus. The others must be impatient, and she was holding them back. She stood and brushed off her tunic. "We must go to them." She took a step.

Aaron placed a hand on her arm. "Wait. Before you go." He stood and kissed her. "We're in this together."

The warm glow spread, and for the first time since Aaron had gotten sick, she knew it was to be all right. She refused to let the fear of what Elam might do enter her mind.

CHAPTER 46

The walk to see Jesus passed much too quickly for Aaron. The streets were filled with people who were going in the same direction. Would they have a chance to talk to the great man? Aaron walked beside Sapphira, but his mind was on what he would ask Jesus. He would gladly take back his consumptive illness if it would spare Sapphira from death. She had killed a man. Part was in self-defense, but part was because she was desperate to save Aaron. Would Elam forgive her? Or hold her responsible legally? It was in his hands. Would God spare her now that Aaron finally had her back?

Had God spared him only to have him lose Sapphira? What kind of life was that? And then he was ashamed. He still had the children, and for their sakes, he needed to solve this predicament.

Sapphira and Elam were quiet, each appearing lost in their own thoughts. The others were talking over each other, excited to finally see Jesus. He squeezed Sapphira's hand, and she squeezed back, smiling timidly. He missed the strong, sure Sapphira she'd been only yesterday. The woman who'd had the strength to kill a man to protect him. He should have been appalled, and part of him was. But another part admired what she had done. Would God forgive him for forgiving her? Jesus had said she was forgiven. Aaron needed to remember that, and he needed to remember that

Jesus had also said he was forgiven. He needed to tell Sapphira what had happened to him before he'd arrived in Naraah all those years ago.

The throng was thick, and they moved more slowly now, inching their way forward. He was no longer deathly ill, but the excitement of the crowd urged them on to see Jesus. They moved past the last of the town and its buildings and saw the hillside stretched before them—and all the people waiting. His heart dropped.

#

Sapphira looked at the multitude of people. She didn't see any way they would see Jesus in this crowd. Not one-on-one. The others stopped talking as they edged forward.

"Now what?" Demetrius asked.

"We see where he is," Elam responded. "I'm not leaving without seeing him."

"I agree. Let's find a place to wait." Demetrius led them through the crowd, searching for a place.

They settled on the side of the hill farthest away from the town of Ephraim where the crowds weren't quite as deep.

"This is the best we can do for now." He sat down, and Sapphira sat beside him. The rest of the group followed his example. "We should have gotten here earlier."

"And what would that have done?" Elam asked. "He's obviously not here yet."

"I was lucky he came to my room."

Sapphira agreed, wondering what he looked like. Would he be tall and broad-shouldered like Aaron? Or shorter and a wild, red-haired man like Elam? She thought of the man she'd talked to in the garden. Would Jesus be soft-spoken and kind like him? Or louder like Demetrius?

"What are you thinking about?" Aaron asked softly.

"About Jesus. What kind of man travels and speaks everywhere, and heals people day after day?"

"I don't know. I can't wait to see him, speak to him again now that I'm properly awake and well."

"Do you think we'll get a chance?" Sapphira looked around doubtfully. "Why would he speak to us out of these thousands of people?"

Aaron looked around. "Have faith, my dear. We've come this far."

"But so have they. I feel so small and insignificant. Look at all those crippled, ill people wanting to get cured." She turned to Aaron. "Thank goodness you're well now."

"God still healed me."

Someone sat behind them on the hillside. She turned and saw the man she had spoken to in the garden. "How on earth did you find us here?" she asked.

"I've known where you were in all your travels."

She was a bit spooked by his words. Had he followed them? She turned to Aaron. "This is the man I spoke to in the garden." She was surprised to see Aaron's mouth drop open. She turned back to the man. "I'm sorry. I don't know your name."

"My name is Jesus."

Shock held her speechless. Jesus? The man they'd come to see? And she'd already spoken to him. She remembered his soft, kind voice.

He turned toward Aaron. "And this is your husband, Aaron."

She frowned. She didn't remember telling him Aaron's name, but then again, he knew it in the garden.

Aaron bowed to him. "I'm pleased to meet you, sir. We were wondering how on earth we'd get to speak with you in all this madness."

"You've traveled a long way to see me. And you are already healed. What more can I do for you?" He turned to Sapphira.

Sapphira still couldn't find her voice.

"What more can you do?" Elam interrupted. "You can tell me who killed my son."

Jesus turned to him. "I'm sorry about your son, Elam. And about your wife."

"You're sorry?" Elam's face turned purple. "Why? Why were they taken from me?" He dissolved into tears.

Sapphira's paralysis subsided, and before Jesus could say anything, she knelt beside Elam. "I'm so, so sorry." She didn't know why she suddenly felt this urge to soothe this man. It was as if something had taken over her. "We'll find the answer."

Jesus caught her eye, and she stared at him. He knew what she had done. She had told him she'd done something horrible. He knew. Something told her he'd always known. He moved away with John, and she went back to soothing Elam. Aaron stayed beside her.

Elam's tears ended abruptly as he gained control of himself. He looked up and saw John and Jesus talking. "I want to talk to him."

"You'll get your chance, Elam," she said, "but I have something to tell you. We must hurry before everyone realizes who he is." She saw a group of men, and they looked as if they knew Jesus. "His men are coming this way."

He looked behind him and turned back to her but kept his eye on Jesus and John. "What is it?"

"I know who killed your son." She saw that she had his full attention now. "I killed Gideon. I'm so sorry."

She watched his face crumple. "You?" He shook his head as if unable to understand what she'd said. "You?"

She quit patting his hand and moved slightly away. "I did." Should she tell him? He deserved the whole truth. "He was blackmailing me. Threatening to tell Aaron something I'd done."

He stared at her as if she were a stranger. "The scrolls?"

She was startled. "You know? Yes, that night when you stopped him from attacking me, I had just given them to him. Then he threatened to tell Aaron what I'd done. Aaron was deathly ill that night, and I wanted every moment with him that I could get. If Gideon had told him, he would have died instantly."

"But Aaron already knew you had done something wrong."

Sapphira shrugged, defeated. "I didn't know what Aaron knew. And I didn't know how he would react about what I had done."

They were interrupted by the others.

Jesus looked at Elam. "You wanted to speak with me? We must hurry." He, too, glanced at the crowd and his men.

Dazed as he was, Elam hurried over to Jesus, and they moved away from hearing range.

CHAPTER 47

"Tell me, Elam, would Gideon's mother have been sympathetic in seeing how her son has behaved as a man?" Jesus asked.

Elam knew Jesus was right. She would have died of a broken heart early on.

"You know who killed Gideon now."

"Yes," Elam said.

"Will you forgive her?"

"I don't know. Sapphira's been like a relative ever since Naomi married Omar, but Gideon was my son."

"Vengeance is never wise. Think about it long and hard before you act. Take care that you don't make a big mistake. Forgiveness of God and of man will give you more joy. Try it," Jesus said.

"I don't know."

"What if you had a daughter, and the daughter killed a man like Gideon. Would you forgive then?" Jesus asked.

Elam thought about it. Would he? Maybe. If it were his daughter. But he didn't have a daughter. The closest thing to a daughter he had was Sapphira. Sapphira and Gideon. Together so much in the past few weeks. Something he'd never expected to see. And unfortunately, it seemed Gideon's bad ways had rubbed off on Sapphira, and Sapphira's good ways hadn't rubbed off on Gideon. She'd been desperate to save Aaron and unaware of what Gideon was capable of until it was too late. "I need to think."

"Give it time and thought. I must go now." Jesus took Elam's hand. "Peace, my friend."

Where Jesus held his hand, a warmth flowed through him. Elam felt peace that he never expected to feel again. Peace that he'd felt when Rebekah was alive and well and they were young and in love. When he'd gathered himself, Jesus was gone.

#

Sapphira felt Aaron's arm around her shoulders as she sat on the grassy hillside. "What do you think Elam will do?"

"I don't know. You just told him, and he's still in shock. We'll have to wait and see."

When Elam returned to them, he was silent and kept his thoughts to himself. He muttered and murmured but didn't look or speak directly to them. Sapphira's heart sank. He was going to condemn her. Aaron went to speak with Jesus.

Many people receded on the hillside as Aaron found himself alone with Jesus. The day had finally come, and he found himself unprepared for the moment.

"I'm happy to see you well, Aaron." The dark brown eyes surveyed him.

"Thank you. I am happy to be well." He knew he must talk quickly, yet he found himself tongue-tied. "What about Sapphira?" he blurted out.

"What about Sapphira?" But a spark of humor and kindness was in his eyes.

"She has done horrible things. What can I do to save her? I would do anything. Can you make me ill again in order to save her?"

Jesus shook his head. "Aaron, I heal people, not make them ill. You have had your miracle. Be satisfied."

"Be satisfied?" Aaron felt a frenzy of dissatisfaction. "How can I be satisfied when the woman I love is in danger of being killed for her desperation. Spare her and make me ill again."

Jesus shook his head. "I cannot do that. And have some faith, Aaron. God has already pulled off a miracle making you well. Can you not have the same faith for Sapphira?"

Aaron felt despair weighing him down. "Sapphira doesn't believe."

"Doesn't she?" Jesus looked over at her. "She is here. With you. She has told you what happened. She almost told me in the garden."

"But can God forgive her?" Aaron asked. "Will she not suffer for all eternity because of what she's done?"

Jesus sighed. "I do not believe so, Aaron. We must see what Sapphira does. She's the only one who can save herself. If it were up to me, she is already saved. But she's got to make her choice."

"She's already made it. She's told Elam. But is Elam capable of forgiving her?" Aaron asked.

"It doesn't matter. It only matters what God wills," Jesus replied.

"What does God will?"

"That I cannot tell you, Aaron. That's between Sapphira and Him."

"I'm not satisfied."

Jesus laughed, but not unkindly. "You have received a miracle. Your body has been made whole, and you are well. And yet, you are not satisfied."

Aaron flushed. What had he done? Come before Jesus and been an ungrateful wretch. "I'm sorry. I'm so worried about Sapphira."

"Do you trust me?" The dark eyes searched his.

He nodded, suddenly feeling a moment of peace. "I trust you."

"Then pray and wait. See what Sapphira does. You are a deserving husband and loyal servant."

"Thank you. I should have said thank you first." Aaron bowed to him and waved Sapphira over. She came slowly.

CHAPTER 49

Jesus stood waiting for her, and she hesitated, unsure what to say now that they were face-to-face again. Her gaze dropped.

"What did you wish to ask me, Sapphira?" His voice was soft and clear, and his eyes were kind and familiar from her earlier conversation with him in the garden.

"Aaron…Why was he healed?" The words stumbled out, but he understood.

"Aaron forgave you."

Her eyes lifted to his in surprise. "But how could you know that he forgave me?" The hope she felt that Aaron still loved her mixed with fascination of Jesus's knowledge. "And what has he forgiven me for?"

"Everything." His eyes were the same kind and loving eyes. "Gideon, turning away from me and my Father, for going to the meeting where they were planning my death at the Friends of Jesus."

Shock burst through her system. "You know?"

He nodded. "Word has come to me."

"And still you speak with me? You are kind to me?" Tears brimmed in her eyes. What had she done? Why had she done it? She remembered sinking the knife into Gideon's side, desperation seething through every fiber of her being. And then vomiting afterward, unable to get the sight of Gideon's shocked expression out of her mind. He had reached for her to attack her, and she'd been prepared this time with a knife she'd brought with her. It had been only to warn him, not to kill him. He'd grabbed hold of her, and she'd used the knife. She wondered now if she'd brought the knife knowing what price it would cost Gideon. She knew she had to protect herself, too. Or maybe she had planned his murder even then. She couldn't remember. It was all so muddled in her mind, as if it had happened in another lifetime.

"You were desperate." He answered, even though she hadn't spoken aloud. "Aaron's near death brought you to despair, and your anger led you into wrongdoing."

Shame kindled deep in her soul. She didn't deserve kindness. She didn't deserve love. Most of all, she didn't deserve forgiveness. She shook her head, unable to believe Aaron knew everything and still loved her. And this Jesus. He also knew everything yet forgave her.

"But he does," Jesus said. "You are loved by the Father, Sapphira. He knows what you need. You've told Elam what you've done. That's a start. Now you must wait to see what Elam does with this knowledge."

She clasped her hands together, trying to stop their shaking.

"Aaron has forgiven you for the subversive meeting and stealing the scrolls." His voice was even with no reproach.

She flushed red at his words. "I'm sorry. I'm not like Aaron." She avoided his gaze, and he didn't seem to mind.

"Aaron is a special man. He will do great things. You are special, too, Sapphira, in your own way."

"But I'm not like him. You don't know what else I have done." She thought of Gideon.

"You've hated God. Killed Gideon to save your husband a few more hours." Again, his voice was calm with no condemnation.

He knew. Somehow, he knew. "You…" She held her hand to her throat, feeling it constrict, and gasped for breath.

"I told you. I know everything. There is not a moment of your journey that I'm unaware of. Aaron knows what you've done, and he's forgiven you. I can do no less. If a man forgives, God forgives a million times over."

"You are saying you are God?" She couldn't believe she asked him, but he was so approachable, something she'd never considered. She had thought of him as some exalted teacher who only spoke with his disciples and apostles. A prophet who could heal. But he had already spoken to John, Leah, and Elam. And herself. The look of love in his eyes was something she'd only seen on Aaron's face. A forgiving love with a mix of…greatness? Knowledge? She had no words to describe it. "And you've forgiven me for everything? Even betraying Aaron's love?"

"Even that." He nodded. His eyes were gentle as they met hers. "Even that. You've learned a great lesson, haven't you?"

Suddenly she was eager, excited. "Yes, I never knew what it would be like to lose Aaron. I thought he might die, but that was less painful than thinking he no longer loved me. That was excruciating. I have been afraid of living with him without his love." She shook her head in wonder. "But you are saying he still loves me." She saw assurance mirrored in his face and eyes. *An incredible man*, she thought. *Or God. She'd spoken to God.*

"One of my apostles murdered someone. I forgave him and asked him to follow me. I chose him anyway. Be sorry. Make amends. Go on with life."

"But what if Elam never forgives me? Then what?"

"Man may not forgive, but God does. What God says, goes. Man does not always understand enough to choose the right way."

"Like I didn't choose the right way."

"No, you didn't. But that moment is over. You can't go back. Only forward. Do what is right now. Talk to Elam. Make amends."

"He won't forgive me. Not after what happened with his wife and son. He is too angry."

"I spoke to him. He will listen and be kind. He's angry now, but he still loves you."

She looked at him doubtfully. Elam was angry. Angry men didn't listen. She knew that much.

"You doubt me."

"I don't doubt that you convinced Elam to think about it."

"You doubt my influence over him."

She nodded mutely.

"Wait and see. I will be gone before you receive your answer, but I can tell you this. You won't be stoned."

She hadn't thought of that, as few people knew of her guilt. But she was relieved at his words of assurance anyway. She was starting to believe him. Starting to believe in him. Aaron would be glad.

"Aaron will be glad."

She jumped when he spoke her thoughts.

"But he will be glad for you, not that he was right."

She didn't know how to respond to his words. Finally, she said the only thing she could think of. "Thank you. Thank you for everything. Aaron being well, my not being stoned. Whatever you had a hand in, thank you."

He smiled and took her hand in his, an unusual liberty for a stranger. "You are welcome."

She felt the warmth clear to her toes and knew he was the Son of God.

CHAPTER 50

They returned to the inn to gather their possessions and to bring Gideon back to Naraah. Demetrius and Aaron fed and watered the horses for traveling, and John and Elam carried Gideon's body to the stable. Once he was situated on the horse, and the women were ready to go, they started back at a swifter speed than they did when traveling to Ephraim.

Elam rode one of the horses, setting the pace while leading the horse that carried Gideon. John and Demetrius walked beside Leah, who rode the third horse a few paces behind Elam. Aaron walked beside Sapphira's horse, and she marveled at the difference in his health from the past days. She rode far enough behind the others to talk privately with him.

"Jesus will be seized by the soldiers. They were talking about it at the inn," Aaron said.

She shuddered in horror. "How sad."

"He shouldn't be killed," Aaron said in frustration.

"There's nothing to be done." She felt angry and sad that this should happen to the man whom she'd talked to. The man who had given her reason to hope for the future in spite of what she'd done. "I don't understand why he doesn't do something. Why his followers don't help him."

"There are too many soldiers, and his followers don't have the authority to stop them. They would only end up in jail beside him."

"It's wrong." She wished there was something they could do to stop them, but they had no power. Jesus had cured Aaron and reassured her about Elam, although she was having a hard time believing Elam would forgive her. Jesus hadn't done anything wrong, so why were they going to kill him?

"What are you thinking about?" Aaron asked her.

"My guilt. My misdeeds." She quirked a wry smile at him. "I've done so many things wrong in the past few months. I used to think of myself as an honest, decent woman. Woe betide anyone who thinks so well of themselves." She didn't say aloud that she had killed Gideon since she didn't want to be overheard. She hadn't spoken to Leah yet since Leah had left Sapphira alone to spend time with Aaron once he'd been healed. She had no idea what the others thought of her killing Gideon. They'd let Elam do the talking and remained respectfully silent.

"I would forgive you for anything, Sapphira. I love you." Aaron reached up his hand to her, and she took it.

"I hope that love continues forever, and that you don't regret everything I've done."

She wanted to believe him, but there were so many ways she had betrayed him. Where would she start, and which was the least of her sins? "I don't deserve you, Aaron."

“There are so many things we need to talk about when we get home.”

She nodded. He was right. Now wasn’t the time.

The ride from Ephraim to Naraah passed swiftly but awkwardly. Demetrius would not look at Sapphira, but Elam sent her frequent sidelong glances. Sapphira didn’t feel comfortable chatting idly with Aaron while under the others’ scrutiny.

John and Demetrius talked with Leah about what Jesus had said to them. That John felt some relief was obvious. His face, while always calm, had a look of peace. From what Sapphira could gather from their conversation, John’s brother’s death had been a sad time here on earth but a reason to celebrate in heaven. John, whose life had been spared, found purpose in his brotherly friendship with Aaron.

Demetrius had learned things, too, but so far had kept them to himself. She wondered if he would ever visit their home again now that Aaron was well.

Elam remained quiet and plodded along.

Sapphira tried not to worry. Tried to have faith as Jesus suggested. But it was difficult because she didn’t know if Elam would turn her over to the law once they returned to Naraah.

Sapphira gazed down at Aaron as they traveled, happy that he was well. She couldn’t wait to get home as the tension rose among them all.

Did John and Leah forgive her? What did Demetrius think of her now? She was only mildly regretful that he might find her reprehensible for killing Gideon. She was more concerned with

Aaron's feelings and with the memory of Jesus's kind, caring eyes. He understood. She still could barely believe it. While she wished the silence were more friendly, she welcomed the quiet and being left to her own thoughts. She had much to think about.

What had happened on that hill with Jesus? Did they all receive what they needed from him? Was he only a man? Or a great healer as Aaron still believed?

Aaron had certainly been healed—he believed by God. She didn't know. Jesus had been raised Jewish, as had she and Aaron. Did Aaron want the children raised in a Jewish household? But if so, why had he never told her he was Jewish until he was so sick? They would probably continue on as they had, without teaching the Jewish faith to their children. She found herself sad at the lack of tradition the children would have.

She longed to be home with the children and Aaron. She wished to go back to life the way it was before Aaron became sick, before she'd made the worst mistake of her life killing Gideon.

They all parted ways at Naraah. Elam with a gruff goodbye.

Leah gave her a parting hug and whispered that they'd talk later. It heartened Sapphira to know that Leah at least was still talking to her. Demetrius offered a grave goodbye to her and shook Aaron's hand, wishing him well. John gave his usual calm smile and shook Aaron's hand as well. That should have reassured her, but instead, reinforced the guilt she felt over killing a man.

CHAPTER 51

The day after they returned home, Sapphira was setting the table with Rachelle when Caleb came home and stood in the kitchen doorway.

"I saw a horse," Caleb said. "It's not one that I recognize. It's out on the road. There's a man riding it, and he's coming this way."

"It's probably Elam or Demetrius on a different mount," Sapphira said. "Where's your father?"

"He had one more thing to do at Uncle Omar's before coming home."

"We're almost out of water. Can you go get some from the well? Everyone will be thirsty." She followed him to the front door.

"Yes, Mama." He looked outside again. "The man is coming here."

"Maybe he's a friend of Demetrius's and is going next door."

"I don't think so."

Sapphira wondered who the rider could be. If the man was coming to their house, she wished Aaron was home. She didn't like the idea of a stranger around when he was gone. "Stay here for a few minutes until we know what he wants. Then bring the water."

"All right." Caleb stood there, watching.

"I wonder who it could be," Sapphira said as she went to the door and looked out. "He looks like your father, but it's not." Her voice pitched higher.

"There's your father now, coming from far behind him."

Rachelle jumped up and down. "He's getting off of his horse."

"Shhh," said her mother. "Please go back to the kitchen."

Rachelle ignored her and pressed against her side.

The man arrived at their doorstep and got down from his horse. He did look a lot like Aaron, except he wasn't quite as tall, his complexion was darker, and he was stockier in build. She got a brief glimpse before Caleb blocked most of the doorway.

"Can we help you?" Caleb asked boldly.

"I'm looking for Aaron. Is he around?"

Aaron appeared behind the man. "Here I am."

The stranger turned swiftly and threw his arms around Aaron. "My brother, what is this I hear?"

Then the man stood back, looked Aaron up and down, and said, "You look good. Much better than that letter you sent led me to believe."

"Noah," Aaron said, hugging him again. He turned to see his family watching him from the doorway. "This is my brother, Noah."

Noah shook Caleb's hand and bowed to Sapphira and Rachelle.

Aaron turned to his Noah. "We'll take your horse around to the back, and you can come in and eat with us. As you can see, I've recovered, but it's a long story. It's so good to see you."

Sapphira's thoughts were reeling. She and Aaron still hadn't talked much about his family, and she needed to find out if any more of his relatives were going to show up on their doorstep. "I'll put more food on the table."

Aaron showed Noah where they kept the horses while Sapphira went to the kitchen with Rachelle. "Caleb, don't forget the water."

He looked like he was going to refuse.

"I know you want to go with your father, but let him have time with his brother now, and you can talk to him later. I think he'll be around a while." At least she knew that's what Aaron would want, based on the greeting he'd given his brother. She had seen the light in her husband's eyes when he'd realized his brother had come. What had happened to separate them for so long?

They returned with Noah's travel bag just as Caleb returned with the water.

Sapphira smiled. Caleb looked hot and sweaty. He must have run all the way.

Aaron was smiling widely, and his brother was laughing. He looked up to see Caleb watching from the doorway.

"Caleb, set the water down in the kitchen and help your mother."

"The food is ready," Sapphira said. "We can wash up and eat. Are you hungry?" she asked Noah.

He patted his stomach. "It's been a long ride. I could eat." His smile was a younger carefree version of Aaron's.

Sapphira looked at the children and then at Aaron. "I think after we eat, you two should catch up with each other."

Aaron threw her a grateful smile. "Thank you, but I'd like you to hear what Noah has to say."

He turned to Noah. "I hope you'll stay with us for a while. You're welcome as long as you want to visit."

"Thank you. I didn't know how long I'd need to be here, so I took time off from work. We'll talk later about how long you can stand to have me visit. There are some things going on at home that I'll talk to you about later."

They sat at the kitchen table to eat, and Aaron couldn't take his eyes off Noah as he ate. "I can't believe you're here."

They finished eating, cleaned the kitchen, and settled in the living area. They talked of Aaron's illness and how Jesus had cured him. Noah was excited to share that he'd also heard Jesus speaking to a large crowd when he'd been in his own part of the country. Sapphira was getting impatient to hear details about Noah and the rest of Aaron's family but knew they had to wait until the children were in bed.

#

Noah leaned forward with his elbows on the kitchen table. The children were sleeping, and the adults finally had some time to talk. "I came because of your illness, but also the situation in Jericho is over. No one in Jericho wants your blood any longer. Those who meant you harm have moved away, and you've been forgotten by the ones who remain."

A multitude of feelings overcame Aaron. He could go home again to see his family. "And Mother and Father? Are they still around?" He meant alive, as he knew they were older now, and Sapphira's parents hadn't lived this long.

"Yes, they are alive." Noah had no trouble reading his mind. "And so are Keziah, Levi, and Daniel. All are doing well, except Father. He has had a hard time lately, and Levi, Daniel, and I have been doing most of the work. Daniel is married with four children, Levi has two, and Keziah is getting married."

Aaron thought about that. Keziah was old enough to be married. "So much time has passed. Keziah and Levi won't know me. Levi was about Rachelle's age, and Keziah was but two years old when I had to run away."

Noah patted him gently on the shoulder. "We kept your memory alive for them. Never did a day go by that we didn't pray for you at night or at mealtimes. Of course, we kept your name quiet in public, not wanting to create problems for the little ones, but we never forgot you, Aaron. Never."

The warmth and caring nearly made him cry. They had loved him, even after what he had done.

He turned to Sapphira, who had been sitting quietly, listening to them. "I killed a man in a fight."

Noah patted his shoulder. "It was an accident. You never meant to harm him."

"No, but he died anyway. I'm lucky you pulled me away and sent me out of town before the townspeople stoned me."

"He pushed you first. You were only defending yourself. It wasn't your fault he fell and hit his head on a rock."

"How do you know?" Aaron asked. "I should have turned and walked away, not pushed back."

"You were only seventeen. Give yourself some leniency."

They were silent while they both absorbed the past, and Aaron thought about the ramifications of the present.

He turned to Sapphira. "I killed a man, so, you see, I understand."

Noah nodded. "You didn't tell her before today?"

"No." He changed the subject. He would need to explain things to Sapphira later and ask her if he could tell Noah about Gideon. "You mentioned praying for me. Does that mean things haven't changed in the household?"

"Not in that regard, no, they haven't. What are you thinking?"

"Do you believe Jesus of Nazareth healed me?"

Noah was nodding before Aaron finished speaking. "Oh, yes, we talked about taking Father Nehemiah to see him, but Father refused."

Aaron's heart sank. "Because he didn't think he would be healed?"

"No, because he thought there were more people sicker than him, and they needed Jesus's healing more than he did."

"Oh, I see." He took a deep breath. "They still practice the Jewish faith, though?"

"Yes, does that concern you?"

"No, but how do they reconcile that with Jesus?"

Noah shrugged. "It's a mystery."

CHAPTER 52

The next morning Aaron and Noah had gone to Omar's place to do chores. Caleb went too, fascinated by his new uncle and the fact that there were cousins near his age and two other uncles besides Noah and an aunt he had yet to meet. Rachelle had a hard time choosing where to go but stayed with Sapphira and clung to her skirt.

She decided to take Rachelle over to Leah's house and leave her to play with Ruth so she could talk to Aaron in private. She wasn't sure how Leah felt toward her but knew she could count on her to watch over Rachelle.

Leah's greeting was subdued, but she agreed to watch Rachelle and said she'd talk to Sapphira when she returned to pick up Rachelle.

Sapphira walked to Naomi and Omar's house and arrived in time to greet Naomi, who stood on her front doorstep. They hugged, and Sapphira felt it was the first genuine hug they'd exchanged.

"I'm glad to see Aaron well," Naomi said.

"Thank you. I'm not quite used to believing it yet."

Naomi nodded. "It will feel normal again soon."

Sapphira hoped so. She decided to share her happy news with Naomi. "I'm having a baby."

A moment of sadness swept across Naomi's face, and then she smiled and hugged Sapphira tightly. "I'm happy for you and Aaron. You deserve it."

Sapphira knew Naomi's wish to have another child was at the back of her mind, but she'd been gracious. "Thank you. I wanted to tell you as soon as possible."

Aaron had seen her on the step talking to Naomi and joined them.

Naomi greeted him with a smile. "I'll let you two talk. I'm sure you haven't had much time alone since your brother arrived as soon as you returned from your trip."

She went into the house, and they walked a little way away from the front door before stopping.

"Is Noah staying for a while yet?" she asked.

"About a week. He wants me to go back with him to visit."

She wanted to go with him but was still waiting for Elam to make his decision about her fate, which left her uncertain about what would happen.

"Would you go by yourself to see them?"

"I haven't had time to think about the details. If my father is dying, I might need to go soon if I want to see him. If he wants to see me." Aaron shrugged. "By killing a man, I thought I'd never see them again. My father was angry. I don't know how he feels about me right now. Noah and I didn't have time to go into many details last night, even though he did say my father wants to see me. There were too many other things to talk about. At least I'm getting to see Noah again."

"Your family lives near Jericho?" she asked.

"Yes."

"I've never been there." She thought it might be interesting to visit his family and take a trip with Aaron and the children. If Elam didn't turn her in to the authorities.

Sapphira had never seen Aaron so unsure of himself. He looked at her, then at the ground.

"What is it?" She grabbed his arm. "What did Noah say to you?" She tried to keep the panic from her voice. She had come so close to losing him, and she didn't know what Noah could possibly have said to Aaron to make him so hesitant.

He took her hand and held it. "My father is really sick. I want to see him before he dies, but I can't leave until Elam makes his decision about you."

"Elam will not do anything." She forced more assurance into her voice than she believed. "He'll take some time to come to terms with Gideon's death, but I don't think he'll want to hurt me after he has had time to think about it. I almost told him about the baby, but I thought he might think I was lying."

"Maybe you should have told him. If he knew about the baby, I know he wouldn't do anything to harm it. He just couldn't do that."

Sapphira knew he was right. She'd been so emotional on their trip, she hadn't been thinking clearly. She'd felt dazed ever since Gideon's death, and even though Aaron was well, she couldn't sleep at night.

"You're right. If he decides to turn me in, I'll let him know. It wouldn't be fair not to tell him."

He touched her cheek gently. "I know we just got back, but I need to go see my father one more time. As soon as Elam gives us his answer, I'll leave."

She leaned away from him to look at his face. "I'll go with you if Elam forgives me. If not, Naomi can watch the children, and you go see your father. You can travel faster without the children."

He pulled her into his arms. "It will work out. Just think about what we've already gone through, and God has been good to us."

She didn't know if he was trying to convince her or himself. How much more would God give them?

She rested against him, praying Elam would forgive her. They had returned home only a few days ago. Now, Aaron wanted to travel again. "If Elam forgives me, we're both going, and we're taking the children with us. Rachelle will not want me out of her sight for a long time."

"We'll all go. Caleb and Rachelle should see their father's family."

CHAPTER 53

Sapphira waited a week for Elam. Every day she waited, wondering if the law would arrive to arrest her. By nighttime she was exhausted, though she was doing less manual work since Aaron was well and taking care of the outside work again. The children were happy to have them home.

Rachelle clung to her and rarely left her side. Caleb stuck to his father and helped with whatever he was doing. Omar had treated the children well while they were gone, for which Sapphira was grateful. He did not say anything to her about Gideon, as their traveling party had all agreed before they returned to Naraah that none of them would reveal what had happened unless Elam chose to tell the authorities. For that, Sapphira was grateful. She feared Omar's reaction if he ever found out what she'd done.

The trip receded in her mind, except for a few memories that robbed her of peace and sleep. Killing Gideon. Remembering his shock and surprise. She shuddered. Would she ever get that memory out of her mind?

The kind eyes of Jesus replaced Gideon's, and she inhaled calm breaths. She believed that kind gaze was the only thing that kept her sane. He'd understood, even if he didn't condone her actions.

Demetrius never came to the house during that week, although Sapphira knew Aaron had visited him and taken Noah with him to meet

Demetrius. She didn't know if he would return. Aaron didn't need a physician any longer, and Demetrius had other patients to attend to. She was surprised to find she didn't miss him.

She did miss Leah, though. She'd become used to their daily talks, but she knew Leah was as busy at home with the children as she was. They'd both been gone and needed to reassure the children that life had returned to normal, and they weren't leaving again.

Sapphira thought about visiting Leah but was afraid of what Leah's opinion of her was now. She couldn't remain afraid and hide out forever, but she allowed herself some time. Leah would come over to see Sapphira when she was ready to talk. If she didn't visit, Sapphira would talk to her as soon as Elam informed her what he intended to do about Gideon.

She was in the middle of making bread when she heard a knock on the door. She opened it to find Elam standing there. Sapphira looked around in dismay. She was alone. Aaron had taken both of the children and gone to the pasture at Omar's earlier. They hadn't returned yet.

Would Elam harm her? That he had come to some conclusion was obvious from his presence, but she couldn't tell from his expression. She stood in the doorway. "Elam." She forced her voice to evenness.

"Sapphira. May I come in?"

She moved aside, and he entered the house. "Can I get you a drink?"

"No, nothing for me."

Stomach churning, she gestured to one of the chairs in the room. "Please, sit down." That way, he wouldn't be looming over her.

He sat, looking around the room.

He'd been there many times before, and nothing had changed. He didn't know how to start, she realized. He was as nervous as she was. "Have you decided what you will do?" she asked gently, no longer afraid of him.

He nodded. "I thought at first that I would tell everyone what you had done." He looked her in the eye. "But then I realized what he had done. I don't want people to know of the wrongs he committed."

She said nothing, waiting for him to have his say.

"Then I thought, how could I make you pay for killing him without anyone knowing why you'd done it? I thought of killing Aaron so you would know how it felt."

Her heart lurched in her breast. *No,* she thought, *please not that.* She'd finally gotten Aaron back, healthy and well. And, miracle of miracles, he still loved her.

Elam closed his eyes and sighed. "But I couldn't do that to you." He opened them again. "I couldn't do that to you."

"Why not?" Would he change his mind later? She had to know.

"Because I realized you'd already been through that with Aaron. We went to Naraah to save him. By some miracle, which I believe was through God, he survived. How could I take his life after that?" He didn't wait for her to answer. "Then I thought about killing you."

His eyes were fierce. She sat up straighter, ready to edge away to protect herself.

"I lived off that image for days. Until one day, I remembered Jesus telling me that forgiving was the best thing to do. He said it would give me joy to forgive. I'm not there yet. I miss Gideon even though I know he did terrible things. Things I already knew in my heart but didn't want to believe. What father wants to believe that of his son? I still don't think it was right of you to take my son's life. That's wrong no matter what. But I understand the desperation a person can go through. I felt it when my wife died. I would have done anything to bring her back. I understand you would have done anything to save Aaron's life. And did so to save his life. You were protecting yourself. I saw my son attack you in the street that night, and I know he would have harmed you in that stable. My son lived a violent life and died a violent death." He stood up. "That's all I came to say."

"And you aren't turning me into the authorities?" she asked, relief surging through her, even though she knew the guilt she felt would be forever in her heart.

"No, it's over." He walked to the door and opened it to leave. "I know we'll continue to see each other as I work on Omar's land. I wish you no harm." He stood for a moment by the door.

"Thank you. I wish I could go back and do things differently, but I can't. I'm sorry."

He nodded. "I've decided to take a trip in a few months to go to see Thomas, one of Jesus's apostles. Jesus told me to see Thomas when I finally decided what to do about you."

After Elam left, Sapphira closed the door gently behind him and leaned against it, tears running down her cheeks. He'd not forgiven her, but he wasn't seeking vengeance. Where was Aaron? She wanted to tell him.

CHAPTER 54

Sapphira ran all the way to Omar's house to find Aaron, waving at him to come to her when she saw him. She told Aaron what happened. "He didn't forgive me, but he's letting it go."

Aaron pulled her into a big hug. "What did he say?"

"He won't pursue it with the authorities. He'll be civil when we meet by chance. Why did I kill Gideon, Aaron? Why did I think it was so necessary? Now it doesn't seem like I had to do it." She didn't know what she wanted from Aaron. He could absolve her, tell her she was forgiven, but what would wipe the stain from her heart? Make her feel good about herself again?

"I would forgive you for anything, Sapphira. I love you." Aaron held her at arm's length to look into her eyes. "Forgive yourself."

She wanted to get over it but didn't know how. Where would she start, and which was the least of her sins? "I don't deserve you, Aaron."

"Remember, I killed someone, too. I believe I'm forgiven because Jesus said so, and he healed me. Didn't Jesus say you are forgiven?"

She remembered his dark, kind eyes. The peace that radiated from him. His gentleness. His strength. "Yes."

"Then believe him. It's over. We're here in this place together."

She felt peace sweeping through her. It was over. Aaron was well. She had the children. She had God. "Thank you, Jesus," she whispered, watching the smile spread across Aaron's face.

"Thank you, God."

ACKNOWLEDGMENTS

Special thanks to the great editing by Michele Mathews at Beach Girl Publishing LLC, who made this book better with her expertise.

Special thanks to the excellent editor, Denise Roeper of Eloquent Edits, LLC, (www.eloquentedits.com), for her great suggestions. They helped create a better book than I could have envisioned on my own.

Considerable thanks to my friends Sally, Ruth, Karen, and Amy, who have been so supportive as we all struggled through 2020. I couldn't have finished this book without your help. Thanks to all of my family, who have encouraged me every step of the way in writing this book.

COPYRIGHT

ABOUT THE AUTHOR

Jean Rezab writes from her home in North Dakota. Having grown up on a farm, she enjoys all things country, especially wildflowers, wheat fields, and winding lanes.

An excerpt of her writing has appeared in Humanities of ND Magazine. She likes to entertain her readers with mysteries and women's fiction containing messages of love and forgiveness.

Visit her website at www.jeanrezab.com for upcoming releases and further information.